I0685203

TURQUOISE
WATERS

SAMOT PRESS

ISBN: 0615526179
ISBN 13: 9780615526171
Library of Congress Control Number: 2011936817
Samot Press, Austin, TX

TURQUOISE WATERS

* * *

BY
LARRY
THOMAS

SAMOT PRESS

This book is dedicated to the memory of my mother, Kitty Thomas.

Acknowledgments

The first person I want to acknowledge is my mother, Kitty Thomas, who was wonderfully supportive and encouraged me to stick with it. Originally, my mother actually served as my editor, but she passed away before I finished. Thank you, Mom, for everything you did for me.

Rebecca Bender then took over the editing duties and was absolutely terrific. I feel so very lucky to have had Rebecca's help on this project.

I appreciate Matt Morehouse, who recommended the services of Rebecca as editor.

I appreciate the help of William (Bill) Hamilton, an ex-FBI agent whose input was invaluable.

I appreciate the encouragement of Mike Sullivan who also introduced me to Bill Hamilton when I needed the technical help.

I appreciate the help of Austin Wampler, a friend and pilot, who offered his flying expertise to help with my project.

I appreciate my buddies from college who provided inspiration: Henry, Roland, Neil, and David.

I am grateful for all the help given me by my publishing team.

I am grateful for the help and encouragement of my friends and co-workers: Sara, Carole, Angela, Stephen, Pam, Monica, and T.

I would like to offer a special word of thanks to my friend Ron (R) Hardcastle, for his encouragement as well as humorous inspirations.

I would like to express my sincere appreciation to Nancy LaSpina for her help with this project.

Finally, a special word of appreciation for the support and encouragement of my family: Darlene, Cliff, Janet and Sean, who helped in so many ways from listening, reading, re-reading, humoring me, and just being there.

When in disgrace with fortune and men's eyes,
I all alone beweep my outcast state
And trouble deaf heaven with my bootless cries
And look upon myself and curse my fate,
Wishing me like to one more rich in hope,
Featured like him, like him with friends possess'd,
Desiring this man's art and that man's scope,
With what I most enjoy contented least;
Yet in these thoughts myself almost despising,
Haply I think on thee, and then my state,
Like to the lark at break of day arising
From sullen earth, sings hymns at heaven's gate;
From thy sweet love remember'd such wealth brings
That then I scorn to change my state with kings.

William Shakespeare

PROLOGUE

Havana, Cuba, 1992

The desire for freedom will drive a man to take desperate risks, Manuel Favela thought. His back and shoulders ached as he allowed himself a brief respite from the loading. Eleven men, seven women, and four children, from four years old to thirteen, had gathered in the shadows where the boats were moored.

He inhaled deeply. The cool breeze brought the scent of salt and seaweed from the long, narrow stretch of beach. The land he would miss, the man ruling it he would not. He glanced over at Omar Cabrillo. Omar was busy loading an identical trunk to the one Manuel was sitting on onto the next boat.

Manuel and Omar were two of Castro's closest generals. For years the two had been operatives in much of the general's drug trafficking, prostitution, and money laundering throughout Central and South America. As Manuel's own daughter grew, he began to regret the lives other girls had been subjected to under his watch. He and Omar had begun to siphon money off the illicit transactions; they were certain their skimming had not been missed from the millions transacted throughout banks in the Caribbean and Europe. Both men knew the risks to themselves and their families of stealing from the dictator, and each had covered for the other. They were in an intractable pact.

With the Mariel boatlift incident more than a decade old and Castro getting older, they felt the time was now right to make a run for freedom.

In their entourage, four twenty-two-foot boats were quietly being loaded for the 145-kilometer trip to America. The night was still, with barely a whisper of a breeze coming in off the harbor. It was still several hours until daylight, but the brightness of the full moon made the loading easier.

The women and children were huddled in the darkness beyond the beach on a low stretch of dunes covered with scrub grass. Far out on the horizon, a cruise ship, a floating island of festive colored lights, slowly made its way south.

Manuel listened to the soft murmur of voices around him. He glanced over at his teenage daughter, so much like her mother, and his young son silhouetted in the shadows. For a split second he wondered if the risk was too great, but he knew that true freedom for his wife and children required taking this chance. He knew he had to get away from Castro, and Cuba, and he accepted the risks.

Omar paused a moment, wiped the sweat from his brow, and looked over at Manuel. They briefly made eye contact, then continued to stow their cargo.

When the last crate had been loaded, the men signaled for the women and children to board, then quietly shoved off, leaving Cuba and their past behind forever.

The first hour passed quietly. Cuba could no longer be seen on the horizon as clouds rolled in. There was only the blackness of the night and the ebony sea around them as they moved out of the chop and into much heavier seas. The four boats stayed close together. Although the darkness covered them like a shroud, once they were forty kilometers from shore, Manuel allowed himself to breathe. *My children will make it to America*, he thought.

Another hour passed. The full moon, clear skies, and calm seas lifted Manuel's spirits. They had covered about seventy-five kilometers and were more than halfway through their journey when he looked off to port and spotted a light out on the horizon. Manuel knew that Castro's navy regularly patrolled these waters, even though they were outside Cuban territorial waters. Unsure if it was a navy vessel or a fishing boat, the only thing he could determine was that it was moving toward them. He offered a silent prayer to God. His hope was that it was Brothers to the Rescue, a group that did reconnaissance flights in the Florida straits looking for Cubans attempting to escape. But it did not take long for Manuel to realize this was no rescue plane. It was a ship, and it was moving toward them quickly.

The four small boats moved close together and shut down their engines. The men knew only too well that if they were intercepted by a Cuban naval ship they would either be killed or imprisoned. Early in the planning stages, Manuel and Omar had agreed that if they were pursued, they would fight.

Manuel stood on the bow and spoke to the women and children. "Stay low and out of sight." He turned to the men. "Ready your weapons." He offered another prayer to God for their protection.

Manuel moved to the stern of the boat, leaned over, and spoke quietly with Guillermo Gonzalez, a close friend who was driving the fastest of the small boats. "If a gun battle erupts, I am depending on you to take our children safely to America."

Within minutes a sixty-foot twin diesel Cuban gunboat throttled down and came to rest ninety feet from the group. The engines sputtered and gurgled in the low gentle swells rolling beneath the boat. Manuel could clearly see several men on the gun deck and three more on the bridge tower. Suddenly, he was blinded by a searchlight from the top of the tower.

A voice boomed in Spanish from a loudspeaker somewhere behind the searchlight, "You and the others are in violation of Cuban waters."

Manuel knew they were clearly outside Cuban waters, but he also knew it made no difference. He remained silent.

The voice again proclaimed, this time in heavily accented English, "You are in violation of Cuban waters. What is the nature of your business here?"

Manuel held his hand up to shield his eyes from the light. He responded in English, "We are in international waters en route to America."

"That will not happen, Manuel Favela."

The blinding light prevented Manuel from seeing details, but he could see motion on the gun deck. And then, out of the silence, he clearly heard the sickening sound of metal against metal—guns being readied.

He turned to the men in the boats on either side of him. "Take out the searchlight first," he cried.

The next few minutes passed in a blur. From somewhere behind the light an automatic weapon opened fire. Shells began thumping wildly against the boats and spitting into the water around him. Men were yelling, women were screaming, and children were crying.

Manuel, Omar, and the other nine men took cover, drew their weapons, and began to return fire. Their return shots spattered against the hull and tower of the gunboat. Manuel steadied his rifle against the rail and took aim at the searchlight. He didn't have an automatic weapon, but on his third shot there was a loud crack and the light exploded, showering sparks down onto the deck of the gunboat. Yellow-blue lights, the weapon fire from both sides, lit up the night.

Manuel grabbed his two children, pushed them to the stern, and yelled for them to get to cover in Guillermo's boat. Guillermo crawled to the bow and pulled Manuel's son aboard. Quickly Manuel reached for his daughter and was hoisting her toward Guillermo when a shot ricocheted off the rail, striking Manuel in the arm. His daughter, screaming and crying, fell to the water below.

Horrified by his daughter's submerging body, Manuel's mind quickly turned to his son. "Guillermo," he yelled in desperation, "go now and get my son to safety."

"But—" Guillermo sputtered.

"Go, now. I will get my daughter and put her on another boat."

Guillermo knew not to second-guess the general. He gunned the engine and sped off as automatic weapons-fire from the gunboat peppered the three remaining boats.

Manuel threw his daughter a line, and the girl grabbed hold and followed her father's ardent pleas to hold on.

Omar and Manuel both leveled their weapons in the direction of the automatic weapons and opened fire, hoping to hit someone and stop the relentless shower of shells. Bullets were flying in both directions when Manuel heard a loud cry of pain and saw a body fall from the gunboat into the water.

Omar was in a good position to see the silhouettes of several figures on the bow of the gunboat. He steadied his pistol and fired several rounds. Two of the figures fell, and one stumbled off into the water. Manuel watched the figure fall, then noticed two men on the bridge. In the glow from the bridge light he could clearly see one man at the helm and another taking aim at Omar. Manuel steadied his rifle and squeezed off a round. The glass from the windscreen shattered, and the man aiming at Omar slumped to the floor.

The man at the helm turned toward the slumping figure next to him and reached for the weapon, but never made it. Manuel had squeezed off a second round; he saw the helmsman's head snap back and blood splatter against the wall behind him. Manuel then looked to see how many of his men were still fighting. As the full moon broke through the clouds he saw several bodies slumped on the decks and several more floating in the water. Omar's boat was quickly taking on water. There were only four men, including Omar, still firing their weapons. Manuel's own boat was also taking on water, and he knew it was now only a matter of time. He turned and saw his wife lying on her back, her blouse covered in bloodstains. He knelt beside her.

She took his hand and looked into his eyes. "Save our daughter," she whispered. "Get her to safety."

Manuel knew he had to grant his wife's dying request. He moved to the stern of the boat, grabbed the line he had thrown his daughter, and pulled her aboard. He then moved to the third boat, the only boat still seaworthy. Only two men, Vincente and Felix, were left onboard the craft.

"Vincente, please get my daughter safely to America," he yelled as he lifted her into the third boat. Manuel hugged his daughter and whispered, "I love you. I promise I will see you again some day."

Omar had made his way to the stern of his boat. "Go, Vincente," he yelled. "Manuel and I will stay behind and keep the gunboat busy so you can get away." Manuel and Omar again grabbed their weapons and took cover.

Obviously outmanned and outgunned, and with their boats slowly sinking, the two generals continued fighting until the boat carrying Manuel's daughter to safety had retreated into the darkness. Shells peppered the remaining two boats. Manuel's arm was covered in blood from the shot he had taken earlier, but he continued firing. Then, out of the darkness, there was a loud crack, a heavy thump, and a cry of pain from across the water. Manuel saw Omar fall back into the water with a loud splash. Manuel jumped into the next boat, looking for his friend, but Omar never surfaced.

Alone, Manuel knew it was over. He dropped his weapon and fell to his knees. The firing had stopped. An eerie silence engulfed him in the darkness. Several seconds passed before the sound of water rushing over the stern brought Manuel back from his thoughts. The boat was about to sink. Manuel crawled back to his own boat just before Omar's boat sank beneath the ebony blackness. He sloshed through the water and knelt next to the still body of his wife. As he took her lifeless body in his arms, he saw the gunboat creeping slowly toward him and began to cry. His boat was fast filling with water and would soon go under. He looked up into the blanket of stars and prayed that God would be with his children.

CHAPTER
1

Monterey, California, 2007

*A*n orange sliver of morning light filtered through the curtains of the forty-six-foot cruiser. Sean Tripp slowly cracked one sleep-blurred eye and peered at the bedside clock. He turned on his side and let his eye close again, trying to will himself back to sleep. Tripp enjoyed mornings aboard the cruiser, especially when he got to sleep in. He enjoyed the peace and quiet and the gentle rocking motion created by the water against the hull.

Failing to will himself back to sleep, Tripp got up and staggered to the galley to start a pot of coffee. After dressing in gray jogging shorts and a sweatshirt, he poured a mug of black coffee and went up on deck. Lounging with his feet up, Tripp took his first long sip and wondered how anyone could survive mornings without coffee. He settled back and watched the sun rise over the blue waters of the Pacific, where his boat was moored in Monterey Bay.

The muscular Tripp, at six foot four inches tall and 210 pounds, was still in excellent physical shape. Several pro teams had shown interest in him before he enlisted in the military.

Tripp's life had been on the fast track since he left home for college. He had received his degree in marine biology on a football scholarship from Texas A&M University. He fully intended to dedicate his life to the sea, but at the urging of his best friend, Neil Manning, whom he had known since childhood, he instead joined Neil and enlisted in the army. He never regretted the choice of serving his country over playing pro ball.

The two buddies, who had played in the same backfield in high school and college, became chopper pilots in the same unit in the Gulf War. By coincidence, they both ended up in intelligence. Tripp had considered reenlisting, but Manning convinced him the FBI needed him more.

Tripp, tan with piercing green eyes, black wavy hair, and a seemingly permanent smile, was what they called a man's man. His good humor and quick wit allowed him to fit in equally with corner-office executives and utility linemen with calloused hands. Women swooned over him, which he didn't discourage. But his life as a playboy had come to an abrupt stop when he met his wife, Katie, a fellow FBI agent. Tripp had known many beautiful women in his life, but Katie possessed something more— the auburn-haired beauty had what he could only describe as grit. She worked in covert operations and never shied away from an assignment. She had been killed in Miami while serving in an undercover sting operation. Tripp was devastated.

The bureau had offered him an extended leave of absence, but he said he was done chasing bad guys and quit. Not sure what to do with his life, he was convinced by an agent who had tried to recruit him for the NFL to take a job with the Dallas Cowboys, rehabilitating a promising quarterback who had been sent to prison on a weapons charge. Tripp worked with the young man upon his release, and the following year the Cowboys won the Super Bowl. Tripp was paid handsomely by a very satisfied team owner.

The only place Tripp found contentment was on the sea. He invested most of the money he earned from the Cowboys, but kept enough to purchase his cruiser, which he christened *Katie's Eyes.*

This particular morning, Tripp sat on the deck trying to decide if he wanted to go fishing or whale watching, when his thoughts were interrupted by a voice from the dock.

"Mr. Tripp, mind if I come aboard?"

Sean recognized Stony Barker's voice. Stony was the starting quarterback of the local high-school football team, the Pacific Grove Dolphins, where Tripp was an assistant coach.

Working with the young Dolphins quarterback was satisfying to Tripp. He liked having a positive influence on the young man's life.

Everyone in town knew Sean Tripp from his glory days as quarterback for the A&M Aggies and his work with the Cowboys' quarterback. Tripp had been in town only a couple weeks when the local head coach convinced him to come down to the field house and be a part of the program. Tripp had spent most of the fall season with the team, offering advice and support. The entire team had grown very close to Tripp and had dedicated the year to him. It was not unusual for the players to come to him with their problems or just to share some time, so Tripp was not entirely surprised to hear Stony's voice.

"Permission to board granted," Tripp replied.

Stony stepped aboard and walked across the deck to where Tripp was sitting.

Stony shook Tripp's hand and said, "Thank you. I hope I'm not intruding."

"Not at all," Tripp replied. "Pull up a chair."

The blond, blue-eyed eighteen-year-old, dressed in khaki shorts and a blue polo shirt, looked troubled. "I wonder if I could talk with you about a problem?" he asked.

"I'll be glad to listen and help if I can. Would you like some water or juice?" Tripp asked.

"Some water would be great," replied Stony.

Tripp went to the galley and grabbed a bottle of water. Returning to the deck, he handed it to Stony. The sun was higher in the sky now, so Tripp pulled the lounge chair around to shade his eyes.

"Now, tell me what's on your mind," he said.

Stony was quiet for a few seconds before he finally spoke. "It's about Tony Casteel. It's about something Tony told me before he...disappeared."

Disappeared? The word sounded melodramatic to Tripp. He wondered if this had something to do with a girl. Tripp knew Tony from the team. A determined and dedicated tight end, Tony was socially shy. Tripp figured it was because Tony was an orphan whom Social Services had placed with the Casteel family when he was four years old. The family knew very little about Tony other than that his family had drowned in some type of boating accident, but they warmly took him in and loved him as if he were their biological child. Tony never asked about his real parents or where he had come from, but Tripp figured the boy had to be curious about his roots.

"What's this about?' Tripp asked Stony.

"Tony and I were supposed to go camping. When we met at my house, he seemed kind of upset. He said a man had called him, claiming to know about his parents—his real parents. The man told Tony he was an investigative reporter working on a story about a Cuban boat incident, and he had information that might help Tony find his family."

"It was my understanding that Tony had lost his entire family in some type of accident at sea," Tripp said. "I didn't know they were trying to escape from Cuba."

"Tony didn't know much either. Anyway, you can see how this phone call upset him," Stony said. "He said he needed to go home, that he forgot some of his gear, but he never came back to my house."

"Have you talked to his parents?"

"The Casteels went to LA for a wedding. I didn't want to upset them."

"They need to know their son is missing. We need to report this to the police," Tripp said.

"Tony made me promise not to say a word. The man on the phone told Tony if the wrong people learned of his investigation they could both be in great danger, and he would never see his sister or parents again. I was afraid to even say anything to you, but I had to tell someone, and I knew you used to be with the FBI. I was hoping you would know what to do."

"When did you talk with him last?" asked Tripp.

"Two days ago. I just know it has something to do with that phone call," Stony said.

Tripp was staring out over the bay. Nearly a minute passed in silence. He wasn't sure what exactly raised the red flag, but something in Stony's words was gnawing at Tripp to look a little deeper. Then, nodding his head as he reached a decision, Tripp promised Stony to do some discreet checking, asking him not to say anything to anyone else for the time being.

CHAPTER 2

*N*eil Manning was assigned to the bureau's regional field office in San Francisco and lived in a two-bedroom townhouse in Santa Cruz. While he tried to see his lifelong friend Sean Tripp on a regular basis, as a member of the antiterrorism task force he had little time for anything but work the entire year. Maybe he could get some time off for Christmas. He missed the camaraderie with Tripp and wished they still worked together. Neil had tried several times to convince Tripp to come back to work, but Tripp had always refused.

Their teammates at A&M used to call them Mutt and Jeff. Neil stood five foot seven inches in his bare feet and weighed 165 pounds. His commitment to boxing and lifting weights allowed him to maintain his muscular fullback physique. While he was no Sean Tripp, he possessed his own rugged attractiveness, with thick broad shoulders, sandy blond hair, and deep blue eyes. He never lost his penchant for beautiful women and Chivas Regal, preferably when it was from Tripp's supply cabinet. It was his friendship and undying sense of humor that had seen Tripp through his darkest hour.

When Manning's cell phone chirped, he immediately recognized the call was from Tripp. "I didn't take it," he answered after the first ring.

Manning had a key to Tripp's boat and lived less than an hour from Monterey. He had a long tradition of pilfering his friend's liquor cabinet.

"I'm not calling about the missing Chivas this time," Tripp answered. "I've got something I want to run by you, if you're not hot on the trail of Mullah Omar, that is."

"Let me guess," Manning interrupted. "The Mullah's moored right next to you, and you think he's after your liquor?"

Tripp ignored the jibe and continued, "Any chance you can break away and drive down to the boat? I'll even throw some steaks on the grill."

Manning could tell by the tone of Tripp's voice that it was something serious.

"I can be there in an hour," he said.

Manning clicked off, grabbed his keys, and headed for his Corvette. An hour later he turned onto Del Monte Avenue and parked next to the dock. He walked down the gangway and stepped onto the deck of the cruiser.

"I hope you remembered I like mine rare."

"If I remember correctly, you like it warmed a bit on each side, but still bleeding," Tripp answered.

"I just don't want to hear it moan when I stick the fork in," said Manning.

"Help yourself to a drink. I think you know where the liquor cabinet is," Tripp said with a smirk in his voice.

Tripp had learned in college that one of the best ways to attract women was to cook for them. What started out as a gimmick to pick up girls had become a lifelong passion. He appreciated the opportunity to cook, even for an old football buddy.

After the steak dinner, which included a Caesar salad and baked potato, Manning poured himself another drink and said, "Okay, so tell me what you've got."

Tripp pushed back from the table and told him about Tony's disappearance and the phone call.

Manning listened quietly, then said, "Sean, you do realize you're talking about a teenage boy here. He may simply be busy being a teenager. What makes you think he's not a typical boy out feeling his oats?"

"I don't know exactly, it's just a gut feeling," Tripp said.

Manning had been around Tripp long enough to trust in his friend's gut-feelings. Finally, Manning asked, "Do the local police have anything?"

"No. I called the chief earlier today. He said all they could do is put him down as a runaway. They need the Casteels to file a missing persons report," Tripp said.

"Have you talked to them?"

"Stony said they're due home tonight. I'd rather talk to them face to face."

"But knowing you, you have a plan," Manning said, draining his glass.

"I was thinking we could start by checking the phone records to see if we can find where the call came from," Tripp said.

"I think we should also get with Social Services and check the records on Tony's adoption to see what we can find out about his family before he was placed here. We'll need court orders, so I'll get to work on those," Manning said.

"Thanks."

"Call me after you talk with the Casteels."

CHAPTER
3

Tony Casteel, his head resting against the window of the bus, watched the countryside drift past. It was early December and a light snow was falling. The flakes swirling past the window added to his sense that this was all a surrealistic dream. Tony, nineteen years old now, had been only four when he lost his parents and sister at sea. After he was placed with his new family, he had managed to block out the few memories he had of his past. However, the snow reminded him of a dream he used to have when he was a little boy. He was curled up in his father's lap—not Armando Casteel, another man, a man who promised to take him to Switzerland and teach him how to ski.

Tony was a bright young man, quiet, intelligent, and liked by his teachers and peers. He was short and lean at five foot five inches and 165 pounds. He had black hair, brown eyes, and dark olive-colored skin. He played practically every sport offered in high school, but he excelled at soccer.

The voice from the telephone kept playing over in his mind: "I can help you find your parents."

Tony couldn't understand how that could be, but the man sounded convincing. The man on the telephone went on to say, "I've been working on this story for weeks and have put myself in great danger, but with your help, Tony, I'm confident I can find them. You do want to see your real parents, don't you, Tony?"

Tony loved the Casteels, but he was curious as to who his real parents were. He could never understand what would have compelled them to take their young child on a risky sea expedition.

"Sure," Tony responded, a lump rising in his throat.

"Tony, it is imperative that you tell no one about our conversation. You must immediately find your way to Miami. Once you arrive, take a taxi to the La Carreta Inn on Calle Ocho in the Little Havana district. I'll meet you there."

"But—" Before Tony could ask another question, the phone went dead. He pressed the caller ID button, but all that showed on the display was "Private," with no number.

His parents were out of town and he was supposed to go camping with Stony. He went to his friend's house and without thinking, still mulling the conversation over, told Stony about the call. Then, remembering the caller's stern warning, Tony stuttered an excuse that he needed to go get some more gear. He ran home and got his backpack. His parents kept a stash of emergency cash in a soup can in the cupboard; he grabbed it, then headed downtown to the bus station.

The bus skidded slightly on the wet road, jolting Tony from his thoughts. He had no idea what he was getting himself into, but he knew he had to see it through. The snow had stopped, replaced by a slow, steady drizzle. Tony grabbed an apple from his backpack, pulled his jacket up tight around his neck, and looked back out the window.

CHAPTER
4

$\mathcal{T}$ripp woke early the following morning. After two cups of black coffee and a breakfast consisting of three eggs, two sausage links, and toast with strawberry jam, he shaved, showered, and dressed in khaki slacks and a teal polo shirt. The Casteels had still not been home when he had gone to Tony's house the previous evening. He hoped they were back now. His plans were to swing by the Casteels' house, then go over to see Chief of Police Jim Taylor. Tripp hopped in his Jeep Cherokee, turned onto Pacific Street, and was at the Casteels' door twenty minutes later.

Tony's adoptive father, Armando Casteel, immediately recognized Tripp and welcomed him in.

"I'd like to speak with you about Tony if you have a few minutes," Tripp said.

"Have you seen him? Have you talked to him?" Armando asked anxiously. "We thought he'd be back from his camping trip by now. We tried to reach him, but he left his cell phone in the kitchen."

"No, I haven't," Tripp answered. "I don't want to alarm you, but you need to go down to the station and file a missing persons report."

"He's camping with Stony."

"No, he's not." Tripp told them about his conversation with Stony. Mrs. Casteel began to sob.

"This could all just be a prank, but we don't want to take any chances," Tripp said, trying to soothe the anxious parents. "If Tony has left for Florida, then this is an interstate matter, which means we can get help from the FBI."

"The FBI—I don't understand," Armando said.

"I used to work for the FBI. My old partner Neil Manning is with the bureau in San Francisco. He is willing to help, and so am I."

"Anything you can do to help find Tony would be appreciated," Tina Casteel replied. "Can I get you some coffee, Mr. Tripp?" she asked.

"No, thank you. Two cups is my limit," Tripp answered.

"We both want you to know how grateful we are," Tina said.

"I don't want to give you false hopes, but I will do what I can," Tripp replied.

"Please have a seat and tell us how we can help," Armando said.

They sat at the table and Tripp said, "Tell me what you know about Tony's past and how you came to adopt him."

There were a few moments of silence before Armando spoke.

"All we were told was that he was rescued when his family was trying to flee from Cuba. The family he arrived with told the authorities that about halfway through their voyage, while they were in international waters, they had come under attack. The people who reached U.S. soil told immigration they were able to rescue Tony and escape partly because the rest of his family stayed behind to fight, allowing Tony and his guardian family time to get away."

"According to U.S. law, if a Cuban refugee touches American soil, he can stay," Tripp said, voicing his understanding of the situation.

"Yes," said Armando. "At some point Social Services became involved and decided it was in Tony's best interest to find him a home with a family who could love him and take care of him properly. The guardian family's only request was that he be placed somewhere on the West Coast. They felt it would be better for Tony to start a new life somewhere far away. So that is how we were able to adopt him. We had been looking to adopt for ages when the Social Services office in San Jose called and told us about Tony."

Armando paused and looked at his wife, whose eyes were red and swollen with tears. He continued, "For months Tony had nightmares. Countless nights we sat up with him, talking him through his fears. We realized it was best to put his past behind him, and we never talked about it again."

There was silence for almost a minute. Then Tripp looked at Tina and said, "But there is more, isn't there?"

Tina looked at Armando, as though searching for approval before she spoke.

"A child never forgets the love of a parent. Tony told me he wished he could find out what really happened to his parents and why they were not in his life anymore."

"Tina, you never told me this before," said Armando.

"He was afraid he would seem ungrateful."

"He will always be our son," Armando said, putting his arms around his tearful wife.

CHAPTER 5

_N_eil Manning pulled into the regional FBI headquarters in San Francisco early Sunday morning. He parked his Corvette at the far end of the covered parking lot, as he always did, to ensure that no one would park too close and possibly scratch the paint.

Manning had called headquarters the night before and found Dana Whitten still at work. Dana was one of the duty officers and a friend he often worked with when he was in the field. He told Dana about Tony Casteel and asked her to pull the phone records of the Casteel home for the last month, and to find a judge who would sign the orders he would need to cut through the red tape at Social Services.

Manning went directly to his office, poured some coffee, and checked his messages. Dana had left a message that she would leave the phone records on his desk, and she had found a judge to sign the court orders. A courier would deliver them to headquarters by 9:00 a.m. Manning called the front security desk and left a message that he was expecting a courier, asking security to buzz him as soon as the documents arrived.

He picked up the phone and pressed a button. "Jenner, I need a favor," he said into the phone.

After a brief discussion, the assistant director, Roland Jenner, agreed to do some research on Cuban defections in 1992. As Manning hung up, the front desk buzzed him that the documents he was expecting had arrived.

He took a sip of coffee and began to scan through the phone log. He decided to start with the long-distance calls first. There were two calls from Denver, a call from Minneapolis, a call from Miami, and one from Phoenix.

The two calls from Denver were from a Romero Casteel, probably a relative, Manning thought. The call from Minneapolis had been placed from an office at the 3M Corporation. The call from Miami was from a pay phone. And finally, the call from Phoenix was from a Hector Alvarez. Manning took another sip of coffee and looked back at the call from Miami. The address, he noted, was placed from a pay phone in a section of town known as Little Havana.

While he was pondering the possible connections, his phone rang. It was Jenner. He told Manning about a reconnaissance report that had been filed regarding Manuel Favela, a top general to Fidel Castro and a suspected drug contact in the Miami area, who had tried to flee Cuba in 1992 with his family. Based on the details in the top-classified report, Manning began to consider the possibility that Manuel Favela might be Tony Casteel's biological father.

CHAPTER 6

The bus pulled into the terminal in Dallas. Tony Casteel had to change buses again and was looking at a three-hour layover this time. It was early December, but as he stepped off the bus he was greeted with an unseasonal blast of Texas heat. They had long since left the snow and cold of New Mexico, and he wondered to himself how hot it must get here during the summer.

This was Tony's second day on the bus, and his legs and rear end were beginning to get sore, so he decided to spend a couple hours exploring downtown Dallas and stretch his legs. Tony passed a restaurant with a sign in the window that read, "Texas' Best BBQ." He had spent the last three days living off apples, pears, and granola bars and had been longing for some real food; he decided to splurge and have a BBQ plate dinner. The meal consisted of sliced beef, pinto beans, potato salad, pickles, onions, saltine crackers, sweet iced tea, and a dessert of banana pudding.

When Tony finished his meal, he continued with his exploration. As he walked along, Christmas shoppers passed with their gifts and packages. Store windows were brightly decorated with ornaments, tinsel, and scenes of families gathered around the Christmas tree. Tony began to feel homesick, thinking about the special times he had spent with his family. He thought about the Christmas they had spent at Keystone, Colorado, skiing and sleigh riding during the day and ice skating around a giant, beautifully lit Christmas tree at night. The memories made him want to turn back and go home.

But he was also beginning to have the sense of other memories—another mother's loving arms; someone, a girl, leaning over him, tickling him; a man throwing him a ball. These memories had been suppressed for so long they were little more than impressions, but they were none the less real.

Tony missed his parents. By now they would be home from LA, and he knew they would be worried. He searched in his backpack for his cell phone but could not find it. He sprinted back to the bus station to see if he had dropped it on the bus, but the bus he had arrived on had already left. Tony glanced up and saw a CVS across Commerce Street. He went to the drugstore and found a prepaid phone and phone cards on an end cap. The prepaid phone and minutes took almost all of the cash he had left.

Tony dialed his parents' number, but as the phone rang a third time, Tony remembered another voice saying, "If anyone finds out about this, we will both be in great danger and you will never see your parents again."

Tony's mother picked up on the fourth ring. He heard her beautiful warm voice answer, "Hello?"

Tony hung up, and the line went dead.

CHAPTER 7

ripp left the Casteels' home, backed the Jeep out of the driveway, and headed to Police Chief Taylor's home. His cell phone rang. "Talk to me, Neil," he said, recognizing the number. Manning filled him in on what he had learned from Jenner.

Tony's father had held a high position in Castro's regime. Could this be true? Tripp wondered.

"What would make a high-ranking general want to flee?" Manning asked Tripp.

"Freedom," Tripp responded.

"Ah, Sean, always the romantic. My guess is money."

"Ah, Neil, always the cynic," Tripp said, then hung up.

Tripp turned north onto Lighthouse Avenue. The view in front of him looked out over the bay, where dozens of expensive sailboats were tacking against the offshore breeze. *Maybe Manning's right*, he mused. *Freedom* and *money*.

Ten minutes later, Tripp pulled into Chief Taylor's driveway. Taylor was in the yard watering what looked like a variety of hearty weeds but was in fact the chief's lawn. Tripp shut off the engine, stepped from the Jeep, and said, "How often do you have to water those weeds to get 'em that healthy?'

Taylor, dressed in jeans and a navy T-shirt, grinned and said, "I'm just waiting for the bureau to send Fox Mulder to check them out. No matter how many times I kill them, they come right back.... I think they're alien."

Taylor laid the hose down, turned the water off, and said, "Come on in, I just made some fresh lemonade."

Chief Taylor lived in a modest, well-kept, three- bedroom frame house painted white with green trim. As he poured two glasses of iced lemonade, Tripp sat on a bar stool facing the kitchen.

Taylor looked at Tripp and said, "So tell me, have you come up with anything on the Casteel kid?"

Tripp told Taylor about the Castro connection, but decided not to mention the suspicion of money. "If Tony's father really is alive and was a part of the Castro regime, and if Tony is trying to find him, he could be walking into a hornet's nest," said Tripp.

Taylor handed Tripp the glass of lemonade, sat on a stool next to him, and mused, "Could be his father's not alive and there's nothing to that telephone call; maybe it's extortion."

"The Casteels aren't rich. What's the motive?"

"Could just be a story Tony made up to get his friend to cover for him. Kids take off all the time."

Tripp took a sip of his drink and said, "You told me you checked with Amtrak, the bus terminal, and the rental agencies, but got nothing?"

"Nothing solid," Taylor replied. "We got zip at Amtrak and the car rentals. There was a kid working at the bus station who recognized Tony's picture. Said he had played soccer with him and may have seen him, but was busy loading luggage and wasn't sure."

Tripp thought a moment and finally asked, "Chief, do they have video monitors at the bus station?"

"As a matter of fact, I believe they do," Taylor answered.

"I think I'd like to have a look at those tapes," Tripp said.

"I think it's a stretch, but I'll make the call and have them give you complete access. If you'd like, I can give you some manpower to go through the tapes," Taylor offered.

"Thank you, Chief," Tripp said. "And one more thing," he continued, "can you get me the name of the kid at the bus station who thought he saw Tony?"

Taylor reached for the phone and said, "It'll only take a minute."

Tripp finished his lemonade while Taylor made the call. Tripp knew it was a long shot, but he also knew it was all they had right now.

Taylor hung up the phone and said, "The kid's name is Oscar Trevino."

Tripp thanked Chief Taylor and said he would let himself out.

As Tripp started for the Jeep, Taylor walked out and returned to his lawn. Tripp got in the Jeep, started the engine, rolled down his window, and said to Chief Taylor, "I'll let Mulder know you're waiting for him."

CHAPTER

*C*nemencio Vargas sat on the edge of his bed at the El Sereno Inn. It had been four days since he had made the call to California, and he was growing tired of the wait. His orders were to stay close and report back when Casteel checked in. At first he was sure Casteel would show, but as the days passed, he began to wonder if he was wrong. His orders were clear, and he did not want to think about failure.

Vargas was well known in the exile community as the man to go to when a *special* kind of help was required. He was equally well known in Havana and was often called upon for his "services." Vargas knew he walked a thin line, working both sides of the exile movement, and he had powerful contacts in both Miami and Havana who often referred to him as "Padron."

Vargas, a muscular man with deep bronze skin, thick black hair, and tattoos covering his upper arms and back, stood and walked to the window. It was a beautiful sunny south Florida morning. The street was crowded with shoppers and tourists all busily going about their business. The Domino Club two doors down, where he had spent much of his time the past several days, was in full swing. He turned and glanced across the street at the La Carreta Inn, wondering if this would be the day, when the phone rang.

The familiar voice on the other end of the line belonged to Rogelio Cruz, an agent of the Direccion General de Intelligencia, or DGI, the Cuban equivalent of America's CIA. The ominous voice, deep and scratchy from years of heavy smoking, asked in clear, precise Spanish, "Do you have anything to report?"

"I have nothing yet," Vargas answered in Spanish with a thick Cuban accent. "I'm watching the entrance and lobby, and I have an understanding with the hotel manager. I paid him a generous tip to let me know if anyone matching Casteel's description checks in. He will be here soon," Vargas said, hoping his voice didn't reveal his growing doubt.

"He better be there soon," Cruz warned. "We have been there for you countless times. I don't need to tell you that should you fail, our arrangement with you will be at great risk."

"The boy's been missing for almost fifteen years. Why this need for urgency now?"

"Only recently, through a series of fortunate circumstances, were we able to locate him. Also, the old man is sick. There may not be much time left," Cruz answered. "But it is not your concern, Enemencio. Your only concern is to get the boy. Just do what you must to cause it to happen."

CHAPTER 9

*N*eil Manning was still looking through the Casteels' phone records when his intercom buzzed. It was his administrative assistant, Karen Turner.

"Mr. Manning, the other documents you've been waiting for are here," she said.

Karen, a tall, slim, and attractive brunette with soft brown eyes, had been with the bureau for twelve years, the last eight working for Neil. While she was intelligent and efficient, Neil most appreciated that she was dependable and had kept him out of trouble on more than one occasion.

Manning asked her to bring the papers in, then clicked off and dialed Tripp's cell number. Tripp answered after the second ring and gave Manning a rundown of his conversation with Armando and Tina Casteel.

"A high position in Castro's regime.... Did they know the father's name?" Manning asked.

"No, but I'm hoping we can get that at Social Services. Did you find a judge to sign the orders that we'll need to check Tony's adoption records?"

"Yes. They arrived only minutes ago, and I found something interesting in the Casteels' phone records. A call was placed a week ago from Miami. A pay phone in Little Havana, to be precise," Manning said.

"I would say that sounds like more than a mere coincidence," Tripp said.

"I'd be willing to bet a bottle of scotch on it," Manning replied.

"I hope you don't bet with scotch too often; I'm not sure I can afford it," Tripp said.

"The Social Services office in San Jose will be closed today. I'll make some calls and see if we can find someone to open up for us," Manning said.

"Call me when you get someone. I've got one more stop to make and I'll meet you at your place. It may be nothing, but I want to run by the bus station."

CHAPTER 10

Tripp turned back onto Lighthouse Avenue, this time heading south. The traffic was light and once again he glanced out over the waters of the Pacific.

The sailboats he had seen earlier were still dancing across the surface. Tripp focused on one of the boats, a thirty-seven-foot Seafarer, white with turquoise trim, similar to the one he and Katie had rented for their honeymoon. They had sailed down to Catalina Island and spent the week diving and swimming with dolphins. He remembered how beautiful Katie was and how she seemed most happy when with the dolphins. After sunset she loved dining on deck under the stars, looking out over the sparkling lights of the coastline. Tripp smiled as he remembered how Katie thought the lights looked like a huge diamond necklace stretched out along the beach. He also remembered how much he had looked forward to the years they would share together.

A car's horn blaring as he approached Del Monte Avenue broke him from his thoughts, and he turned left toward the bus station. Five minutes later he parked the Jeep and walked inside. It was noisy, with some of the crowd huddled together waiting to board while others excitedly looked for friends and family getting off of the arriving buses. Most were carrying colorful bags decorated for the season.

Tripp walked to the ticket window and asked to speak with the station manager. While waiting, he looked around the station and toward the ceiling. He spotted a video camera in the corner next to a sparsely decorated Christmas tree.

A few minutes later a tall, wiry man with pale skin and bushy eyebrows opened an office door, extended his hand, and said, "Mr. Tripp, my name is Sam Friedman. Chief Taylor called and said you'd be dropping by. I don't know the Casteels, but I will help you any way I can."

Tripp shook his hand and said, "Thank you, and please call me Sean. I'm sure you're busy, so I won't take a lot of your time."

Friedman said, "Follow me, Sean; we can talk in my office."

They walked down a cramped corridor to a surprisingly big paneled office. Friedman sat at his desk and offered Tripp a chair.

He pointed to an oak cabinet and said, "The video tapes Taylor called about are in that cabinet, and you're welcome to use the monitor here in my office."

Thanking Friedman again for his courtesy, Tripp said, "That would be great, but first I was hoping to speak with one of your employees. I understand Oscar Trevino works for you?"

"Yes, Oscar has been with us for almost a year. Would you like me to call him in?"

"Yes, if you will."

Friedman left the room and Tripp walked over to the cabinet where the tapes were stored. They were all in order and labeled by date, going back two weeks.

A few minutes later Friedman returned, accompanied by a young man.

"Mr. Tripp, this is Oscar Trevino."

Oscar was twenty years old, clean-shaven, and neatly dressed in tan overalls. He was wearing earphones around his neck and an Ipod was clipped to his belt.

Tripp walked over, shook Oscar's hand, and said, "Hi, Oscar, I understand you know Tony Casteel?"

Oscar smiled and said, "Yes, sir, we played soccer together when I was in high school."

"Chief Taylor told me you may have seen him here at the station recently."

"It may have been Tony. As I told the police, I was busy, and the station was crowded, so I'm not really sure."

"Do you remember what day that was, Oscar?"

"Well, I was off yesterday, so it had to have been Friday."

"And do you remember what time it was when you saw him?"

"I'm not sure, sir, but I know it was midmorning. My shift started at 8:00 and I hadn't had a break yet. I remember I was going to talk to him on my break, but he was gone by then."

Tripp walked to the cabinet, pulled out the video with Friday's date on it, and said, "Oscar, I want us to view this tape together, and I want you tell me if you see the boy that looked like Tony."

Friedman set the monitor on the conference table and put the tape in. The tape started at 6:00 a.m., so Tripp fast-forwarded it until the counter read 9:00 a.m.

They had been watching for about forty-five minutes when Oscar pointed to the screen and said, "That's him!"

Tripp paused the tape and asked, "Which one do you think is Tony?"

Oscar walked over to the monitor and pointed to a young man sitting near a soda machine.

"That's him there; it's Tony, I'm sure of it."

Tripp focused on the fuzzy image; he agreed with Oscar's identification.

"Thank you, Oscar, you've been a terrific help."

"I hope you find him," Oscar replied. "I don't know him well, but he was always kind to me."

As Oscar left to go back to work, Tripp turned to Friedman and said, "Now, let's see where our young Mr. Casteel was off to."

They watched the video for another twenty minutes before Tony finally got up and boarded a bus.

Tripp once again paused the video and said, "I need to know where that bus was headed."

Friedman moved to his desk, clicked on his computer, and said, "Read me the number on the bus."

Tripp looked close and said, "Looks like N1200."

Friedman punched some more keys and finally said, "Bus N1200 left here Friday morning, headed for Dallas. The manifest shows that the passengers on that bus were transferring to Chicago, San Antonio, and Atlanta, and one was headed to Miami, Florida."

CHAPTER
11

*M*anning left his office, caught the elevator up one floor, walked to the end of the hall, and entered Assistant Director Jenner's outer office.

Roland Jenner was a heavyset man with an intelligent face and a ring of silver-white hair circling his head. He had begun his long career with the FBI at Quantico, where he finished first in his training class. He was then assigned to the New York office and spent most of his time working with security at the United Nations. After New York, he moved on to Washington, D.C., to head a newly formed crimes unit to fight drug trafficking, his primary focus Latin America. Over the years, he worked throughout the country, including an extended stint in Miami, and eventually landed in San Francisco as assistant director, concentrating on terrorism.

Like Tripp, his true passion was for the water. Whenever he wasn't in his office, which was most days, including weekends, he'd be either hip deep in a cold stream fly-fishing for trout or out deep-sea fishing for marlin. While others decorated their offices with family photos, his office walls were filled with photos and relics of his fishing exploits.

Manning waited only a couple of minutes before he was buzzed in.

Jenner stood and met Manning halfway from the door, shook his hand, and said, "I'm glad you came by, Neil. How is everything?"

"Everything is great," Manning replied.

"How's Tripp coming along? Have you seen him lately?"

"He's doing well, moving on with his life. As a matter of fact, I saw him only yesterday. That's why I came to see you. He's the one that got the tip."

"The Cuban connection you asked me to drop everything for a couple of hours ago?"

Manning told Jenner what he and Tripp had found so far. Both men were well aware of the implications all this could have for Tripp. Tripp's wife Katie had been killed in Miami while working on a drug sting that was closely tied to a Cuban drug lord.

When he finished, Jenner said, "I want you to work with Tripp and see if you can find out who Tony's father really is, then get with our Cuban bureau in Miami to see what they have on him."

Manning left the federal building, returned to the parking lot, and frowned when he saw someone had parked on his end of the lot. They were several spaces from his Corvette, but still too close. He got in his car, peeled out of the parking lot, and headed toward Santa Cruz. Once he was on U.S. 101 he punched in Tripp's cell number.

Tripp answered after the first ring and asked Manning where he was.

"I'll be in Santa Cruz in about an hour. I've got a contact in San Jose who can meet us at Social Services. Can you meet me at the house? We can grab a bite and drive over."

"I'll be there, and I've got another bit of information. Tony boarded a bus Friday bound for Miami."

"When is he scheduled to arrive?"

"Tomorrow morning."

CHAPTER
12

$\mathcal{T}$ ripp left the bus terminal, pulled back onto Del Monte Avenue, and merged onto Highway 1 north toward Santa Cruz. Traffic was light on this Sunday afternoon, and in less than an hour he turned onto West Cliff Drive, pulled into Manning's circular drive, and parked behind the familiar red Corvette.

Tripp let himself in and called out, "Anybody home?"

"I'm in the kitchen. Come on in," Manning replied.

Tripp made his way to the kitchen and found Manning standing over the stove. Smelling spaghetti sauce, he queried, "I cook a steak dinner for you and you give me spaghetti?"

"This is a special recipe handed down from my grandmother. She was Italian and took great pride in her sauce. What I'm preparing for you is a part of my family heritage…. Besides, it's quick and easy, and we've got to get over to San Jose pronto. There's some red wine in the cabinet; how about making yourself useful and pouring us a glass."

Tripp found a corkscrew in the cabinet, pulled the cork, and poured two glasses. He stepped to the closet to toss the cork away and noticed the Ragu spaghetti sauce jar in the trash bin, but decided not to mention it.

They had dinner on the patio overlooking the ocean. It was midafternoon and there was a slight breeze coming in off the Pacific. They ate quietly for a few minutes before Manning took a sip of wine and said, "Assistant Director Jenner sends his regards."

"So how is Jenner? I haven't talked with him in months."

"He's well. I spoke to him this morning about this situation with Tony. He wants me to work with you and see where this thing leads."

"I guess he's wondering about the Cuban connection?" Tripp asked.

"Actually, I think he just wanted me to keep an eye on you, but let's give him the benefit of the doubt."

"Well, if you're going to keep an eye on me, you better finish up. I want to get over to San Jose and look at those records," Tripp said. Twenty minutes later Tripp turned the Jeep onto Highway 17 toward San Jose. Earlier that morning, Manning had spoken with Bernice Johnson, an adoption caseworker, and she had agreed to meet them at the office. Manning pulled out his cell phone and made a short call.

"Ms. Johnson is at the office now and is expecting us," Manning said.

In another twenty minutes, Tripp parked the Jeep in front of the adoption agency and shut off the engine. The office door was locked, so Manning dialed the cell phone number his connection at Social Services had given him. A few seconds later an older black woman appeared at the door, unlocked it, and let them in.

Manning said, "Ms. Johnson, I'm Neil Manning and this is Sean Tripp. I want to thank you for seeing us today."

Bernice Johnson, a pleasant, motherly lady dressed in a black and white pants suit, shook Manning's and Tripp's hands and said, "You're quite welcome. I had some work to catch up on anyway. I pulled the file you asked about. Do you have the court orders allowing me to show it to you?"

Manning pulled the orders from his suit pocket and handed them to her. She looked them over, then locked the outer door and asked them to follow her to the conference room.

The room was sparsely decorated with artificial flowers and various pictures of rural scenes. Bernice invited them to sit at the conference table and pulled a file from a desk. She sat at the table across from Tripp and Manning and pushed the file across the desk.

Manning opened the file and began to leaf through the documents. Tripp pulled up closer and looked on. The first document was the record of adoption. It announced the adoption of

Tony Arollo Favela
to
Mr. Armando Leon Casteel
and
Mrs. Tina Elaine Casteel

The following page was a decree showing the adoptee's change of name. Attached to it was a copy of a new birth certificate with the name Tony Arollo Casteel.

The next several pages were psychological reports on Tony, Armando, and Tina. Then there were several copies of the Casteels' financial records. Following this was a lengthy report from the Social Services office in Miami. Manning and Tripp quickly scanned the report. It included a detailed account of how one Guillermo Gonzalez had come to have custody of Tony.

The following account was Guillermo Gonzalez's testimony:

*My family and I were on one of four small boats that left Cuba
for Miami. Tony and his family were on one of the other boats.
Many miles into the voyage we came under attack. We were
armed and initially tried to fend off the attack. It soon became
obvious we were outgunned, and it was decided we would split
up. Three of the boats would stay behind and continue the fight,
while the other would make for Miami to get the children to
safety. Tony's father began to pass his children over to my boat,
but I was only able to get Tony aboard before I was forced to leave.
The fighting was fierce and I left at full speed. I watched the scene
until it disappeared behind me, and I never saw the others again.*

The account was interesting but unhelpful, and both Tripp
and Manning were growing increasingly frustrated. They had
gone through almost the entire file without finding the names of
Tony's true parents. Finally, on the last page, they found what
they had been looking for. It was a single, double-spaced page
that listed four names:

- - - *Tony Arollo Favela* - - - *Adoptee*
- - - *Manuel Ramon Favela* - - - *Father (deceased)*
- - - *Amalia Arollo Favela* - - - *Mother (deceased)*
- - - *Carmen Rene Favela* - - - *Sister (deceased)*

So there it was. Both men instantly recognized the Favela
name. Manuel Favela was believed to be connected with the
same drug lord at the center of the failed sting that Katie Tripp
had been working on. The two men stared at the page in silence.

Finally Manning looked up and asked, "When did you say
Tony's bus is scheduled to arrive in Miami?"

Tripp closed the file and said, "Tomorrow morning."

CHAPTER 13

$\mathcal{T}$ony was lying back in the seat half asleep when he glanced out the window and saw the sign he'd been waiting for: "Miami City Limits." His heart raced as he realized his long journey was almost over and he would find his parents after all these years.

He was wide awake now, his eyes glued to the window. Like a child eager to get to grandma's house at Christmas, Tony watched as they passed exits for Bay Harbor Islands, Miami Shores, and Bayshore. Tony saw the IH 195 exit for Miami Beach ahead, and when the bus slowed down to exit he thought he might get to see the celebrated beach he'd heard so much about, but the bus instead turned right onto Highway 112 toward the airport and bus terminal. Ten minutes later the bus slowed, pulled into the terminal, and came to the final stop.

Tony grabbed his backpack, slung a strap over one shoulder, and joined the line to file off the bus. The terminal was noisy and crowded as he fought his way through. He spotted a map of Miami half covered with notices and business cards, and began looking for Eighth Street. Tony found the street, and although it wasn't terribly far, he decided not to walk. He was hesitant to use what money he had, but decided a cab would be best since he wasn't sure where the hotel was anyway. He made his way outside, found a taxi, tossed his backpack into the backseat, hopped in, and closed the door behind him.

The driver, an amiable young Hispanic man, asked Tony, "*Donde va?* Where are you going, *amigo?*"

Tony said, "I need to get to the La Carreta Inn on Calle Ocho."

The driver started the meter, smiled at Tony, and said, "Sit back, *amigo*, I know it well. I'll have you there in no time."

Tony was quietly looking out the window when the driver asked him, "Are you new to Miami?"

"Yes, this is my first time here," Tony answered.

"Where are you from?"

"I'm from Monterey, California."

The driver turned left on 386, whistled, and said, "Monterey Bay…you're a long way from home, *amigo*. What brings you to our city?"

"I'm hoping to meet some family I haven't seen in a while."

"I see," he said. "A Christmas reunion, *amigo?*"

"Yeah…. A Christmas reunion," Tony said, his voice trailing off.

"Miami *esta ven bonito de la Navida*…a beautiful city at Christmas. I hope you have a nice stay."

Tony didn't respond.

The cabbie continued, "There are many places to visit right there on Calle Ocho." He turned right onto SW 17th Street and said, "Maximo Gomez Park is close. You can see the giant mural that portrays the Summit of the Americas. It is also known as Domino Park and you'll know why—it's where the old men gather to play dominoes. And not far from there is Little Havana's Paseo de las Estrellas, the walk of stars. It's similar to the one in your California, except the stars are given to Latin American actors. I think you would enjoy it very much, *amigo.*"

"What I'd really like is a place to eat," Tony said.

They made a left turn onto Eighth Street, and the cab driver said, "Then I know just the place for you, *amigo.* El Pescador is one of the best restaurants in Miami, and it's right here on Calle Ocho."

"I'll remember to try it," Tony answered.

The driver pulled into the hotel's drive and said, "Here we are, *amigo*, La Carreta Inn. I hope you have a pleasant stay, and I wish you a happy Christmas."

Tony reached for his money, but the cabbie said, "There is no charge this time, *amigo.* You're a long way from home. I hope you meet your family. That is my Christmas wish for you." Tony paused a moment, grabbed his backpack, and stepped out of the cab. Before closing the door he looked at the driver and said, "Thank you, and Merry Christmas to you too, *amigo.*"

The cab pulled away and Tony stood there looking at the marquee. "La Carreta Inn," he read aloud. He slipped the backpack over his shoulder, walked through the portico, and entered the hotel. The huge lobby was decorated in a Latin American motif, with high vaulted ceilings, marble tile floors, and plush sectional sofas backed by massive floor-to-ceiling gilded mirrors. As Tony looked around the lobby he listened to the soft shuffle and murmur of guests as they milled about. He could also hear the rhythmic sound of Latin music coming from the club room somewhere behind a tall, colorfully decorated Christmas tree at the rear of the lobby.

The day was quickly fading to evening and Tony was hungry, having not eaten since a quick bus stop at breakfast. He crossed the lobby to the desk, stepped up to a clerk, and told him he needed a room for the night, possibly longer.

The clerk eyed him suspiciously, but remembered he was to be on the lookout for a Cuban American teenager traveling alone. "Welcome. *Feliz Navidad*," the clerk welcomed Tony, handing him a registration form.

While Tony filled out the form, the desk clerk stepped into a side office. He dialed a number, spoke softly into the receiver, and then returned to the desk, where he informed Tony he would be in room 315. Tony asked where he could get a bite to eat, and the clerk told Tony the hotel had a fine restaurant just down the corridor past the clubroom. Tony thanked him and reached into his pocket, his remaining cash wadded in his palm.

"We'll settle up at the end of your stay," the clerk said. "Just put your room number on any bill you get from the waiter."

Tony thanked him and collected his room key. He then turned and headed toward the restaurant.

Tony was quickly seated, and soon a waitress brought him a menu and glass of water. She smiled and said she would give him a few minutes and be right back.

While Tony was studying the menu, a man entered the restaurant and began to study the diners. Without waiting to be seated, he took a table near the back with a clear view of Tony. The man's eyes never left Tony, even when the waitress brought him a menu; he told her he was waiting for a friend and wouldn't be ordering right away.

When Tony's waitress returned, Tony ordered a club sandwich, a pasta salad, and an iced tea. It wasn't long before his dinner arrived, and Tony ate slowly, thinking about what his future was to bring. He had no idea who he was to meet or how or when. The voice on the phone had only told him to check in and that he would be contacted. Fatigue suddenly overtook him, and he decided he would think about it all later; what he wanted immediately was a hot shower and a real bed. Tony left a tip, signed his bill, and walked back toward the lobby.

The bank of elevators was next to a flowing fountain shaped to look like a tall breaking wave with two dolphins riding the crest. The bottom of the fountain was covered with conch shells, starfish, and assorted reef formations. Tony pushed the elevator button and walked over to the fountain while he waited. The man from the restaurant followed Tony out of the restaurant and watched him walk to the elevators, then over to the fountain. He watched Tony close his eyes and toss in a coin. Then the elevator opened and Tony stepped inside.

After the doors closed, the man walked over and watched the elevator stop on the third floor.

The man whispered, "Have a nice rest, Tony Favela. I will see you in the morning."

Enemencio Vargas then turned, walked out the front door, and disappeared into the night.

CHAPTER
14

*I*t was late Sunday evening when Tripp and Manning returned home from their meeting with Bernice Johnson. On the drive back, Manning phoned Jenner and confirmed Tony's birth father's name. The assistant director was very familiar with the name Manuel Ramon Favela. Fully aware of the implications, he informed Manning he would contact the Miami office to let them know the situation.

Tripp and Manning made plans to meet at the airport the following morning to fly out to Miami. This would give Tripp time to file a flight plan, move his plane from the hangar, fuel up, and do a final visual inspection.

Tripp always moved his plane himself. He never allowed airport personnel to move the Beechcraft Bonanza G36 because it was parked next to his most prized possession: a 1957 Chevy Bel Air, two door, hard top, equipped with the original 283 eight-cylinder engine. He had upgraded it with a four-speed transmission, power steering, and air conditioning and restored the paint to its original colors of silver and black.

Tripp awoke before the alarm sounded the next morning. The sun had yet to rise, and the only light filtering into the cabin was from the full moon. During his time with the bureau, Tripp often woke before dawn, especially on mornings prior to going out on assignment. On those mornings he would look over at Katie as she slept, watching her chest rise and fall with each breath; he had never imagined she would be taken from him. As he turned his head to her side of the bed, a slit of moonlight fell across her picture on the nightstand. They had never caught the drug runners who had shot her and left her to die. Maybe this trip to Miami to rescue Tony, the same city where Katie had been taken from him, would give him an opportunity to bring closure, one way or another, to her death.

Tripp slipped on his robe, stumbled to the galley, and started a pot of coffee. He put some biscuits and breakfast sausage in the oven to warm, poured himself a cup of black coffee, and went up on deck. It was still dark except for the moon that had dipped farther down on the horizon and the strings of Christmas lights that had been strung around the marina. Tripp sipped his coffee and watched the multicolored lights flicker against the early morning blackness. He again thought about Katie and the Christmases they had spent together. It was times like this when he would vow to someday find those responsible for taking her from him and make them pay.

Tripp finished his breakfast of sausage, eggs, biscuits, and orange juice and returned to his cabin to shower and pack. After toweling off, Tripp shaved and put his toiletries into a leather Dop kit. He then packed a few changes of clothes into a matching leather bag. Next he stepped to the back of his closet, entered the combination to his safe, twisted the handle, and opened the heavy door. He briefly studied the contents. There were bundles of hundred-dollar bills, his passport and other personal documents, and his personal arsenal: a dozen various handguns and an assortment of shells. He chose the Glock and the smaller Kel-Tec, both of which used the same 9-mm shells. He also took a box of shells and three magazines. The magazines were stored empty to preserve their spring; he took a few minutes to load them. Finally he put the weapons, shoulder holster, leg holster, magazines, and a full box of ammo into the bag under his clothes. Dressing in a pair of lightweight khaki trousers, a sky-blue polo shirt, and a pair of walnut Top-Siders, he pulled on a navy sport jacket, grabbed his bag, and left for the airport.

Tripp turned into the airport parking lot and pulled up to his hangar just as the sun was beginning to break the horizon. He parked the Jeep, walked to the hangar, unlocked the door, and stepped inside, flipping on the lights and engaging the switch to raise the huge hangar door. The early morning sun bathed the hangar in a burnt orange glow, and a small smile formed on Tripp's lips as he turned to admire his '57 Chevy.

After calling in his flight plan, Tripp hopped on the golf cart he kept parked next to the Chevy, drove around facing the Bonanza, and attached the tow clip. He carefully backed the aircraft out and pulled it over for fueling. Finally, he pulled it back to the front of his hangar, unhooked the tow clip, and parked the golf cart back inside.

Tripp had been flying since his days in the army and had logged thousands of hours. He currently owned a Beechcraft Bonanza G36 variable pitch prop with a 300-horsepower TCM engine and retractable gear, with a top speed of 200 mph and a range of 1,100 miles. It seated six. The plane was equipped with a fully integrated GFC 700 autopilot, XM satellite with weather and terrain displays, and air conditioning. But what Tripp liked best was the relatively short distance it needed for takeoff and landing.

Tripp returned to the plane to do a visual inspection. He walked along the port side, running his hand along the fuselage, touching, stroking, feeling every inch of surface. He ran his hand along the flaps and leaned in to stroke the wing. He checked the engine cowling, looking for any sign of oil or fluids. Next, he knelt down to touch the tires and landing gear. Finally, he repeated the familiar preflight routine along the starboard side, the same routine he had followed for more than twenty years of piloting. He was almost finished when he looked up and saw Manning pull up and park his Corvette in the usual spot at the far end of the lot.

A few minutes later Manning strode up, stood behind Tripp, and said, "Do you need help winding up the rubber band?"

Tripp turned and smiled, his turquoise eyes beaming. "You know I'd let you, but I'm afraid you would wind it the wrong way, then we'd have to fly to Miami backwards."

With the preflight inspection complete, Tripp offered to let Manning park the Corvette in the hangar next to the Chevy. While Manning was parking the Corvette, Tripp grabbed his leather bag from the Jeep, climbed into the pilot's seat, and began the preflight systems check. Manning parked his car, closed and locked the hangar door, stowed his bag, and climbed into the copilot's seat. Once Manning was aboard, Tripp switched the engine tab to ON and cranked the engine. The engine immediately came to life. Tripp feathered the props and the engine settled into a smooth, deep growl.

With the systems check complete, Tripp and Manning buckled in and Tripp said, "All systems are go!"

Manning replied, "Take me to Miami, Jeeves."

Tripp taxied to the runway, checked the flaps, pointed the nose into the wind, and increased the throttle. The aircraft shot down the runway and lifted off. Tripp retracted the landing gear and began a slow, steady climb.

CHAPTER
15

The first light of dawn was breaking over Miami, and shafts of pale orange light began to filter through the window of the El Sereno Inn. Enemencio Vargas woke up and sat on the edge of his bed. He lit a cigarette, inhaled deeply, and grinned to himself as he thought about how well his plan to lure the boy to him had worked.

Vargas had called Havana the previous evening to report with confidence that Tony Favela was in Miami—alone. He was across the street at the La Carreta Inn. He would be delivered to Rogelio Cruz as promised.

The pale orange glow from Vargas' window morphed into streaks of gold. He walked to the window and looked across the street. A sense of relief came over him as he knew he would be free from the room that had imprisoned him for days—as soon as he delivered the boy. There was much to do, but he was ready. Two of his men were in position on the boat. Two would meet him here at his room. Now all he had to do was make the call.

An hour later there was a knock at the door. Vargas, dressed in a beige guayabera shirt with four pockets, brown trousers, and a matching brown sports jacket, was wiping down his gun. He checked to see that there was a shell in the chamber, walked to the door, and in his gruff voice asked, *"Quien es?* Who's there?"

"Juan and Benito," a voice replied.

Vargas let his men in, then closed and locked the door behind them.

"Is everything ready at the boat?" Vargas barked.

"*Si, todo esta bien.* Everything is set." Juan assured him.

"Okay, here's how we will do this. Park the car at the end of the block. You will both be in the front seat. When you see me walk out with the boy, pull to the front of the hotel. You, Benito, will step out and open the back door. When we are both in the car, drive directly to the dock."

"And if the boy refuses to enter the car?" Benito asked.

"You and I will see that he accepts our ride, but I do not expect a problem. The boy wants to see his parents again, and we are the ones trying to make that happen for him. That is what he believes. No more talk. It is time."

Vargas put his gun in his shoulder holster, walked to the desk, and dialed the number to the La Carreta Inn. After the second ring, the desk picked up. Vargas asked them to ring room 315.

Tony was still asleep, but he woke quickly when his phone rang. He rolled over and looked at the phone. He tried to imagine who could be calling him. No one here knew him, and no one knew he was here. The phone rang a second time, and his heart began to race. The voice he had heard on the phone a week ago in Monterey had said to check into the hotel and wait to be contacted.

"Could this be it?" he whispered to himself.

On the third ring Tony sat up and reached for the receiver.

"Hello," he said tentatively.

"I see you made it, Tony. Who knows you're here?" Vargas asked.

Tony recognized the voice. It was the same one he had heard a week earlier.

"Yes, I made it fine and I told no one, just as you said."

"That is good, Tony. You did well."

"Tell me about my parents. I did just as you said. Do you know where they are? Can you take me to them?"

"Yes, I can take you to them, but we must be very careful. I don't want to say any more on the phone. Can you be ready in thirty minutes?"

"Yes, I will be ready," Tony said.

"*Bueno*, it is now 8:30. I will meet you in the lobby at 9:00. You might want to bring a light jacket if you have one; we will be taking a short boat trip."

"What is your name? How will I know you?" Tony asked.

"I will find you. Be in the lobby in thirty minutes."

The line went dead and Tony returned the phone to the cradle. He scribbled a note on the hotel pad next to the phone to remember a light jacket for the boat trip...then put a question mark after it. He sat up in bed, rubbed his eyes, and looked around the room.

The room was simply furnished with wicker chairs and a table, a bamboo desk, and artificial palmetto plants. Several framed pastel pictures featuring beaches and seascapes hung from the walls. On the table sat a basket of fresh fruit.

Tony hopped off the bed, grabbed and peeled a banana, and walked to the window as he ate. The window overlooked the pool and courtyard. He was excited, but anxious; he finished the banana in three bites. Tony closed the curtain and turned and went into the bathroom. He stood under the hot water, and for the first time began to seriously consider this whole ordeal. Why the need for all the secrecy? Why should he be in great danger if he talked? And who was this mysterious contact? He briefly considered turning back and going home, but the hope of seeing his birth parents again was stronger than his anxiety. He had to see this through and find the truth.

Tony finished his shower and dressed. He wore a blue and gold pullover with "San Diego Chargers" across the front and the NFL logo on the collar, blue jeans, tennis shoes, and a denim jacket. He put everything back in his backpack and set it in the closet. He checked the time and found he had five minutes. He grabbed an apple from the fruit basket and headed for the lobby.

Vargas stood near the rear of the lobby behind a tall palm plant and watched as the elevator opened and Tony stepped out. He watched Tony walk past the fountain, turn toward the front door, and stop in front of a bay window facing the street. Vargas waited a minute longer to see if anyone was following. When he was satisfied that Tony was alone, he moved from behind the palm plant and turned toward the front of the lobby. He stopped a couple steps behind Tony, but his eyes were focused outside the window, looking for anything that didn't seem right.

After another minute, Vargas said in a low tone, "You're right on time, Tony. I hope you had a good rest after your journey."

Tony turned and looked at Vargas, finally able to put a face with the voice.

"I slept well, thank you. Tell me—you know my name, what is yours? And how do you know my parents?"

"My name is Enemencio Vargas. I am a reporter, and I am working on a story about your father."

"Can you tell me about my parents?"

"I will answer all your questions, but not here. This is a very delicate matter. My associates will meet us outside, and I will answer all your questions once we are in the car. Now, if you are ready, please follow me."

Tony and Vargas walked to the lobby door, through the portico, and stopped near the marquee. Ten seconds later, a black Cadillac with tinted windows pulled up in front of them and stopped. The passenger door opened and Benito stepped out.

He said *"Buenos dias"* to Tony and Vargas and then opened the rear door. Vargas motioned for Tony to slide in, but Tony paused. He looked at Vargas and said, "Where are you taking me?"

Vargas looked at Tony and said, "If we are not too late, I am taking you to your father."

Tony stood still for several seconds, then finally turned and slid into the backseat, closely followed by Vargas. Benito shut the door, got back in the front seat, and they sped off.

After a few minutes Tony said, "Now tell me what you know about my parents."

Vargas sat back, lit a cigarette, and said, "As I told you, I am a reporter. A while back, I was working on a story about Cuban refugees who sneak to America on small boats. In my background research I learned that your father—and you, for that matter—left Cuba that same way. I learned your father was once a very important man in Cuba, one of Castro's top generals. Not long after I began to research your father, I was cornered outside my apartment and quite firmly told to drop it. You see, it seems your father took something from El Presidente Castro, and Castro is not too keen on the embarrassment this would cause if word got out that his top general had betrayed him."

"Who told you to drop your story?"

"Let's just say they are comrades of Castro's."

"But you didn't drop it?"

"No, and that is why we must be very careful. You see, Castro has many *orejas*—ears—in America."

"And you found my parents?"

"I found your father. I was thinking he could tell you where your mother is."

"And how did you find me?"

"That was not hard. I am a reporter. I used my sources to check the records for you and your sister."

"You know where my sister is too?"

"No, not yet, but I am still working on it."

Tony sat quietly. His mind raced and his heart pounded. He wondered if he was actually close to finding his birth family again after all these years.

Finally he looked over at Vargas and said, "Where are you taking me now?"

"El Castillo del Morro."

"What is that, and where is it?"

"It is a small island fortress near Cuba. We will board my boat and should be there in a few hours."

"And my father is there? You have seen him?"

"No, I have not seen him, but my sources have been good so far."

Vargas snubbed out his cigarette just as the car began to turn onto the dock. The "boat," as Vargas called it, was a fifty-three-foot Navigator Pilothouse yacht, named *El Diablo Rojo*. The ship had three staterooms and was powered by twin 370 Volvo engines that could reach a top speed of forty-two knots.

Juan stopped the car in front of the ship. Benito stepped out, opened the rear door, and Vargas and Tony stepped out. Vargas saw two of his men in the pilothouse; they already had the engines running. As Vargas and Tony walked toward the ship, Juan and Benito left to park the car.

Vargas ushered Tony up the gangplank and said, "This is my little boat, Tony. There's food and drink in the galley below. And if you wish to rest, there are rooms below you can use. Make yourself comfortable and I'll have you there in no time."

Juan and Benito returned to the boat, released the mooring lines, and climbed aboard. As soon as they stepped aboard, the ship began to move slowly up the channel toward open seas. The tropical sun had begun to climb higher and now bathed the ship in rays of bright golden sunlight. The aqua blue waters of the Atlantic glistened around them as they began to throttle up. Within minutes they had moved into the open sea. Vargas climbed to the pilothouse and instructed the pilot to set a course for El Castillo del Morro. He then returned to the deck and his favorite leather chair, put on his Armani sunglasses, and sat back for the five-hour ride.

Tony sat near the stern and watched the long white wake stream up behind the boat. He thought about his father, his mother, and his sister, and about the last time they had all been together in these waters. Then he thought about his family in Monterey, remembering something his mother in Monterey often said, about how life goes in circles. He prayed that God was watching over his family and would allow him to complete the circle.

CHAPTER
16

As the Bonanza G36 neared Miami International Airport, Tripp reached down to disengage the autopilot. He then reached over and woke Manning, who had fallen asleep shortly after they refueled in San Antonio, Texas.

"We'll be landing soon. I thought you might want to watch my landing skills," Tripp said over the headset.

Manning opened one eye and said, "I'll appreciate your landing skills once we're safely on the ground."

"You know, you could have stayed awake and helped me out here."

"My faults are why you like me. Besides, you had it on autopilot the whole way. What could I have done to help?" Manning asked.

"Well, you could have kept me company and reported in as the control towers passed us off."

"I wanted to conserve my energy in case we need it in Miami."

Tripp contacted the control tower, reported who they were, announced their intention to land, and requested landing instructions. The tower confirmed their intention to land, informed them of the wind conditions, and gave them the squawk code, instructing Tripp to reduce altitude to one thousand feet. The runways were one and one-niner. Tripp entered the squawk code, leveled off at one thousand feet, checked his compass heading, and watched for the runway. Finally he was cleared for landing. Tripp dropped the landing gear, lined up for the runway, and pulled back to reduce airspeed to sixty knots. A few minutes later they were on the runway, taxiing to a private hangar used by the FBI.

Manning checked a car out from the motor pool, put their luggage in the trunk, turned south on NW 42nd Avenue, and merged onto 836 East toward downtown. The traffic was relatively light for a Monday morning, and five minutes later they merged onto Highway 95 North. Traffic was a bit heavier on Highway 95, but they still made good time, and within twenty minutes they were taking the exit for 826 East. Manning was at the wheel and stayed on the freeways, deliberately steering clear of the area where Katie Tripp's body had been found. Very little was said on the trip to headquarters, and they soon turned right onto NW Second Avenue and pulled into FBI headquarters.

Tripp and Manning knew the Miami FBI offices well, having spent many days there after Katie's death. Ten minutes later Tripp and Manning had passed through security and were in the elevator. A soft bell sounded and the door swished open. The reception area could easily have passed for a New York City Park Avenue high-rise executive suite. The men stepped out onto a shiny slate-gray marble floor with the FBI crest inlaid with cobalt blue and gold trim. Beyond the expansive reception area was a huge mahogany desk. Intricately carved into the desk was another gold-trimmed FBI crest. The only Christmas decorations were two red candles encircled by wreaths on each side of the desk.

Cecelia Salazar was an attractive, middle-aged Hispanic woman with skin that could have belonged to a teenager. She had long black hair that was tied back with a blue scrunchy, and she wore a navy jacket over a khaki blouse with a navy faille skirt. When she saw Tripp and Manning, she beamed a smile that could have lit up the entire complex.

She stood and said, "Sean and Neil, my two favorite agents. Welcome back to Miami—it's been way too long." She stood, came around the desk, and hugged them both.

Manning held the hug, looked her in the eyes, and said, "You're right. It has been too long, far too long."

She smiled, kissed him on the cheek, and said, "Still the same Neil, I see."

Then she turned to Tripp, took his hand, and asked, "How have you been? I heard you had retired. Are things getting any better, Sean?"

Tripp smiled warmly and said, "I'm fine, Cecelia. It's a slow process, but yes, things are getting better."

Cecelia said, "I'm glad. We've all been thinking of you."

She then walked back behind the desk and said, "Henry Powell is waiting for you."

She pushed a button somewhere behind the desk and said, "He's in the conference room. You better go on back."

The conference room was comfortable, with a long, polished oak table in the center, surrounded by twelve leather chairs. On the table sat a silver tray with a pitcher of water and twelve glasses. Along the wall was an oak cabinet with a decanter of coffee, a plate of bagels, and a mini fridge. Sitting in the room were two men, Henry Powell and Ben Hagle.

Powell was forty-five, clean-cut, with thick black hair and penetrating dark eyes. He was a black man, with a big barrel chest and forearms like jackhammers. He had been with the bureau for seventeen years, specifically dealing with Cuban issues, and he knew Tripp and Manning well. When Tripp and Manning entered the conference room, Powell rose and met them at the door. They shook hands and exchanged pleasantries. Powell then introduced Ben Hagle.

Hagle was a career man who had been with the Central Intelligence Agency in Washington for some forty years. He was an older man whose build was on the light side. Thick glasses covered his pale blue eyes, and on top of his head was a mat of white hair. Hagle did not get up or reach to shake hands, but simply nodded and gave a slight wave.

After the men sat down, Powell continued, "Ben runs the Cuba desk at the Central Intelligence Agency." He looked at Manning and continued, "Yesterday I received a call from your boss, Assistant Director Jenner. He told me you were on your way to Miami and why. When I heard the name Manuel Favela, I called Ben. He immediately flew down to be here this morning. I think this would be a good time to turn it over to Ben."

"Gentlemen," Hagle began, "as Agent Powell said, I run the Cuba desk at the Central Intelligence Agency. My job is to gather military and economic intelligence on Cuba. I stay informed on Castro's top officers, the drug trafficking, and the Cuban economy, specifically with respect to our sanctions and how they are working. As I'm sure you know, Manuel Favela was at one time the top general under Castro. His drug trafficking throughout Latin America was well known before he disappeared. It was believed he used contacts in the exile community to run drugs into the United States. We believe these same contacts are still trafficking now, but with a new boss in Havana."

Tripp winced as the words were spoken, then said, "I do know something about this." He continued, "How is this connected to Tony?"

"Recently our intelligence sources have been hearing Favela's name again."

Hagle looked at Powell and Powell pushed a button on the table. Two large panels on the wall slid open and a screen lit up with a picture of a man in a Cuban military uniform.

"The man on the screen is Manuel Ramon Favela," Hagle said. "As I'm sure you know, some fifteen years ago he disappeared from Cuba without a trace. It was assumed he abandoned Castro and took millions of Castro's dollars with him. Our guess at the time was that Castro had discovered Favela's plan, had his boat followed to open sea, and executed him. Apparently, however, he was captured and imprisoned. At least, that's what our sources are now saying."

Hagle looked at Powell again and another slide flashed onto the screen. It was the image of an island off the coast of Cuba.

"This island is the Isla de la Juventud, or Isle of Youth. It is known as the island of a thousand names. The Indians called it Camargo, Guanaja, and Siguanea. Christopher Columbus discovered it in 1494, named it La Evangelista, and claimed it for Spain. For a brief time the United States claimed ownership when Spain dropped all claims following the United States' victory in the Spanish-American War. However, in 1907 the United States Supreme Court ruled that the island did not belong to the United States, and a treaty was signed in 1925 recognizing Cuban ownership. Other names the island came to be known as are Santiago; Isla de Cotorros, or Isle of Parrots; and Isla de Tesoros, or Treasure Island. Most recently, until 1978, it was known as the Isla de Pinos, or Isle of Pines. It is the largest island off Cuba proper and lies almost directly south of Havana across the Batabano Gulf."

Once again Hagle looked at Powell and another image appeared. "This, gentlemen, is Prison El Guayabo. It is a maximum-security prison located on the Isla de la Juventud, and according to sources in Havana, it is where Manuel Favela is currently being held."

Manning looked at Trip, then to Hagle, and said, "We assume this is all tied to Tony's disappearance."

Hagle looked at Powell, then back to Manning, and said, "Yes, we believe so. We believe the only reason Manuel Favela is alive today is because Castro wants the millions that are still missing and believes Manuel knows where they are."

Tripp looked at Hagle and said, "And you believe that somehow he plans to use Tony to get Manuel to talk."

Hagle was quiet for a few seconds before he spoke.

"We believe that is the most likely scenario."

Tripp looked at Manning and said, "It does make sense. Tony gets a call that his father has been found, and then he's told to come to Miami, but warned not to say anything to anyone."

A few seconds passed in silence before Manning spoke up.

"If they get their hands on Tony, it won't be for a reunion."

"So, what are the plans?" Tripp asked.

"Right now we're checking all the hotels and motels in Miami to see if anyone matching Tony's description has checked in," Powell answered. "We're also leaning on several of our sources within the exile community to see what the word is on the street."

"Any news yet?" Tripp asked.

"Not yet," Hagle said. "But we're asking our contacts in Havana to see what they can come up with on their end."

Tripp turned to Powell and said, "The man Tony arrived with when he reached the states was Guillermo Gonzalez. We've read a report he gave to authorities soon after they arrived here. Can you find him? I'd like to talk with him."

Powell pushed an intercom button on the table. A man's voice answered and Powell asked for all the information they had on Guillermo Gonzalez, a Cuban refugee linked to the Favela family.

Tripp stood and walked behind the table to the mini fridge. He took out a Sprite and reached for a bagel, but stopped.

He returned to his seat and Manning said, "You have something against bagels?"

"I have a policy not to eat anything that looks older than me," Tripp answered.

A minute later, a man entered and handed Powell a file folder. Powell opened the file and leafed through it.

"Guillermo Gonzalez lives in Little Havana with his wife and four children."

Powell gave Tripp the address and said he would contact Manning if they came up with anything new.

CHAPTER 17

*R*olando Prieto Zavala sat alone in his cell at the maximum-security facility in El Paso, Texas. Zavala, a Cuban-born native, now a naturalized citizen of Brazil, was an older man, tall, lean, and wiry, with a rich head of white hair and a weathered face. He had been arrested on immigration charges which claimed he had lied on his application to become a United States citizen. The CIA file on Zavala was three inches thick. Zavala had actually worked with the CIA in several covert operations throughout the United States and South America, including the ill-fated Bay of Pigs.

Zavala's childhood in Cuba was scarred with the images of his parents' murder and the imprisonment and torture of other family members. As a teen he had escaped Cuba by hiding in the hold of a ship. He ended up in Brazil.

Zavala had worked odd jobs around the docks and shipyards of Rio to support himself, but his anger and hatred of Castro never waned. A dockmaster whose uncle was imprisoned in Cuba was sympathetic to the Cuban plight and took a liking to Zavala. He took Zavala into his family and eventually helped him get his Brazilian citizenship.

He also introduced Zavala to a group of men with similar backgrounds who used their "special talents" to thwart Castro's

Communist regime as often as possible. This secret militant group, which came to be known as Los Vengadores, had sprung from the anti-Communist sentiment in Uruguay, Brazil, and Argentina prior to World War II. After the war, wealthy German industrialists, along with their billions, immigrated to Argentina and Brazil. The industrialists employed a man by the name of Otto Skorzeny, who at one time was considered to be Hitler's favorite commando, to smuggle their money out of Germany and into South America. Skorzeny's talent at organizing and training special agents in sabotage, espionage, and paramilitary skills was legendary. Later, Skorzeny served as an advisor to the Peron government in Argentina and trained anti-Communist forces. Funded with millions from the German industrialists, these forces eventually broke into small paramilitary organizations. Los Vengadores was one such group, led by a man known only as "Grouper." Zavala soon became one of Grouper's right-hand men and a key member of Los Vengadores.

The door at the far end of the cell block clanged open, and Zavala heard footsteps moving toward his cell.

"Zavala, you have a visitor," the guard shouted.

The guard waved to another guard at the end of the cell block and the cell door slid open. Zavala followed the guard through the runway, and they made their way down a dimly lit corridor to a secure visitors' room where the inmates and their visitors were separated by thick reinforced glass. The guard left Zavala, then shut and locked the door behind him. Zavala sat and stared at the visitor.

The man in the pin-striped navy suit, cream-colored shirt, and matching tie looking back was no stranger. He was Zavala's attorney, Henrique Fernandez. They had first met at a meeting of Los Vengadores, where they had planned the bombing of a

Cuban jetliner that was to carry several members of Castro's family; although the attempt failed, they had since worked together many times.

"*Buenos dias*, Rolando...good morning. How are you holding out?" Fernandez began.

"How do you think I'm doing in this stinkhole? Every day is like the next. When are you getting me out of here?"

Fernandez was not what one would call a prominent lawyer, but he was feisty. He had been born and raised in the Texas Rio Grande Valley. As a child, his family was poor, and Fernandez often found himself in and out of trouble with the law. He clawed and scratched his way through college and law school, and relished every opportunity his practice gave him to fight the system. He was a lightly muscled, thick-set man of medium height, with black hair, brown eyes, and an easy smile. A baseball fanatic, he occasionally played on a local coed softball team. His practice focused on criminal law, but he often worked immigration cases if the money was good, and the money was very good when he worked for Rolando Zavala.

"Your situation is difficult, Rolando. You have become a political liability to everyone involved. As you know, I finally convinced the judge to let you out on bail with the stipulation that you agree to electronic surveillance, but that was overruled on appeal. They know you worked as a covert operative for the United States, and they know you're wanted in Brazil for organized criminal activity. They're worried you could become a political embarrassment should they deport you, and a political nightmare if they set you free here."

Zavala stared back with hard, cold eyes.

Fernandez, looking into a window of pure hatred, swallowed hard and continued, "I do, however, have an interesting message for you from our friend Grouper."

The window of Zavala's eyes opened wider, as though some-one had lifted the blinds. "Tell me this message," Zavala barked.

"He said to tell you the boy is missing. Do you know what this means?" Fernandez asked.

Zavala did not answer, but Fernandez could tell he knew. The anger in his face was replaced with a look of helpless despair.

"I have not given up, Rolando," Fernandez said. "We still have cards to play. I will get you out, my friend. Remember, you worked as a covert operative for the United States, and you're only in here for political reasons. Politics is a game. We just have to play the right card. Trust me, I will get you out."

Fernandez watched as Zavala was led back to his cell. He knew what he needed was leverage—now he just had to find it.

Zavala entered his cell and heard the heavy steel door slam shut behind him. He sat on his bed, staring into nowhere, and thought about his friends in Los Vengadores, about the work he had done for the United States government, about his family members who had been tortured and murdered, and about Tony and Carmen Favela. All the anger he felt focused on one person: Castro.

CHAPTER
18

*G*uillermo Gonzalez lived off Flagler Street, which was not far from the airport, so Tripp and Manning headed back the way they had come. They parked across the street and shut off the car's engine. Situated on a corner lot, the house was a small single-family dwelling with two front façades, one facing the front, the other facing the side street. The once-white paint was now cracked and peeling, and the street numbers over the door were faded to the point of being almost illegible. To the side and behind the house was an unattached garage with what looked like an older-model Oldsmobile '98 inside.

After a few minutes Manning said, "It doesn't look like he's going to come out to greet us."

They stepped out of the car, walked across the lawn, and stepped onto the wood-framed porch. Some of the boards were missing or rotted, and they had to carefully step around them. Latin music could be heard from a radio somewhere in the house. Tripp knocked on the door, and almost immediately they heard heavy footsteps approaching.

A short, husky, dark-skinned man with brown eyes and wavy brown hair opened the door. He was middle-aged and clean-shaven, with a kind but care-worn face, a man who had seen many hardships.

"Yes?" the man asked.

"Are you Guillermo Gonzalez?" Manning asked.

"Yes, who are you?"

"My name is Neil Manning, and this is Sean Tripp."

Manning held out his ID and continued, "I am with the FBI. We would like to speak to you a few minutes.

Gonzalez hesitated a moment, then said, "What is this about?"

"We have some questions we'd like to ask you about the statement you gave several years back regarding your incident at sea."

Gonzalez looked at Tripp and Manning, but did not invite them in. Finally his tone dropped and he said, "That was a long time ago. I gave a statement. I thought that was over."

"We have your statement, Mr. Gonzalez, but something has come up that we hope you can help us with," Tripp said.

Guillermo opened the door and stepped back, allowing Tripp and Manning to enter. He closed the door and led them into a large living room with windows facing the front street. The décor was run-of-the-mill, with a light-brown couch and matching recliner. It appeared the couch might fold out into a sleeper. The coffee table was an oak square covered with a stack of well-read *Sports Illustrated* magazines. The room had a hardwood floor with a beige rug in the center. On the floor in the corner was a three-foot artificial Christmas tree adorned with angels and blue lights. In front of the tree was a small manger scene complete with camels, donkeys, and sheep.

Gonzalez asked them to be seated as he sat in the recliner.

"Are you alone, Mr. Gonzalez?" Tripp asked.

"Yes, my wife is at work. What do you want with me?"

Gonzalez spoke excellent English, with only a trace of his native accent.

"As I said, we read the statement you provided when you arrived in America. We'd like to hear more about the actual attack you fortunately survived on your escape from Cuba," Manning said.

"Not much to tell, really. We were a small group, including women and children. One of Castro's gunboats approached and opened fire. As you say, I was fortunate to get away."

"That was you, your family, and Tony Favela?" Tripp asked.

"Yes."

Tripp could see that Gonzalez was nervous. He tried to make eye contact with the man and failed.

"Did anyone else survive?"

Guillermo hesitated a moment, then said, "No one else survived."

Several moments passed in silence before Tripp continued.

"Tony Favela had a mother, father, and sister. Did you see them die, Guillermo?"

Again Gonzalez hesitated. He shifted in his seat and his eyes dropped to the floor.

"Yes, there were bullets flying everywhere.... They were shot."

Tripp and Manning looked at each other and again there was silence. Finally, Tripp stood, walked over to a bookshelf, and picked up a baseball. Written on the ball were the words "State Champions." Also on the shelf was a picture of a young man holding a trophy.

"Your son?" Tripp asked, holding the picture out.

"Yes, it is my son Jaime. They won the state championship his senior year."

"He's a fine-looking young man. You must be very proud of him."

"Yes, he is a fine boy and I am very proud of him. He honors my family name."

"There's a young man who attends the high school where I live who is also a fine young man and a gifted athlete."

Tripp placed the picture on the shelf, turned to stare Gonzalez in the eyes, and said, "His name is Tony."

Tripp paused a few seconds, then continued, "I think Manuel Favela would be very proud of him."

Gonzalez shifted in his seat and broke eye contact, but said nothing.

Tripp looked at Manning, who nodded slowly. He'd caught it too.

Tripp walked over, sat on the coffee table in front of Gonzalez, and said, "He is in great danger right now, Guillermo."

"You do not understand. I crossed Castro once and lived. Most do not. Castro's men have killed several defectors in Miami over the last few years. He has long arms. If he feels he has been betrayed, he will come after you no matter where you are or how long it takes. I have spent fifteen years staying low, hiding, protecting my family, and looking over my shoulder. Now you ask me to cross Castro again?"

Several seconds passed and Tripp said, "Fifteen years ago you saved Tony Favela. You now have the chance to save him again."

Gonzalez looked up, made eye contact with Tripp, and said, "I once made a promise to Manuel Favela to take care of Tony and see to his safety. What is this danger Tony is facing?"

"Tony is missing and we think Castro is behind it," Tripp said.

"I was afraid someday this would happen. Castro is not one to forget." Gonzalez paused a moment, his face now defined with resolve, and continued, "How can I help Tony?"

Tripp nodded at Manning.

Manning turned to Gonzalez and said, "Tell us more about this promise you made to Manuel Favela."

"Manuel loved his children very much. He knew Castro would use every resource he had to hunt them down. I promised to get them to America and find them homes where Castro would not find them."

"What happened to Tony's sister Carmen?"

"It was a dark night and we were under attack. Manuel brought both children to my boat for me to take to safety as planned. He handed me Tony, and when he was safely aboard, I reached for Carmen. I was helping her aboard when Manuel was hit in the arm."

Gonzalez closed his eyes and wiped tears from his face with his sleeve.

In a low, trembling voice, he continued, "Manuel lost her grip and she fell into the sea. I saw her fall into the ocean, but there was nothing I could do; we were under attack. I had to leave her."

"So when you made it to America, you had Tony put up for adoption?" Manning asked.

"No...not at first. We had planned to keep Tony with us and raise him as our own. Several months later, we received a call from a man who said he was a family friend of Manuel's. He said Tony was in great danger. He said that Castro would not stop until he had Tony, and it was vital that he not be found."

"Why would one small boy be so important to Castro?" Manning asked.

"Castro is a madman. He controls all the drug money and laundering operations in Central America, among other things. If he finds someone has stolen from him, he will do whatever it takes to find him and get his money back. Castro needs Tony to get Manuel to talk."

"So Manuel is still alive?"

"Yes. The man who called only identified himself as Grouper, and he claimed to have been in contact with Manuel."

"What else did he say?" Manning asked.

"He said Castro was sending men to find the children. He said that must not happen and that a man would contact me on what to do."

"And someone did contact you?"

"Yes. A week later a man came to my home. This man also told me Castro would never give up until he had both of the children. It was then that I learned that Carmen had survived. The man said the children would need to be sent to opposite coasts, and for their own protection they should not know of each other. He told me to send Tony to the West Coast for adoption. I don't know where they sent Carmen."

Tripp and Manning stared at each other. Then Tripp asked, "So you are telling us that Carmen Favela is alive as well?"

"Yes, the man told me what happened that night. He said Manuel pulled Carmen out of the water and put her on another boat with Vincente; he sent them away while they held off the gunboat. It was pure suicide. Only Manuel and Omar against a military gunboat.... Suicide to save his daughter."

"Do you have any idea where she is, Guillermo?"

"No...but the man who came to my house would know."

"What is his name?" Tripp asked.

"His name is Rolando Zavala."

Tripp and Manning knew the name and knew of Zavala's background. They also knew it would be a long shot to get him to talk.

"Looks like we're going to be flying out again," Tripp said.

After checking with headquarters to see if they had anything new, and to let them know what Gonzalez had had to say, Manning called the FBI hangar to have the plane fueled and made ready to fly out the following morning. This gave them time to clear things at the prison, have some dinner, and find a hotel for the night.

CHAPTER
19

The transcontinental flight into John F. Kennedy International Airport was on time and had just received clearance to land. It was a gorgeous winter morning in New York City; the skyline looked like a picture postcard. The air was crisp and cool, the sun warm and bright, with not a cloud in the sky.

The terminal was bustling with travelers steeped in holiday spirit. Christmas trees, tinsel, and strings of colorful lights were on display throughout the terminal. Children, parents, and grandparents were smiling, laughing, and hugging.

Flight 109 touched down and taxied to the gate. As the passengers prepared to exit, Carmen Tully took her place at the cabin door to welcome the travelers to New York City and wish them happy holidays. When the aircraft was empty, Carmen completed her final duties and retrieved her rolling flight case.

Carmen Tully was twenty-eight years old. It had been fifteen years since her name was Carmen Rene Favela. She had been adopted by Julie and Ron Tully and spent her second life with them in a home in Syracuse, New York. Carmen was breathtakingly beautiful, with shoulder-length jet-black hair, green-brown eyes, graceful features, and the kind of perfect, delicate skin every woman dreams about. At five foot eight inches tall, she had a shapely figure and a smile that could mesmerize anyone—male or female.

As she was preparing to leave the aircraft, her fellow flight attendant and friend Nancy Parker came up behind her and said, "Two days off, Carmen. You have any plans?"

"I'm going to put up my tree and do some last-minute Christmas shopping. What about you?"

"Our tree's already up and I finished my shopping weeks ago. Why don't you come over and have dinner with us?"

"That sounds nice, but I may go up to Syracuse and see my parents. I'll call you."

"I know your parents would love that. Tell them hi for me, will you?"

"I will, and thank you."

They left the aircraft and walked down the jetway that led to the gate.

They were unaware of the man leaning against the wall outside a small bookshop just beyond the security checkpoint. He held a magazine as though he was reading, but he watched as Carmen and Nancy walked by, pulling their wheeled cases behind them. As they made their way to the door, he tossed the magazine in a trash bin and followed, careful to keep his distance.

Outside, Carmen said good-bye to Nancy and stepped into a taxi. She gave the driver her address, then sat back and looked out at the beautiful morning. She was unaware of the man in the taxi that was following hers.

Carmen lived in a comfortable two-bedroom apartment on the upper east side of Manhattan. It was a good forty-minute drive by taxi from the airport, but over an hour by subway. She loved living there and being near Central Park, the museums, and Broadway. Carmen had gone to college at Syracuse, where her adoptive parents were professors. Her father had invented an integrated circuit and sold the patent to IBM in the 1970s, allowing his family to live a comfortable life.

After Carmen graduated from college, she got a job with an international carrier and moved in with a friend she had met at college. Her friend soon married and moved out, subletting the apartment to Carmen.

As the taxi left JFK International and turned onto the Van Wyck Expressway, Carmen was thinking about what Christmas gifts she should get her mom and dad. The day was absolutely splendid, and the ride passed quickly.

Her mind was on her upcoming trip home to Syracuse when they turned onto the Long Island Expressway toward Manhattan. Christmas at home was a very special time. She could almost smell the homemade cookies baking in the oven and the scent of pine wafting from the living room tree. Her dad would spend countless hours getting every Christmas light to work, both inside the house and out, while her mother would bake her famous cookies and candy, much of which would be taken to church for families who were less fortunate.

When they crossed the Queensboro Bridge, Carmen looked out at the East River shimmering in the morning sunlight. Carmen rarely looked back in life. Her motto was "Keep moving forward." Her new family had been so loving and encouraging that she came to accept all that had happened, and she became determined to not let her past slow her down. But on this morning, just days before Christmas, she found herself thinking back. She thought about her mother, who had held her close on that dark night, and about her father, who had thrown her a line to hold onto while bullets were flying all around him. She vividly remembered watching them both until they faded into the darkness.

As the taxi turned right onto Park Avenue, she thought about the brother she had loved so much and wondered if he had made it to safety. Tears began to form as she remembered how she was only inches away from joining him on that boat. Then she remembered falling, almost in slow motion, into the cold blackness as the sea closed in around her.

Moments later, the taxi turned left on East Eighty-First Street toward Central Park, then left again on Fifth Avenue, past the Met, the Metropolitan Museum of Art. The museum was almost a quarter mile long, and Carmen had spent countless hours perusing each room and aisle in it. She smiled as she recalled the musty scent and the beauty and serenity she always felt there. Carmen closed her eyes, wiped her tears away, and whispered a silent prayer of thanks for the blessings God had given her.

The taxi turned left onto Eightieth Street and pulled to a stop in front of her apartment building. She collected her case, tipped the driver, and walked toward the door.

A block back, another cab stopped and a man stepped out. As his cab pulled away, he watched Carmen enter her building.

CHAPTER 20

The Bonanza G36 sat on the tarmac, fueled and ready. It was a perfect day for flying, with clear, sunny skies and only a trace of wind. Tripp had filed the flight plan before leaving the hotel, so when they arrived at the airport everything was ready to go. While Manning returned the car to the motor pool, Tripp began his familiar preflight inspection.

By the time Manning returned the car and made it to the aircraft, Tripp had almost completed the inspection. They crawled into the cockpit, buckled up, and began the systems check. Soon after, Tripp was cleared for takeoff, and ten minutes later, they lifted off and turned west toward El Paso. They made a steep climb to ten thousand feet, hitting turbulence at just over a thousand feet.

When they finally leveled off, Manning said, "I hope the flight attendant gets here quickly; I could use a drink!"

"You'll need the correct change," Tripp quipped.

"I thought drinks were included on this flight."

"You seem to have a knack for getting your drinks included."

"I think this is where I say, Of all the crazy gin joints in the world, I have to find one with a surly captain."

"Humphrey Bogart wouldn't appreciate the way you butcher his lines."

"Humphrey Bogart never flew with you."

Tripp entered the El Paso airport identifier code into the GPS system and set the plane on autopilot. The skies were crystal clear and Manning was looking out over the waters of the gulf when his cell phone chirped. He pulled the phone from his jacket pocket, saw that the call was from Henry Powell at FBI headquarters, and pushed the answer key.

"We've got some new developments on the Favela case," Powell said.

"Something good, I hope," Manning answered.

"We found the hotel where Tony is registered—the La Carreta Inn. He checked in Sunday evening."

"Is he there?"

"No, but we checked his room, and he was definitely there last night. His backpack is in the room, and the maid said the bed had been slept in."

"Anybody see him leave the hotel?"

"We passed Tony's picture around; the concierge thinks it was Tony he saw leaving with a guy he only knew as El Padron."

"Do you know this Padron?" Manning asked.

"We know him well. His name is Enemencio Vargas, and we've dealt with him on several occasions. He has no real visible means of support, yet he lives well and even owns a fifty-three-foot yacht. We've never been able to pin anything solid on him, but he's pretty much into everything one way or another. He's well known throughout the exile community, too. He claims to work for the exiles, but not all the people trust him, and probably for good reason. Our sources tell us he somehow has a lot of contact with the Cuban government."

"Sounds like a great guy," Manning said dryly.

"There's something else," Powell said.

"What's that?"

"Tony had scribbled a note on a pad on the nightstand, reminding himself to bring a light jacket for a boat trip."

"As in a boat trip to Cuba, maybe?"

"Could be. As I said, Vargas does own a yacht. I have a man on his way to the docks now to see if the yacht is there."

"And if it's not?"

"The best we can do is notify the Coast Guard to be on the lookout, and check satellite surveillance photos to see if we can track him down."

"Thanks, Ben. Keep us informed."

Manning went over the conversation with Tripp. After he finished they sat quiet. They both knew what this could mean for Tony.

Twenty minutes after they touched down in El Paso, Tripp and Manning were in a rental car headed for the El Paso Federal Correctional Facility.

After another twenty minutes they parked the car, stored their weapons in the trunk, and entered the prison. They had called ahead, so the administration was expecting them. Manning presented his FBI credentials and told the guard they were there to see Rolando Zavala. While Manning and Tripp signed in, the guard called a duty guard to escort them to the interview room. Five minutes later a side door opened and Jim Sanders, the prison warden, walked into the waiting room, shook hands, and invited Tripp and Manning back to his office.

Sanders was not an imposing figure, at perhaps five seven, but he was the type to demand respect. He was in his early fifties, lean and wiry, with salt-and-pepper hair that was close cropped and dark eyes under heavy eyebrows.

Sanders' office was huge, with wall-to-wall pictures of him shaking hands with various dignitaries and elected officials. There were at least a dozen plaques displaying honors and citations Sanders had received during his law enforcement career. Without asking, Sanders poured Tripp and Manning cups of coffee, then sat behind his huge eight-foot oak desk and asked them to be seated. Tripp and Manning took seats in two leather chairs opposite the desk.

"I spoke with Henry Powell. He filled me in a little on what you've got and asked me to help facilitate your meeting with Zavala. I'm sure you're both aware Mr. Zavala is a high-security inmate. We have specific directives from the Justice Department and U.S. Intelligence as to who he can speak with. Also, his attorney, Mr. Henrique Fernandez, has ordered that he be present any time Zavala is being questioned," Sanders said.

"Has he been notified?" Manning asked.

"Yes, I called him right after I spoke with Henry Powell. He and Zavala are in the interview room now."

Tripp took a sip of his coffee and said, "I want to thank you for your assistance. We're a bit under the gun on this one, so we'd like to see him as soon as possible."

"As I said, they are waiting for you now. I just wanted to speak with you a moment. I'm sure you've both heard of Zavala." Sanders paused a moment, looked first at Tripp, then at Manning, and continued, "What I don't think you've heard is Zavala's story."

Tripp and Manning looked at each other but said nothing.

"When you meet Rolando, you will see an angry man. You will see a cold man. But if you ever have the opportunity to sit with him and listen to him, as I have in this very office, you will understand why he's that way."

No one spoke for a moment, then Sanders said, "Look, gentlemen, he's no angel. He's in my prison and the Justice Department has told me in no uncertain terms that he will be here awhile, and I will enforce those orders to the letter. But I've been in this business a long time. I've heard all the stories. What I'm telling you is that I don't think any of us sitting here would be any less angry or cold if we had been through what he has."

He paused a few seconds, and when nobody spoke, he continued, "Now, if you will follow me, I'll take you to the interview room."

Before Sanders left them, he said, "Good luck, and let me know if there is anything I can do to help you."

They entered the interview room, made their introductions, and sat at the table; Tripp and Manning on one side and Zavala and Fernandez opposite them. Tripp looked carefully at the two men across the table, trying to read them. Zavala had cold, hard, deep-set eyes. His leathery face was scored and seamed. Tripp also caught a vision of a man who had lived a long life with a heavy burden—a man who had suffered tremendous loss. It was as though life had sucked out his dreams and hopes of youth and left only bitterness and hate.

Tripp also saw a small camera attached to the wall near the door. He knew that all interviews in a federal prison were taped.

Zavala sat in his orange prison-issued jumpsuit and stared back, never blinking.

Fernandez, dressed in an impeccable navy-blue pin-striped suit and conservative silk tie, looked back with a confident, wry smile. He was the first to speak.

"Gentlemen, how can my client help you today?"

"Actually, our hope today is that Mr. Zavala can help two other people who we have reason to believe are in great danger."

"As I'm sure you know, Mr. Zavala has spent much of his life helping other people...including the United States government. I'm sure my client will be glad to hear you out and see if he can continue to be of service," Fernandez answered with the same wry smile.

Tripp watched Zavala intently, but the man's expression never changed.

"Fifteen years ago a family left Cuba in a small boat, hoping to reach freedom in America. Two of the family members, a young boy and a teenage girl, made it safely and have lived a relatively quiet life here," Manning said. Zavala continued to stare impassively. Manning continued, "A few days ago the boy disappeared. We believe he has been kidnapped, and we suspect he is now being taken back to Cuba. We may be too late to help him, but we're hoping we can get to his sister before Castro's men do."

Zavala's expression remained as still as granite and his eyes did not blink.

"Gentlemen, there are Cuban exiles throughout this country," Fernandez said. "I don't believe Mr. Castro is going to comb the country to bring every Cuban child back home, and I don't see how this concerns my client."

There was silence as Fernandez looked at Manning and Tripp. Then he said, "Tell me, what are the names of these children?"

"The boy's name is Tony Casteel and the girl is Carmen," Manning said.

Tripp finally spoke up. "Fifteen years ago when they left Cuba, their names were Tony and Carmen Favela."

This time Tripp saw a reaction from Zavala. It was ever so slight, he could easily have missed it, but it was there. Fernandez, however, clearly understood the significance of the name.

"I see," Fernandez finally said. He looked at his client and paused a few seconds in thought. He then continued, "True, Castro might be intent on returning these two to Cuba."

"We don't have to tell you the fate these children face should Castro get them," Tripp said.

"If the boy has already been taken, perhaps you could use your time more wisely protecting the girl," Fernandez said.

"We don't know where she is, or even her name. That is why we are here. We have information that leads us to believe Mr. Zavala could help us find her."

No one spoke for several seconds. Zavala was still silent, but now his eyes had dropped and were focused far away, as though he had been taken back to another place in time.

Finally Fernandez said, "Gentlemen, could you excuse us? I'd like to speak with my client alone."

Tripp and Manning left the interview room. A guard escorted them to an adjoining room where they could wait.

Fernandez, who knew their every word was being recorded, leaned near Zavala and spoke in a low hushed tone, tapping his pen on the table. "Listen to me, my friend. You and I both know you are here for one reason—politics. Do you remember me telling you how politics is a game and we just had to find the right card to play?"

"Yes, I remember," Zavala said, his eyes still focused far away.

"You've just been dealt that card."

Zavala looked up at Fernandez, but said nothing.

"I remember the last message our friend Grouper sent to you. He said I should tell you the boy is missing."

Fernandez paused, trying to read Zavala. Then his voice dropped even lower.

"You know about this girl Carmen, don't you?"

"Yes."

"I think it is time to play that card and get you out of here."

Zavala looked up and said, "I will not betray Grouper."

"You do not have to betray Grouper. I wouldn't expect you to, but you need to get out of here."

"He told me I was never to tell anyone about the boy and girl."

"He was trying to protect the children, but they are in danger now. He would want you to help them. I will contact Grouper, tell him what has developed. He will understand."

Zavala nodded.

Fernandez stood, knocked on the door, and told the guard they were ready to see Manning and Tripp again.

Manning and Tripp reentered the room and took their seats opposite Zavala.

Fernandez said, "Gentlemen, my client would like to speak with you, but in private...with the cameras off."

Manning said, "I think I know just the person to help us with that."

Once again Manning left the room, this time to speak with Warden Sanders about his offer to help in any way he could. When Manning returned to the interview room, the cameras were off.

"Now, gentlemen," Fernandez began, "as I said, my client would like to speak with you. He would like to help you find your missing girl." He paused, then continued, "There is, however, one more matter we will need to address first."

Tripp looked at Zavala and said, "What is it you want in return, Rolando?"

Zavala looked at Tripp, but before he could speak, Fernandez said, "My client is being held here ostensibly for an immigration violation. The truth is, as we all know, he is a potential embarrassment to the United States government. My client wants his release. You get him that release and he gives you the girl."

"Do you really think they will grant him his release for possibly helping us find a missing Cuban girl?" Manning said.

Before Fernandez could respond, Zavala finally spoke for the first time.

"I can give you much more than one Cuban girl. I can give you Carmen, and Tony, and Manuel."

The room was quiet. Manning looked at Tripp, who was staring at Zavala.

"You have contact with Manuel Favela?" Tripp asked.

"Yes, I can contact him."

Fernandez reached out, put his hand on Zavala's shoulder, and said, "My client will say nothing more until we have assurance of his release."

Tripp sat back, his mind racing. He knew it was still a long shot, but there just might be a way.

Finally he said, "What if we were able to work something out with the Federal Witness Protection Program?"

Fernandez looked at Zavala and said, "We're listening."

"It would mean Rolando would get a new identity, a job, and a place to live. Rolando Zavala would basically disappear."

Zavala looked at his attorney, then turned to Tripp and said, "You get me this new identity and get me out of here, and I will help you."

Tripp and Manning once again left the interview room and returned to Warden Sanders' office.

Tripp called Henry Powell and asked him to get Ben Hagle on the line. He told them what Zavala had said, what he wanted, and what they had proposed. If they could use Zavala to get

Manuel Favela, the NSA might agree to the witness protection plan. It would help them get crucial information on Castro and solve their problem with Zavala at the same time. Hagle agreed, promising to make some calls to Washington and get back with them.

An hour later Hagle called back and spoke with Tripp. "I talked with the vice president and he has tentatively agreed to your proposal, with the assurance that Zavala cooperates fully. As you know, this process will take awhile, but I am flying back to Washington to see that things are set in motion. You can tell Mr. Zavala it will be done."

Henry Powell then got on the line and said, "We have an update on Tony. Vargas' yacht is gone. The Coast Guard has been notified, and they are watching for it. I have also requested satellite photos. We should have them shortly."

"Thank you. Call us if you find anything," Tripp said.

He clicked off and summarized the conversation for Manning. Once again they returned to the interview room and sat across from Zavala.

"They have agreed, on the condition that you cooperate fully," Tripp said.

"My client has always cooperated with the government," Fernandez said. "I'm sure he will continue to do so. When will he begin his new life outside these walls?"

"The process has already begun. It will take awhile, but a CIA agent is on his way to Washington as we speak to see that the process moves quickly."

Zavala looked up at Tripp and said, "I will cooperate. What do you need to know?"

"Tell us where Carmen is, and what her name is now."

"Her name is Carmen Tully. She lives in New York City." He paused a second, then said, "If Castro has Tony, he will surely go for Carmen."

Tripp and Manning left the prison, retrieved their weapons from the car trunk, and headed back to the airport. As they were leaving the parking lot, Manning's cell phone chirped. He checked the ID and saw the call was from Henry Powell.

"What have you got, Henry?" Manning asked.

"I just received the satellite images and we got him. The yacht left this morning for open waters."

"Were you able to see where he went?"

"Yes, he docked at Castillo del Morro. It's an island fortress across the bay from Havana. Tourists from Europe and Scandinavia are allowed to travel there."

"Thanks, Henry, we're on our way back now."

"There's one more thing, Neil. The photo was taken from an Onyx 9 satellite, a satellite that can zoom down far enough to read the name off the boat. I had the image enlarged, and it clearly shows the yacht and everyone on it. Vargas is there, and so is Tony."

Manning clicked off and told Tripp the news.

"I'm going to drop you off at Miami and refuel," Tripp said. "See what you can find out about getting Tony back. I'm going on to New York."

CHAPTER
21

Castillo del Morro, Cuba, 2007

Enemencio Vargas was at the helm as he guided *El Diablo Rojo* into the berth at El Castillo del Morro. Juan and Benito jumped out and began to tie down the yacht as Vargas shut down the twin 370 engines.

"Welcome to El Castillo del Morro," Vargas shouted to Tony.

The castle loomed before them, and Tony stared in amazement at the huge structure rising four stories high. Above the walls stood a lighthouse made of cut stone blocks standing over ten meters high.

El Castillo del Morro, whose correct name is Castillo de Los Tres Reyes del Morro, or the Castle of the Three Kings on the Bluff, is a picturesque fortress guarding the entrance to Havana Bay. When it was initially built in 1589, Cuba was under the control of Spain. Strategically located on the opposite side of the harbor from Old Havana, it defended the city against pirates and other invaders. In 1762 the castle was captured by the British and became the most important fort in colonial times, not only for its strategic military value, but also for its effectiveness as a lighthouse and as a symbol of the city. In later years, Castillo del Morro became a prison. It has four levels, and the lowest level is still guarded to keep out tourists.

"This is a real castle?" Tony asked.

"Yes, it even has a moat and drawbridge," Vargas said. He turned left, pointed, and continued, "And over there is Cuba."

Tony stepped onto the dock and looked over the bay at the island of Cuba. He searched his memory, trying to get an impression about the last time he was there. Out on the curve of the bay dozens of small fishing boats were making their way through the swells, each hoping to bring in big catches to sell. It was a warm tropical morning, and the humid sea breeze smelled of salt and seaweed, a smell Tony remembered from long ago.

"And my father is here?"

Vargas stepped onto the dock and said, "This is where my sources tell me he is. We are to meet them here so they can take us to him."

Tony's heart raced as he said, "When will we meet these sources?"

"They will be along shortly. We have some time. El Morro is quite a beautiful place, full of history, and it has fantastic views. We will have lunch now and listen to some music while we wait. And if we still have time, I will show you around."

Juan and Benito finished mooring the yacht and followed Vargas and Tony up the path toward El Morro. The other two men stayed behind with the ship.

The four men climbed the path, crossed the moat, and entered the irregular walls of the fortress. Inside the gate they passed an exhibition on the lighthouses of Cuba. They climbed a set of stairs to the El Morro restaurant and sat outside at a wooden table with stools. The view of the bay from their table was fantastic. Palm trees framed a battery of cannons along the castle wall, and in the background was a view of Havana. The sky was a bright robin's-egg blue, with lightly scattered clouds and a warm breeze that made the temperature comfortable. The waiter came out and in Spanish welcomed them to El Morro. His Cuban accent was unfamiliar to Tony, who was more accustomed to the Spanglish accent used by his teachers and friends in California. Before passing out menus, the waiter told them about the house specialty, delicias del Morro, or delights of Morro, a dish of fish and prawns with a grated cheese topping. He then recommended the popular house drink, pina delicia, or pineapple delight, which was made with Havana Club Anejo, a seven-year-old rum. Tony understood very little of the waiter's Spanish, so he was somewhat relieved when Vargas told the waiter they would all have the house specialty and house drink.

The meals arrived shortly, each dish decorated in a festive colonial style with ample portions. As they ate, a small band played Cuban standards. Other diners, speaking in different European languages, laughed and enjoyed their meals and the music. Tony said very little; his mind was on his father. He also watched for the contacts they were supposed to meet. Vargas enjoyed the music and spoke occasionally in Spanish with Juan and Benito. As they were finishing their meal, Vargas looked across the table at Tony.

"Visitors are allowed to climb to the top of the lighthouse. I think you would enjoy the view. Would you like to see it?"

"Yes, I would like that. Do you expect your contacts to be here soon?"

"It will not be long now. When you are ready I will show you around the lighthouse."

They finished up and pushed their plates back. Vargas stood, left some cash on the table, and led the way to the lighthouse. Juan and Benito waited outside while Vargas and Tony entered and began the climb. They were welcomed by the lighthouse keeper, a short, thick-set, dark-skinned man with short black hair, wearing a pressed khaki uniform. As if the words had been preprogrammed, he began to explain how the lighthouse worked.

"Unlike many lighthouses that are fully automated, this one is operated manually," the keeper began in a proud voice. "The lighthouse is equipped with a bivalve lens and an electrically driven rotating mechanism."

When Vargas didn't respond, he continued, "The lighthouse displays two white flashes every fifteen seconds. It guides ships safely into the harbor. And at the top is an emergency light that is displayed if there is a mechanical failure. It is a very important job."

When Vargas still did not respond, the keeper said in a somewhat defeated tone, "Please let me know if I can help you with anything. Enjoy your visit."

When Tony reached the top he was amazed. The view was truly awesome. He looked west along the coastline and saw many quiet beaches; a few people walked across the sand. He could see the whole port, with ships coming and going, and a sweeping view of Cojimar and Old Havana. On his right were the Sierra Maestra Mountains. He felt as if he could almost reach out and touch them. And below, he saw the sea crashing into the rocks and the huge moat, some twenty meters deep.

As they stood and looked at the beautiful panoramic view, Vargas noticed five men wearing dark fatigues enter and begin to cross the garrison. The man in front, whom he knew well, was

Rogelio Cruz of the Direccion General de Intelligencia. All but Cruz had assault rifles slung over their shoulders.

Vargas turned to Tony and said, "And now it is time to go. The men we've been waiting for are here."

Tony was excited as they descended the stairs. When they exited the lighthouse and stepped into the bright afternoon light, Vargas found Cruz standing next to Juan and Benito. Cruz, a man of about five eight, had a frame that was compact and wiry. Beneath dark-colored sunglasses was a clean-shaven, lean face with thin tight lips that looked as though their only purpose was to conceal secrets.

"Señor Cruz, it is good to see you," Vargas said.

Cruz, who was focused on Tony, did not remove his sunglasses, nor did he answer.

Vargas continued, "I would like to introduce you to Tony Casteel."

In precise English, Cruz finally spoke. "I am glad to finally see you, Tony." The voice was cold and flat, and held not a trace of inflection or humanity.

Tony looked at Cruz, then at the other men, and asked, "Do you know where my father is?"

"Yes, I know where he is, but first we must talk. If you will follow me, I will take us to a place where we can speak in private."

Cruz led Vargas and Tony down the steps to what had at one time housed prison cells. The rest of the men followed a few paces behind. As they continued to descend, Tony grew more and more apprehensive. He wanted to see his father, but something didn't feel right. He wondered why Cruz and his men were dressed in fatigues and why they carried automatic rifles. He began to regret not telling anyone where he was going. He considered getting out and looked around, but realized there was no place to go. Vargas and Cruz were in front of him and armed men were behind. And even if he could run, where would he go? He was on an island, he knew no one, and he spoke limited Spanish. There was nothing to do now but go on.

When they reached the lowest level, a single guard saluted and stepped aside. Vargas and Cruz entered the dark corridor. Tony stood still. His legs felt paralyzed. He did not want to enter; he wanted to run. But before he could move, one of the men behind him lowered his rifle, and using the barrel of the weapon, pushed Tony along. The corridor was dimly lit and seemed to grow darker and colder the farther they went. The air smelled musty and stale. On each side of the corridor were cell doors. The cells were dark and empty, and Tony wondered how many men had come here never to be seen again. Finally they stopped at an open cell.

Cruz removed his sunglasses and said, "I think this will prove to be very private. We shall talk here."

He motioned for Tony to enter, but Tony stood still. The man behind Tony shoved him roughly into the cell. Tony stumbled in and fell, rolling across the floor.

Cruz closed and locked the cell door, turned to Vargas, and in a dismissive tone told him his job was done and he should go. He then told his men to take shifts watching the entrance and to keep two men there at all times.

As the men turned to leave, Tony said, "I thought we were going to talk."

"I will be back, and we will have plenty of time to talk."

"Am I going to see my father?"

"That depends on how much your father talks."

As he walked away from Tony, he continued, "But I can promise you your father will see you... even if it's a piece at a time."

Tony sat alone on the floor. As the walls seemed to close in around him, he thought with a sinking feeling that no one in the world knew where he was.

CHAPTER 22

*C*armen Tully emptied two cups of whole-grain rice into a copper pan along with four tablespoons of butter and one tablespoon of olive oil. She let it simmer until it was well coated, then added a can of cream of mushroom soup, a can of cream of chicken soup, and a small jar of cheese whiz. Several minutes later she added steamed broccoli and stirred. Halfway through this process she brushed a boneless chicken breast with soy sauce, sprinkled it with garlic powder, salt, and pepper, and coated it with breadcrumbs. Finally, she put both dishes in the oven to bake, walked back to the living room, sat in her favorite recliner, and returned to her book.

Carmen lived in a small two-bedroom apartment. The apartment was in an older pre-World War II building with a limestone façade, but it was comfortable and in a great location, only a couple blocks from Central Park and close to the subways. She lived on an upper floor, which gave her excellent views and plenty of warm, natural sunlight. Upstairs were two bedrooms and a bath. Downstairs was the kitchen, painted white with black and white tiles, another bathroom, a large living room with a Deco fireplace, and a doorway leading to a balcony.

Carmen stopped reading to reach for a blanket she kept draped over the back of the couch. As she pulled the blanket around her, she glanced at the four- foot Christmas tree next to the fireplace. She thought to herself that it looked nice, if a bit bare at the bottom. She hoped when she finally got the gifts wrapped and put under the tree it would look better. Hanging from the fireplace mantel was the personalized stocking her mother had made her with a scene of Santa in his sleigh flying above a snow-covered home and her name in glitter. On the mantel, along with a small manger scene and two red candles, were family pictures. The picture she focused on was the only one she had of her real family. It was an enlarged picture made from a photo she had had in a locket she managed to save on the terrifying trip from Cuba. She looked at her mother, her father, and her brother and whispered, "Merry Christmas." She pulled the blanket up tighter and returned to her book.

Several minutes later the oven timer sounded. She finished the page she was on, folded the corner, and set the book down. As she walked to the kitchen, she heard a soft knock at the door. She yelled, "Just a minute," went into the kitchen, put a pair of oven mitts on, turned off the timer and oven, and removed the two dishes from the oven. She set them on top of the stove and removed the mitts.

Without checking the spy hole on her door, Carmen opened the door. Standing there was a short, sour-looking man with an unshaven, irregular face and hooded, lifeless eyes, the kind of eyes that give one the feeling that they're looking into a dark, empty well. He had dark skin, and his nose was bent from being broken too many times.

"May I help you?" Carmen asked.

"Are you Carmen Tully?" the man asked in a flat voice with a strong Spanish accent.

"Yes, what do you want?"

The man didn't answer at first, and Carmen started to close the door. Quickly the man shoved his foot in the door to prevent it from closing.

"I am here to convince you to come with me," he said.

"I'm not going anywhere with you, and if you don't move your foot, I will call the police."

It was at that moment the man put his shoulder against the door and shoved hard, knocking Carmen to the floor. He entered the apartment, then closed and locked the door behind him. Carmen sat up, then looked over at the small hutch where she kept her keys. On the keychain was a canister of pepper spray. She jumped up to make a dash for the spray, but the man grabbed her by the hair and pulled her near him.

"Pepper spray doesn't agree with me," the man said in an ominous voice.

When Carmen began to scream she felt his fist slam against her head, and she fell back. She was dizzy when she finally focused on the man who was now sitting astride her, his face only inches away. Her ear was ringing and his breath smelled of alcohol and stale cigarettes. Carmen tried to fight back, to roll over and get away, but once again she felt his fist slam into her face. This time her nose started bleeding, the blood running down into her mouth and onto her chin, and she could feel her left eye starting to swell.

The man pinned her arms back, leaned down close, and said, "I'm starting to enjoy this. Do you wish to continue?"

Just then there was a knock at the door. The man quickly covered her mouth, pulled a pistol from his waist, and shoved the barrel against her temple.

A few seconds passed before she heard the building super say, "Ms. Tully, are you there? I need to speak with you about the exterminators. They'll be coming out next week."

Carmen hoped when she didn't answer that he would let himself in, but seconds passed and she heard his footsteps moving away from the door.

Finally the man pulled the gun away from her head, crawled off of her, and told her to sit on the couch. She got up, grabbed some tissue from the coffee table, sat on the couch, and wiped the blood from her face. The man put the gun back in his waistband, shoved the coffee table away with his foot, pulled a straight-backed chair in front of her, and sat down.

"Now, we're going to wait for my friends, and then you're going to come with us."

Carmen said nothing and he continued, "Something smells good in here. I think while we're waiting we should have something to eat. You go fix us some dinner."

Carmen stared at him. What she saw was a man who was clearly no stranger to violence. When she didn't move, he jumped up, knocked the chair away, grabbed her by the hair, and pulled her to her feet. She wanted to scream but held back, knowing what would happen if she did.

He shoved her toward the kitchen, pulled the gun, and grinned. Through tobacco-stained teeth he said, "Now, fix us some dinner."

Carmen turned her back to him and retrieved a plate. She opened a drawer to get some flatware and saw a large knife. She paused and looked at it, then pulled out a fork and spoon. The man started to walk toward her and she partially closed the drawer. She put the chicken on his plate and was spooning out some broccoli and rice when he moved closer.

Still holding the gun, he put his hands on her shoulders and said, "We're going to have a nice sit-down meal, and then maybe we will go upstairs and entertain each other...just me and you."

She said nothing, but continued with the broccoli and rice. Then his hands began to move down, reaching around, feeling her breasts. Her jaw tightened with anger and she felt a surge of electric current run down her neck and back. She dropped the spoon, grabbed the knife from the drawer, and swung it around at him. But he was ready. He hit her in the back of the head with the butt of the gun, and she was out cold before she hit the floor.

The man kicked the knife across the floor, into the living room. He looked in the refrigerator, spotted a Heineken, grabbed the beer, opened it, and took a large pull. He then grabbed his plate and a fork, left her lying there, and went into the living room. He sat at the table and began to eat. Halfway through his meal, Carmen began to stir. Without missing a bite, the man barked, "Come over here and sit on the couch. Keep me company while I eat."

Carmen opened her eyes. Her head was throbbing and her legs felt weak, but she slowly pulled herself up. She was scared, but she was also angry. Without looking at him, she made her way to the couch and sat.

The man coughed out a sickening laugh and said, "I will be finished soon. Then we will see about going upstairs and having time for each other."

CHAPTER 23

Air traffic at New York's JFK International Airport had been relatively light. While JFK would normally require forty-eight-hour notice for small aircraft, Tripp was given clearance due to a phone call placed by Henry Powell from FBI headquarters in Miami. Careful to avoid restricted airspace in the New York area, Tripp followed the air traffic landing instructions to the letter. He had been fortunate in getting a quick turnaround in Miami after dropping Manning off, allowing him to quickly continue on to New York.

The flight into New York was uneventful. Tripp spent much of the time on the phone with Henry Powell getting information on Carmen Tully. Powell was able to get her address, apartment number, and telephone number. Tripp was now in a rental car following the same course Carmen's taxi had taken earlier that morning.

The shadows were growing long as he passed the Met, turned onto Eightieth Street, and began looking for Carmen's building. Tripp found the building a couple of blocks down and began looking for a parking spot—a task he wasn't too optimistic about. As luck would have it, a car pulled away from the curb only a block past the building, and he turned in. Before leaving the car he put his sports jacket on to cover the shoulder holster that held his Glock. He then got out, locked the door, and began walking back toward Carmen's building.

The late afternoon was beginning to grow cold, and somewhere in the distance Tripp could hear Bing Crosby singing "White Christmas." He walked up the steps to Carmen's building and buzzed her apartment. A minute passed and no one answered. He was about to buzz again when a couple opened the door and walked out with gifts in hand, apparently on their way to a Christmas party. Tripp took advantage of their carelessness and stepped inside; he walked across the foyer and pushed the elevator button. The building was quiet and he looked around. The entrance hall was basically bare, with a small table and chair along the wall. A solitary picture of the Brooklyn Bridge, which looked as though it had been hung there in the 1800s when the bridge opened, adorned the wall above the table. A bulletin board covered with notices and business cards hung on the opposite wall, and on the table were a lamp and a realty magazine. A bell sounded, breaking the silence, and the elevator door slid open. Tripp stepped inside, pushed a button, and felt the lift begin to rise. The door opened on Carmen's floor and Tripp began to make his way down the hall, looking for her apartment. He found it near the end of the hallway and knocked on the door.

Inside the apartment, Carmen's captor immediately dropped his fork and pulled the gun from his waistband. This time Carmen didn't hesitate.

"Please help me!" she screamed.

The man was too far from Carmen to restrain her, so he pointed the gun at her and yelled, "Shut up—now."

With the gun pointed at her, Carmen stopped screaming and held her breath. The man turned and started toward the door. Carmen grabbed the lamp next to the couch and hurled it at him. The lamp crashed into the wall behind him. When the man turned toward her, she dove behind the couch.

Tripp heard the scream and pulled the Glock from his shoulder holster. He clicked the safety off, stood beside the door with his ear against the frame, listening, and held the weapon pointed up. When he heard the lamp crash, he braced himself and kicked the door with his full weight. The door crashed open with wood splintering and slammed against the wall. Tripp dove in, rolled across the floor, and came up in a firing position.

Caught off guard, the man was startled and dove over the couch.

Instinctively, Tripp yelled, "FBI. Drop your weapon."

The man grabbed Carmen, pointed the gun at her head, and said, "I don't think so, *amigo.*"

He pulled her in front of him, keeping the gun against her head, and slowly stood, using her as a shield.

Tripp held his weapon out, but the man kept himself shielded with Carmen.

"Drop the weapon and let the girl go. I will let you walk out of here," Tripp said.

"I'm afraid you have it wrong. You will drop your weapon, and the girl walks out with me."

The man shoved the barrel into her neck and waited.

Tripp knew if he let them leave she was as good as dead already. He would have only one shot. He kept his finger on the trigger and slowly started to let his weapon drop. The Glock was a 9 mm. There was no room for error. The room grew deathly silent. Everything seeming to move in slow motion. Tripp had been here before. The man moved his head over a few inches, just enough to see that Tripp had lowered the weapon.

The man smiled and said, "Now, we're going to walk out of here, and you're going to let us. If you make any move to stop us, I pull the trigger."

Carmen was shaking and crying, her eyes closed in resignation.

Tripp knew it was now or never. In a split-second, he raised his gun and squeezed the trigger.

The man never saw it coming. The report was deafening as the bullet entered his forehead a half-inch above his right eyebrow and inches from Carmen's head. The force blew him back against the wall. He fell to the floor, blood smearing down the wall behind him.

Carmen, screaming and crying, fell to the floor into a fetal position. Holding his gun in a firing position, arms extended in front of him, Tripp moved to where the man had fallen. He kicked the man's weapon out of reach and knelt to check for a pulse. Assured that the man was no longer a threat, Tripp holstered his weapon and moved over to Carmen.

Tripp knelt down, took Carmen's hand, and said, "It's okay now. He won't hurt you again."

Carmen turned over, gazed into a pair of big turquoise-green eyes, and said, "Thank you."

Tripp beamed a broad, warm smile and said, "I thought you could use some help."

After lifting Carmen onto the couch, he brought an ice pack for her eye and a blanket. He then called Henry Powell to report what had happened.

Within minutes, the New York City police, along with the FBI, were at the apartment, taking statements and gathering evidence.

When the last officer left, Tripp sat at the table with Rodney Blaine, an FBI agent from the New York office whom Tripp knew well. Tripp and Blaine had attended the academy at the same time and become friends. Carmen had been treated by a doctor and was resting on the couch.

"So, what was his name?" Tripp asked.

"Hector Guerra," Blaine said. "He's a Cuban national. He's been linked to everything from drugs and kidnapping to rape and murder, but he's never been caught...until now."

Tripp stood, walked to the balcony door, opened it, and said, "I appreciate your help this evening, Rodney."

Blaine followed Tripp onto the balcony and said, "I was sorry to hear about Katie. Are you holding up okay?"

It was a cold and clear evening as they looked out into the night toward Central Park.

"I'm okay. Sometimes it's hard."

Blaine looked at the Christmas lights on the building across the street and said, "Why don't you spend Christmas here with us? I know Janie would love to have you, and I would too."

"I might just take you up on that offer. I've got to see this thing through right now, though."

They turned and walked back into the apartment. The super had repaired the door earlier in the evening before the officers left.

"I guess I'm going to head out, Sean," Blaine said. "You call me if you need anything, though."

"Thank you. The NYPD has offered to post a couple of men outside the building in case Hector has a friend out there. I'm going to stay here with Carmen."

Blaine left and Tripp walked over to the couch where Carmen was resting.

Carmen opened her eyes and said, "Thank you for everything."

"I'm glad I was able to help."

"That man said he had a friend. I don't know if I can stay here tonight."

"There are two officers outside, and I am going to stay here. You will be safe."

"Who are you, and where did you come from?"

"That is a long story. You get some rest, and I'll tell you everything in the morning."

Carmen closed her eyes and drifted off to sleep.

CHAPTER 24

$\mathcal{T}$ony awoke from a restless night. The bed in his cell was nothing more than a steel frame with mesh wiring covered with a soiled wool blanket. The cell was fairly large, and at one time had been used as a break room for the guards. At the rear of the twelve-foot-by-twenty-five-foot cell were a small table and several crates the guards had used as chairs. The cell was dirty and as dark as a graveyard. The toilet was just a hole in the corner of the earthen floor. Tony did not see another person during his long night, but in the distance he could hear music. He couldn't hear voices, and apparently no one could hear him, because he spent much of the night yelling, hoping that someone from the restaurant or lighthouse would hear him, but his efforts were in vain.

Eventually the early morning light began to filter down the corridor, lifting the veil of darkness. Tony began to hear voices, and he sat up on the edge of his bunk. The voices grew louder and he could now hear two sets of footsteps. When the footsteps stopped, Tony looked up into the face of Rogelio Cruz. Standing next to Rogelio was a huge bear of a man whose head was bald, but his jaws were covered in a thick black beard. Tony knew he was not Cuban, but he didn't think he was American either. He had dark, lifeless eyes, deep-set in a crater-lined face, and a small ring in his left earlobe. Tony thought he looked like a sinister version of Mr. Clean, and his gut instinct told him this was a man who would enjoy inflicting pain.

Without a word, Cruz stepped back as Mr. Clean unlocked and opened the cell door. They escorted Tony down the corridor to a nearby cell where there was a straight-backed metal chair, two banks of lights on tall stands pointing at the chair, a tripod with a video camera, and a folding chair behind the lights. They sat Tony in the straight-backed chair and walked behind the lights.

"Tony, this is an associate of mine, Comrade Igor Petroff. He will be joining us for our talk today. Igor doesn't say a lot himself, but he has a talent for causing others to."

Igor Petroff had been a member of the Soviet KGB, but after the collapse of the Soviet Union there were few opportunities for his skills, so he stayed behind in Cuba and found work with the Cuban DGI. While the old Soviet KGB doesn't exist anymore, the former members do. All the KGB training and instincts were still very much a part of Petroff, who lived by the KGB code: "Never forget, never forgive!"

"Why do you have me here?" Tony asked.

"There are some answers we need. You are going to help us get them."

"Is my father here?"

"He is not far."

Tony wanted to ask if he could see him, but he remembered the answer he had gotten the last time he asked and decided to wait.

"How can I help you get these answers?"

"Just be yourself and answer my questions truthfully."

Petroff snapped the lights on and stood next to Cruz. The bright, hot lights stung Tony's eyes.

"Now, let's begin, shall we," Cruz said.

Tony held a hand up, trying to shield his eyes from the light so he could see Cruz.

"Tell us your name."

"Tony Casteel."

"What is your full name?"

"Tony Arollo Casteel."

"What was the name given you at birth?"

Tony hesitated a moment, then said, "Tony Arollo Favela."

"What is your nationality?"

"I am American."

"Were you born in America?"

"No."

"What was your nationality at birth?"

"Cuban."

"How did you come to live in America?"

Tony again hesitated a moment. His eyes were adjusting to the light, but not the heat. Beads of sweat had begun to form on his forehead and were running down his face.

Finally he answered, "We came in a boat when I was small."

"You said *we*. Do you mean your family?"

"Yes."

"Including yourself, how many were in your family?"

"There were four of us—my mother, father, and sister."

"What were their names?"

"My mother's name is Amalia, my father's name is Manuel, and my sister's name is Carmen."

Cruz paused a moment, looking at Tony. The effects of the heat, lack of sleep, and fear were beginning to have the desired effect on the boy. Cruz whispered to Petroff and the huge man left the cell, only to return shortly with a pitcher of ice water. He poured Cruz a glass, and Cruz took it and drank slowly. He then set the glass on the floor next to his chair.

"I need a drink of water," Tony said.

Cruz ignored Tony and continued, "Now, tell me about your boat trip to America."

"What about it? What do you want to know?"

"Tell me what you know."

"I don't remember too much. I was very little. I remember we left at night... It was dark. I think there were several boats.... My family and I were in one." Tony closed his eyes, trying to pull some memory forward. Most of his memories were not from what he had witnessed as a toddler, but from recurring dreams he had had over the past fifteen years. "I remember another big ship came along and began shooting at us. My father put my sister and me on another boat...only my sister fell into the sea. Then we left, and that's about it."

"So you left your family behind while you made it safely to America."

Tony could feel anger welling up inside as he said, "I did not desert my family. I was only—"

"But here you are, safe and sound, while your family..." Cruz interrupted, allowing his voice to trail off.

Tony was tired, hot, thirsty, and angry.

He finally said, "I'm not saying anything more until I get some water."

This was exactly what Cruz was waiting for. He got up, folded his chair, nodded at Petroff, and left the cell.

Petroff left the video camera running and walked over to Tony. The thick stone walls absorbed much of the screams, but Cruz could hear the tortured cries echo from far down the corridor. Before Cruz left the prison chamber, he stopped and listened to the wails, somehow comforted in knowing Castro would be pleased. He listened to the piercing shrieks for several more minutes, then turned and walked out of the tunnel.

He passed the guards, turned, and said, "Be sure no one enters, and tell Comrade Petroff to meet me on top when he's finished with his work."

A half hour later, Tony lay unconscious on the dirt floor. Petroff looked down at Tony, smiled, and flicked off the video camera and lights. He dragged Tony to his cell and closed and locked the door, then returned to the nearby cell, collected the videotape, and left the prison chamber.

Cruz was standing by the south wall of the castle, looking out over the bay. It was a crisp, clear morning, and Cruz was enjoying the cool breeze.

When Petroff approached, Cruz said, "Did you bring me the videotape?"

"Yes, I have it for you." He handed the video to Cruz.

"He is still alive, isn't he?"

"Yes."

"That is good. We may have to make another visit this evening. I will see if the video will cause Manuel Favela's tongue to loosen."

Cruz looked toward Havana and watched the flow of daily life along the Malecon.

"Fidel will not be around much longer. After he's gone, I don't believe Raul's power will last. In which case, it will fall to the strongest man. I intend that man to be me.... And you, Comrade Petroff, will be my general. But it will also take money, and if Castro is right, this video may be the piece I need to solve that problem."

He turned back toward Petroff and said, "That will be all for now. I may contact you this evening should I have further need of your assistance."

Without another word Petroff turned and walked away. Cruz stuffed the videotape into his jacket and turned his attention back to the bay.

CHAPTER
25

*M*anning was in the elevator at FBI headquarters. A bell chimed and the doors slid open. He stepped out into the reception area and was greeted by Cecelia Salazar.

"Good morning, Agent Manning."

Manning walked over to the reception desk, flashed one of his patented smiles, and said, "What a great way to start the morning. I could really get used to working here."

Cecelia smiled, looked into his deep blue eyes, and said, "Thank you, but you better go on back."

Manning entered the conference room and was greeted by Henry Powell.

"Good morning, Neil. I hope you had a better night's sleep than I did. A lot has happened since yesterday. Help yourself to some coffee or juice and have a seat."

Manning walked behind the conference table, chose grapefruit juice and a bagel, and sat in one of the leather chairs.

"Did Tripp find Carmen?" Manning asked.

"Yes. Fortunately he got there in time. One of Castro's men, a Hector Guerra, had already paid her a visit and worked her over pretty good. Tripp took him out and Carmen will be fine with a little rest."

"Looks like our visit to Zavala paid off," Manning said between bites.

"Yes, and none too soon either. But there's more."

Manning finished the bagel, opened the can of grapefruit juice, and waited.

"Hector Guerra told Carmen he was waiting on some friends. NYPD posted two men at the door to her building and Tripp stayed in her apartment last night, so we weren't too worried about Carmen's safety. Nevertheless, we had a surveillance team set up. Shortly after two this morning, our surveillance team spotted two men watching the building. Agent Rodney Blaine was part of the surveillance team, and he thought he recognized the men, so he had them followed, hoping to get a positive ID."

"Did he get one?'

"Yes."

"Who were they?"

"The Soto brothers."

There was complete silence for several seconds before Manning finally spoke.

"Does Tripp know?"

"Blaine will be meeting with Tripp today to tell him."

The Soto brothers were well known throughout the intelligence community as the leaders of an organized crime ring that specialized in prostitution, gambling, and drugs. The bureau had evidence that they filtered their money through the Grand Cayman Islands, where it ended up in accounts connected to Castro. They were the same men Katie Tripp had been trying to apprehend when she was shot and left to die while working undercover.

Manning, staring off into space, said, "This is going to open some old wounds."

"There's still more. They followed Raul and José Soto into Central Park, where the two met with a man we have identified as Yuri Petroff. Do you recognize the name?"

"If I recall, he's tied in with the Russian Mafia."

"Yes, he has quite the history too. As a young man he was a member of Vorovskoy Mir, or the Thieves' World. The Thieves World was an underground criminal organization that Stalin often used for his own cruel and devious purposes. When the organization was outlawed, Yuri Petroff, along with a great many of his fellow members, was imprisoned. When World War II came along, he was offered a deal for his freedom if he would join the fight against the Nazis. He fulfilled his end of the deal, but after the war the czar reneged and returned him to prison. Back in prison, Petroff was ostracized by the Thieves' World for cooperating with the authorities. The Thieves' World had a code, and Petroff broke the code when he cooperated with the authorities and served in the military. Yuri now found himself having to side with the prison guards in order to survive. He was labeled a bitch. Somehow Yuri survived the infamous Bitch Wars and was eventually released, only to become a lord in organized crime. However, as you might expect, he now had many enemies, and began to look for a way to leave the Soviet Union. Somewhere along the way, Petroff broke another of the organization's codes when he had a son. The codes allowed for lovers, but no wives or children. Anyway, his son grew older and eventually became a member of the Soviet KGB. As a KGB agent, this son used his contacts to help his father escape to the United States, where he settled at Brighton Beach, also known as Little Odessa. In Little Odessa, Yuri eventually led the Red Mafia, dealing in drugs, weapons, and prostitution."

"And this Yuri Petroff is the old man who met with José and Raul Soto?"

"Yes, but there's more, and this is where it gets very interesting. After the breakup of the Soviet Union, Yuri's son, the KGB agent, seems to have found employment in Cuba. Our sources in Cuba tell us that his son, Igor Petroff, now works for the DGI, which as you know is the equivalent to the CIA. They tell us he works in several capacities, one of which is as liaison between his father and Castro to broker drug deals. He also serves as a hit man or strongman as the needs arise."

"How were these thugs able to find Carmen and Tony after all these years?"

"We're not sure—not yet, anyway. It's suspected that Yuri and his Mafia have members of the NYPD and ATF on their payrolls. It's possible they have someone inside Intelligence working for them as well. Both the FBI and CIA are investigating. We're checking everything from e-mails to phone records to find a connection to Yuri."

"Sounds like our intelligence may need to be tightened up."

Powell opened a folder and pulled out the enlarged images from the Onyx 9 satellite.

"Now that Carmen is safe, our immediate concern is Tony. My guess is Castro's people know by now that they missed on Carmen, so that leaves Tony as their last hope to get Manuel to talk. They're going to turn up the heat on him unless we can get him out."

Powell handed Manning one of the satellite images.

"This photo is a shot of Tony, Vargas, and his men on his yacht, the *El Diablo Rojo.*"

He handed Manning the next photo.

"This shot is the same yacht docked at El Castillo del Morro."

Manning stared at the image.

"This image shows Tony, Vargas, and two of his men inside the walls of Morro."

Powell handed Manning the last photo.

"And this is *El Diablo Rojo* leaving Morro. If you will notice, Tony is not aboard."

"So Tony is still on Morro," Manning said.

"Yes. And we're going to have to get him out."

CHAPTER
26

Tripp awoke to the smell of bacon frying and the sound of coffee brewing. He had spent an uncomfortable night stretched out on a recliner next to the couch in Carmen's apartment. He glanced at the couch, found it empty, and looked toward the kitchen. Carmen was standing at the oven with her back to him. He picked up the Glock he had kept next to him on the end table and checked to see that the safety was on. He then reached for the shoulder holster and slipped the weapon into the pocket. Morning sunlight was filtering in through the drawn curtains, slowly erasing the darkness of night and spreading the warmth of a new day. Tripp removed the blanket someone had draped over him and stretched.

Carmen, who was now mixing a pitcher of frozen orange juice, heard Tripp beginning to stir and looked over at him.

"Good morning. I hope I didn't wake you," she said.

"Good morning. Coffee and bacon will do it every time."

"How do you like yours?"

"Coffee black, bacon crisp."

Carmen took the bacon off the burner, poured Tripp a cup of black coffee, and walked into the living room to hand him the cup.

Tripp took a sip and said, "How does that commercial go... the best part of waking up? Thank you, it's perfect."

Carmen sat on the couch next to the recliner.

"Thank you for coming to my rescue, Sean."

She was dressed in black slacks and a matching wool sweater, which worked to highlight her shoulder-length black hair that was pulled back into a ponytail. Sean looked into Carmen's greenish-brown eyes and realized how strikingly beautiful she was. Some of the swelling in her face had gone down, and makeup covered the bruises.

"How are you feeling?" Tripp asked.

"A little sore. I slept well and spent a good part of an hour soaking in a hot bath."

Tripp smiled; his turquoise eyes were warm and comforting.

"I'm glad you're safe and I was able to help."

"Will you tell me now what this is all about?"

"How about I tell you everything over some breakfast?"

"Coming right up," Carmen said with a smile.

While Carmen set the table for breakfast, which included scrambled eggs, bacon, toast, and orange juice, Tripp excused himself to the restroom to clean up.

When he returned, Carmen had breakfast on the table and invited Tripp to have a seat. She opened the curtains on the windows leading to the balcony. It was a beautiful morning, and a light snow had begun to fall, with huge flakes that looked like big puffs of cotton floating past the window. Tripp pulled the chair back for Carmen, then sat opposite her in the chair facing the window.

They ate in silence for a couple of minutes before Tripp broke the silence.

"I like your apartment, it's very comfortable."

"Even the recliner?" Carmen asked with a sheepish grin.

"Well, perhaps you could replace it with one of those sleep number units."

"Is the bacon crisp enough?"

"It's perfect," Tripp said, making eye contact.

There was another minute of silence, this time broken by Carmen.

"So tell me who Sean Tripp is. You weren't wearing a cape, so I'm guessing you're not a superhero."

"My cape is at the cleaners," Tripp said with a grin.

Carmen took a sip of orange juice, looked at him, and began again.

"I haven't seen you around the building before. Do you live here?"

"No, I live in Monterey, California."

"I see, and you just happened to be in my neighborhood."

The disarming smile left Tripp's face as he began, "I live on a cruiser docked in Monterey Bay. Most of the locals know I am a retired FBI agent. Five days ago, a young man I have known for a while came aboard my cruiser asking for my help. A friend of his was missing, and he asked if I would look into it. The missing boy's name is Tony Casteel."

"And you thought the missing boy was in my apartment?" Carmen asked with a playful smile.

Tripp put his fork down, wiped the napkin over his mouth, and continued, "No, it was his sister I was looking for."

Carmen smiled and said, "Well, I do hope you find the boy, but I must say I'm glad you happened into the wrong apartment."

Tripp knew what he was about to say would completely change Carmen's life. He stood, pulled his chair around, and sat down adjacent to her.

He looked into her eyes, paused, and said, "Carmen, I didn't come to the wrong apartment. Tony Casteel's given name is Tony Favela."

Carmen dropped her fork. It clinked against the plate and fell to the floor. Her expression changed from a smile to one of confusion.

"My brother is alive?" Carmen asked, almost in a whisper.

"Yes, your brother is alive, Carmen. Tony was adopted by Armando and Tina Casteel and has been living in Monterey until he disappeared about a week ago. We think Tony was taken by the same group of men who were here last night to abduct you. They've taken him to Cuba, and we're pretty sure that's what they had planned for you as well."

Tripp pulled Tony's picture from his shirt pocket and handed it to Carmen.

Carmen looked at the picture, then glanced at the photo of her family on the mantel. Tears began to form as she recognized Tony.

"Who are these men, and why did they take Tony to Cuba?"

"They are Castro's men. They've taken him because they're hoping to use him to get your father to talk."

Carmen's head jerked up and she looked Tripp square in the eyes.

"My father is alive?"

"Yes, we believe he is being held in Guayabo Prison, on a small island near Cuba."

"What about my mother?"

"There have been no reports about her. We can only guess she must have died."

"What do they want from Tony?"

"It seems when your family left Cuba your father took along some of Castro's money."

Carmen's eyes dropped to the table. She stared blankly for several seconds before speaking again.

"Why was I kept in the dark about Tony?"

"Here things get a little more cloudy, but it seems there is a somewhat influential man called Grouper who is a friend of your father's and has somehow maintained contact with him. He knew Castro would be looking for the two of you, so for your own protection he kept you separated. He arranged to have each of you placed with a family on opposite sides of the country, and if my guess is right, his actions are what have kept you alive for fifteen years."

"Who is this Grouper?"

"We don't know. Do you ever remember your father mentioning the name?"

"No, but I don't allow myself to remember a lot from my past. I remember my father used to play word games with names, but that one doesn't ring a bell."

"Think about it. If something should come to you, no mater how insignificant you may think it is, I want you to tell me."

Carmen nodded and asked, "How did they finally find us?"

"We don't know that either...not yet."

Tripp's cell phone chirped and he walked to the base of the stairs where his jacket hung on a coat rack. He reached out and slipped the phone from a pocket.

"This is Sean Tripp," he answered.

"Good morning, Sean. How is our girl this morning?" Rodney Blaine asked.

"Good morning, Rodney. She is fine, considering."

"Listen, there have been some developments since I left you last night. We think Carmen was about to have some more visitors around two this morning, but they saw the two NYPD officers and left. The NYPD intends to pull their men today, so you should probably move Carmen somewhere safe. Also, we need to meet so I can bring you up to date on other developments."

"Thank you, Rodney, I will do that this morning."

"Call me when she's safe and we'll get together. When you call, don't tell me where she is."

Tripp clicked off and turned toward the kitchen. Carmen had cleared the table and was in the kitchen rinsing the dishes.

"Carmen, we need to move you out of here for a while. I want you to go pack some things. I will finish up in here."

"Tell me something, Sean. Is anything being done to help Tony?"

"My partner is trying to find where they have him. Once we know his exact location we'll come up with a plan. I'm going to meet with Agent Blaine in a little while, so I'll know more later."

Carmen dried her hands and turned to go upstairs.

"You don't need to pack too many things. It shouldn't be more than a couple of days," Tripp said.

"It may take *us* longer than that to rescue Tony," Carmen said with an edge to her voice.

Tripp started to respond, but Carmen had disappeared up the stairs.

An hour later Tripp was checking into the Hotel on Rivington, located in the historic lower east side of Manhattan. The hotel wasn't far from Carmen's apartment, and was the first luxury high-rise in the once-dilapidated neighborhood whose former tenement buildings now housed the trendiest boutiques and bars.

Although it was only a few blocks from Carmen's apartment, Tripp had made at least a dozen turns, each time doubling back to assure himself he wasn't being followed. When he was confident he didn't have a tail, he turned into the hotel, left the car with a valet, and hurried through the cave-like entrance. Carmen was wearing dark sunglasses and had a scarf pulled over her head and tied under her chin.

She sat in the corner of the egg-shaped lobby with her face stuffed in a magazine while Tripp checked in. Tripp signed the form while the desk clerk ran his credit card. With key in hand, Tripp grabbed their luggage and escorted Carmen to the elevator. They were the only two on the glass elevator, and Carmen removed her sunglasses as it began to rise.

"Do you really think all this cloak-and-dagger stuff is necessary? I feel like a married woman sneaking into a hotel with another man."

"I wouldn't know anything about that, but you may want to keep your sunglasses on until we reach the room," Tripp said with a playful grin.

Carmen slapped him on the shoulder as the elevator came to a stop on the sixteenth floor.

The spacious suite was gorgeous. Its floor-to-ceiling windows and private terrace provided an unobstructed, stunning view of the Manhattan skyline. The living area had a leather sofa and chair, a coffee table, and a large flat-screen television. Next to the kitchenette was a round glass dining table with two chairs. Amenities included a DVD movie library, an assortment of gourmet snacks, a full-bottle wine selection, and a large under-counter refrigerator. The restroom had a large two-person tub, a shower with glass walls and windows, and a floor covered in stylish mosaic tiles.

Tripp set the luggage on the floor and locked the door.

"I'm going to have to leave for a while to meet with Agent Blaine, but you will be safe here. I don't want you to leave the room," Tripp said, "and do not call anyone, not even your parents."

Carmen didn't respond, but walked onto the terrace and looked out over the peaks of Wall Street. The light morning snow had turned heavier, and the sky looked more like buttermilk now. Tripp followed her onto the terrace.

"Are you okay?" he asked.

"Considering my life has been turned upside down, I guess so. Yesterday my main concern was what to buy my parents for Christmas. Today I'm hiding in this hotel, wishing I could do something to find my brother."

Tripp put his hands on her shoulders and turned her to face him. What he saw in her eyes was not fear or sorrow, but resolve.

"I will do everything I can, and there are many others helping," he promised. "Just hold on."

CHAPTER
27

Isla de la Juventud, Cuba, 2007

There are more than 350 islands in the Canarreos Archipelago. El Guayabo Prison sits on the largest of these islands, the Isla de la Juventud, which lies about sixty miles almost directly south of Havana and Castillo del Morro.

Within the walls of Guayabo, men are held for violent crimes and for crimes against the state, which usually means speaking out against Castro or the inhumane conditions brought about by his Communist regime. Manuel Favela was one of the prisoners held at Guayabo.

For some ten years he suffered the atrocious conditions at Boniato Prison in Santiago de Cuba, in the southeastern province of the island nation, the same prison in which Fidel Castro was once imprisoned. He had been held in an isolation cell that could only be described as filthy. The cell was very small, with no running water, a latrine that was little more than a hole in the floor, and a dirty, hard mattress on the floor that was torn and soiled. In strong rains the roof leaked, and the cell would flood with residual water from the hallway. Rats would enter his cell from the latrine, along with the pervasive stench, but there was no light. The only thing provided by the prison was a pair of shorts and a T-shirt. Provisions such as sheets, toothbrush and toothpaste, towels, and mosquito netting were allowed if provided by the families, but Manuel had no one. The food was foul smelling and rotten, which often led to dysentery. Occasionally Manuel would be allowed a few minutes of sun out in the yard, which was surrounded by barbed wire and armed guards, but he was taken out separately so as to maintain his isolation. He knew he would never get out of prison alive, but he also knew he could have avoided the torture and died quickly if he had told what he knew about the money. Manuel never said a word; the hope that his children were alive and that he might someday see them again kept him going. As the years passed the torture subsided, and his existence became the endless day-to-day routine of life in prison.

Then he was transferred to Guayabo. While the cells were still cramped and dirty, he was no longer in isolation, and the food was tolerable. After being in hell for ten years, it was an improvement. He had no access to newspapers, radio, or television, so he knew little of what was happening in the world, but fortunately, some of the guards knew of Manuel's plight, and at great risk to themselves, they helped him whenever possible. Most of the guards were poor, helpless, and frightened, and he knew they must follow orders or might very well find themselves behind the same bars they guarded.

One day, one of the guards who had actually served with Manuel and Omar before they fled smuggled a message to him from the outside. The message said his children had been adopted and were doing well; it was signed only by the name "Grouper." As the years passed, more messages came periodically and kept him updated. Although he had no hope of getting out of prison alive, the messages served to greatly improve his spirit. Now he was resigned to spending his remaining years behind bars, comforted in knowing his children were safe.

Manuel sat alone on a bench in the courtyard, thinking about the last message he had received from Grouper. The message said Castro had located his children and had already taken Tony. For fifteen years Manuel had rotted away in prison and survived the torture and indignities without speaking a word about the money by clinging to the hope that his children were safe. Now that hope was dashed. He thought about the last time he had seen his family. After all the years, that night was still vivid in his mind. He could feel the boat rocking in the Gulf Stream, hear the gunshots, smell the salty brine, and see the lifeless body of his wife in his arms and the blackness of the night closing around him. Though he had managed to live through the ubiquitous anguish of Castro's prisons, that misery paled in comparison to the fear of what they would put Tony through. Grouper told him to just hold on; he said Fidel would be gone soon, and there might be reforms that could bring Manuel's freedom. Now Manuel was no longer sure his resolve was strong enough, not if Tony was the one having to suffer.

As he sat considering all this, a guard began walking towards him. Manuel looked up just as the guard stopped in front of him.

"You are to come with me," the guard said.

"Where are you taking me?"

"The commandant's office. You have a visitor."

Manuel followed the guard through the courtyard, past the barbed wire, through a massive steel gate, and into the facility that housed the prison offices. He was escorted down a long corridor and into the commandant's quarters, where the commandant sat behind his desk. Standing near the wall to his left was Rogelio Cruz.

The office was small and dreary. There was a desk and chair, a bookshelf cluttered with reams of paper stacked helter-skelter, a straight-backed wooden chair opposite the desk, and a three-foot-by-six-foot safe in the corner of the office. On the far wall hung a map of Cuba and a framed photo of El Presidente Castro. A small table with a television and video cassette player had been rolled in and stood squarely in the middle of the office.

"Be seated, Manuel," the commandant began.

When Manuel was seated in the small wooden chair, the commandant continued, "I believe you know Señor Cruz. He has some matters to discuss with you."

Manuel stared straight ahead and said nothing. He knew Cruz very well, having spent many days with him, and his KGB friend, in his small cell, where they tortured him, trying to get him to talk.

"Mr. Favela, you have some information we need. So far we have been unsuccessful in causing you to share your secrets," Cruz began.

Cruz paused a few seconds, watching Manuel, then walked around the desk and stood behind the prisoner.

"This morning I met someone I believe you know."

Manuel still said nothing, and Cruz circled around until he was facing Manuel again.

"This morning I had the opportunity to meet a young man named Tony Casteel. You may know him by the name Tony Favela. He actually looks a bit like you. He is anxious to see his father. Could that be you, by chance?"

This time Cruz got a reaction.

"Where is he?"

"He is not far from here."

"Leave him out of this. He knows nothing."

"Perhaps not, but you do."

Manuel sat silent, his eyes straight ahead.

"It's been awhile since you've seen him, Manuel. Maybe you would like to see how he's changed."

Cruz pulled a remote from his pocket and pushed a button. As Manuel turned around to face the television, it lit up with the video of Tony from earlier that morning.

Manuel's eyes began to well up when he saw his son for the first time in fifteen years. He watched closely as they began the interview, watched his son's face, listened to every word, listened to his accent and the way he formed his words. He heard Cruz ask him his name, and heard his son answer, "Tony Casteel." He thought how strong and handsome Tony looked, and then he heard Cruz ask Tony his birth name. He listened closely as his son answered, "Tony Favela." He then heard his son give the names of his family: Manuel Favela, Amalia Favela, and Carmen Favela.

Manuel not only felt sadness, he felt anger. He knew all too well that Cruz was using Tony against him. He knew he could not show weakness; if Cruz saw any sign of weakness, things would only get worse for Tony. Manuel watched as Cruz left and the Russian KGB agent approached Tony. He sat in silence, watching Petroff beat his son and listening to his cries. It took every ounce of courage and strength Manuel could muster to show no sign of anger or resentment. When it was finally over Manuel turned back toward Cruz, his face stoic, and stared straight ahead.

"Perhaps your memory is clearer now?" Cruz asked.

In a voice as indifferent as he could muster, Manuel said, "I hardly remember him. That was many years ago. He means nothing to me."

Cruz took a step toward Manuel, violently slammed his fist on the desk, and in an enraged voice said, "You will tell me where the money is, Favela, or you will not see your son again."

"I thought he was already dead. And besides, I'm not even sure that boy is really my son."

Cruz was furious now. He pulled his sidearm from his holster, shoved it against Manuel's temple, and said, "He *is* your son, and you *will* tell me where the money is. I will give you some time to think about it before I visit your son again. Just know that anything that happens to the boy is on your hands."

With that, Cruz shoved Manuel to the floor, holstered his weapon, and left the office.

CHAPTER 28

*W*ith Carmen settled into her hotel room, Tripp stepped out onto the terrace, pulled out his cell phone, and punched in the number for Rodney Blaine.

"Agent Blaine."

"Rodney, our girl has been safely moved."

"How is she doing?"

"She's doing well, actually. She's mostly concerned about her brother. You said there were some new developments?" Tripp asked.

"Yes, we need to get together so I can bring you up to date."

Tripp looked out over the Manhattan skyline. His eyes focused on the Woolworth Building.

"How about the Woolworth Building in thirty minutes?" Tripp asked.

"I'll meet you in the lobby," Blaine said.

Tripp clicked off and walked back into the hotel room. Carmen was sitting on the sofa drinking orange juice and leafing through a magazine she had found on the coffee table.

"I'm going to have to go out for a while, Carmen. I'm going to meet with Agent Blaine to find out what the status is with Tony. You will be safe here."

Carmen looked at Tripp, her eyes set and determined.

"I want to go with you. Tony is my brother."

"And I want you to see your brother again. We don't believe the man in your apartment last night was alone. I need to find out where we stand, Carmen."

"I don't like being stuck here, hidden away, doing nothing."

Tripp watched Carmen as she spoke, watched the way the morning sun framed her face, bringing out her Latin features. Her eyes and mouth were serious and determined, yet still warm and delicate. He found himself drawn to her in a way he hadn't known in a long time. Tripp smiled warmly and sat beside her.

"I'm not going to leave you stuck in here, hidden away. Tell you what, you make us some reservations for dinner tonight—anywhere you want—and over dinner I'll fill you in on what I find out and what the plan is to get Tony back."

"Anywhere I want?" Carmen asked, the corners of her mouth turning up in a grin.

Tripp stood, walked to the door, then turned back and smiled. "Anywhere."

"I hope you brought your tux." She returned to her magazine.

Tripp left, checked to see that the door was locked behind him, and headed for the lobby.

A light snow was still falling when Tripp stepped out of the hotel. The Woolworth Building was only a few minutes away and Tripp briefly considered walking, but time was running short. To avoid the task of finding a parking spot, Tripp decided to leave his rental where it was and waved down a taxi. The taxi turned right on Delancey, then left on Lafayette. When they turned onto Broadway Tripp could see the fifty-five-story Woolworth Building looming in front of them. The cab pulled over and stopped at 233 Broadway. Tripp tipped the driver, stepped out into the snow, and entered the lobby. The lobby was decorated for the season with a giant eight-foot Christmas tree and streams of red lights and silver tinsel.

Five minutes later Agent Blaine, wearing an impeccable gray suit, button-down white shirt, solid blue silk tie, and a light wool overcoat, entered the lobby, shook hands with Tripp, and suggested they take a walk across the street to historic City Hall Park.

The nine-acre park, surrounded by brownstones, bookstores, and cafés and criss-crossed with walkways, is an oasis from the bustle of the city. As the two men strolled slowly through the park, Tripp told Blaine where Carmen was and how she desperately wanted news on Tony.

"Tell me about these new developments," Tripp said.

"As I mentioned this morning, we believe Carmen was about to have some more visitors early this morning, around two, but they were probably dissuaded by the NYPD officers outside her building."

"Do you know who they were?"

"We weren't sure at first. I thought they looked familiar, so I had them followed."

The snow had stopped when they reached the fountain, and Blaine suggested they sit down. The men wiped a thin layer of snow from a bench and sat facing an ornate fountain. Water flowed freely in the chilled winter morning and cascaded over two levels, where it was caught by a square retaining wall before spurting out and emptying into smaller frosty ponds on each side. An elaborate lamp with five globes cast in glass cages stood in the corner closest to them. In the background, looming above the trees, stood the City Hall building.

"Our agents followed the two men into Central Park. The agents had to stay well back to keep from being spotted, but when the two men stopped to talk to a third man who was waiting for them, our agents got close enough for some infrared digital photos."

He pulled some photos from his inside breast pocket and handed them to Tripp.

Tripp instantly recognized two of the men as the Soto brothers. His eyes narrowed and his jaw tightened as he saw visions of his wife Katie.

"Sean, I knew this wouldn't be easy for you. That's why I wanted to meet with you in person."

There was a long pause before Tripp spoke. "Did you arrest them?"

"No, our agents didn't recognize them. It wasn't until we downloaded the digital photos that I knew," Blaine answered.

There was another long pause as Tripp looked into the fountain. "Who is the old guy in the picture?" he finally asked.

"His name is Yuri Petroff. He is a leader in the Red Mafia."

"That explains his ties to Raul and José Soto."

"Yes, and an interesting side note is that his son is a former KGB agent who now works with the DGI in Cuba."

"So where are we with Tony?"

"The Coast Guard stopped and arrested Enemencio Vargas shortly after he left Castillo del Morro. He said a DGI agent by the name of Rogelio Cruz has Tony and is holding him in a cell at Morro. Neil Manning and Michael Juarez are going over to get him back."

Tripp knew Agent Juarez well and felt confident that he and Manning could do the job.

"Please let me know if you hear anything," Tripp said.

"I will. I've got to go. Are you all right, Sean?"

Tripp's eyes were focused on the fountain. He answered that he was fine, but his thoughts were far away. Carmen was safe with him, and Manning would hopefully get Tony back, but his mind was on José and Raul Soto and the promise he had made to Katie to find those who were responsible for her death.

CHAPTER 29

Rio de Janeiro, 2007

*R*io de Janeiro, with its picturesque placement between lush, forest-covered mountains and breathtaking beaches, is one of the most beautiful and spectacular cities in the world. Nestled against Guanabara Bay, the city is commonly known as Rio and is nicknamed a Cidade Maravilhosa, or the Marvelous City. Guanabara Bay is connected to the Atlantic Ocean by a deep channel that's less than a mile wide and provides a natural landlocked harbor, which allows ocean-going vessels to berth almost in the center of the city. Out of the harbor rises the famous landmark Sugar Loaf, a huge rock over one thousand feet high that's shaped like an old-fashioned loaf of sugar. Another famous landmark standing atop Corcovado Mountain is the giant statue of Christ with open arms, making the shape of the cross. The statue of Jesus, known as Cristo Redentor, or Christ the Redeemer, stands some thirty-eight meters tall and is considered one of the wonders of the modern world. Rio de Janeiro, or River of January, got its name from Spanish navigators in honor of the month they arrived. It is famous for its spectacular natural setting, its annual Carnival celebration, and the gorgeous hotel-lined beaches of Copacabana and Ipanema.

Sitting on the patio of the Coconut Hut, Amado Fuentes held a fat cigar in his left hand, sipped on an ice-cold beer, and looked out over Ipanema Beach. It was a gorgeous setting, with crystal-clear aqua blue water and dazzling white powder sand. It was late afternoon, but it was still cool and comfortable. Temperatures at Ipanema, moderated by the cool sea breezes from the ocean, average between seventy and eighty degrees Fahrenheit, and Fuentes knew he was truly in his element.

As Cuban finance minister, Fuentes used his diplomatic status to its full advantage. He stayed at the finest hotels, drank the best beer, and entertained the most expensive women. Amado Fuentes was a heavyset man in his mid-fifties, and he had been Castro's finance minister for almost twenty-five years. His hair, combed straight back, was mostly white, and his skin was deeply tanned. He wore shorts, sandals, and a light guayabera shirt with the top three buttons open, exposing a thick mat of salt-and-pepper chest hair. Behind a set of steel-framed sunglasses resting on a big fleshy nose was a pair of dark eyes that missed nothing.

From somewhere in the background, "The Girl From Ipanema" was playing, and Fuentes smiled as he watched Thereza, the lady he had selected for the evening's entertainment, step out of the water and begin to towel off. He listened to the lyrics of the song—"Tall and tan and young and lovely, the girl from Ipanema goes walking, and when she passes, each one she passes goes a-a-ah"—and thought to himself that those words perfectly described Thereza. He took a long pull on his cigar, blew out a dense cloud, and was satisfied that she was well worth the money he had paid for her services.

Thereza, wearing a blue and white tropical print Asha Couture bikini, walked over to Fuentes, gave him a quick kiss on his forehead, her blond hair falling from her shoulders, and sat in a lounge chair next to him.

"The water is wonderful. You should go for a swim and enjoy yourself, Amado," Thereza said in Portuguese.

Fuentes looked into her almond-brown eyes and responded in Spanish, "I am very much enjoying myself by watching you."

"Thank you! You are sweet, Amado."

"And anyway, I am expecting a visit from an old friend. Would you like a drink, my love?" Fuentes asked.

"Some pineapple juice would be nice," she said as she stretched out to get some sun.

After several minutes and another ice-cold beer, Fuentes was intently rubbing tanning oil onto Thereza's back and shoulders when he heard a familiar voice.

"Minister Fuentes, it looks as though you're enjoying your visit to Brazil."

Fuentes turned to see his old friend standing a few feet away.

"General, my friend, it's good to see you!" He stood, picked up a towel, wiped the oil from his hands, and continued, "I always enjoy my visits abroad."

Fuentes had established commercial accounts in several South American and European countries, held by various shell corporations, to launder money for Castro and the drug syndicates. He regularly transferred funds to other accounts around the world, creating a long and intricate trail before the money eventually ended up in Castro's hands. As finance minister, Fuentes made regular "diplomatic" trips to these countries to check on the accounts.

He walked over, shook hands with the general, and added, "I enjoy any chance to get out of Cuba."

"You mean to get away from the people who fight daily battles to get enough food and basic necessities to survive?" the general said in a tone that was less than convivial.

"Are you forgetting, General, these people were fighting the same battles when you stood next to Fidel?"

The general looked down, his voice softening, and said, "I have not forgotten, but I am fighting for them now."

Attempting to lighten the mood again, Fuentes walked over, sat next to Thereza, and said, "So too am I, my friend, but in the meantime, I choose to enjoy myself when I can."

Fuentes kissed Thereza on the top of her head and said, "Thereza, my dear, I would like to introduce the general, an old and dear friend of mine from long ago."

The general walked over, took her hand, and said, "It is a pleasure to meet you, Thereza. My friends call me Grouper, and I hope you will too."

"I'm pleased to meet you, Grouper," Thereza said with a smile.

"Thereza, I need to speak with the general alone. Could you excuse us for a while?"

"Of course, Amado, I was about to go for another swim anyway."

Thereza gave Amado a kiss on the cheek, said her good-byes to Grouper, and jogged toward the surf.

The men watched Thereza running and Amado said, "She is lovely, is she not?"

"Yes, she is. Now, tell me how things are going in Cuba, Amado."

"Not much has changed since we last spoke. Fidel is old and sick, and is not expected to last much longer."

"Do you have the support you need to take control?" Grouper asked.

"I have assurances from the military of their support—as long as the money continues. I have been paying them the money you send me, and when Castro dies, I will have access to the millions Castro has in banks around the world. I know all the bank codes and my signature is on file."

"And what of Raul?" Grouper asked.

"Raul's power comes to him because he is Fidel's brother, but most of the people are miserable and are looking for a change. When Fidel is gone, he will not be able to maintain his power."

"I too want change for the people of Cuba. That is why Los Vengadores and I have been helping you."

"I know that, and I will not let you down, my friend."

Grouper pulled a letter from his pocket, handed it to Fuentes, and said, "Please see that Manuel gets this."

"I will deliver it to him personally," Fuentes said.

CHAPTER
30

*L*ess than an hour after leaving Castillo del Morro, Enemencio Vargas and the other men aboard *El Diablo Rojo* were in handcuffs aboard a United States Coast Guard cutter, with their yacht in tow.

When the cutter made port, Vargas and his men were separated and held in isolation cells. Manning and Powell were there waiting. At first Vargas refused to talk and demanded his lawyer. When he was informed that his men were spilling their guts to save themselves and he was facing life in prison for kidnapping, or, should Tony be killed, the death penalty, he became as loquacious as a green parrot. He gave Manning and Powell the name of the man who had Tony and described where they were keeping him, drawing a map showing how to get to the cell and the position of the guards at the entrance to the chamber.

The plan was for Manning and Agent Michael Juarez, a field agent of Cuban descent whom Manning had worked with on several assignments, to use the confiscated yacht, *El Diablo Rojo*, and return to Castillo Del Morro to retrieve Tony. The thought was that by using *El Diablo Rojo*, should they happen upon a Cuban patrol boat, the Cubans would be less likely to stop them, as they were used to seeing the yacht in Cuban waters. Both men understood their tenuous situation as FBI agents working outside

United States borders. Powell had made it clear that should they be caught, any help from the United States would be limited at best.

With the yacht modified to include a scrambled communications system, a global positioning system, a radar tracking system, and a supply of hidden but easy to retrieve weapons, Manning and Juarez left United States waters late that afternoon, heading for Morro.

Waters along the Intracoastal Waterway were rougher than normal, but the yacht cut its way through with little problem. The sun had begun to fall low in the sky when they reached the Florida Strait. The wind had picked up, and the waters of the Gulf Stream were choppy, causing Manning to slow their pace, but with no sign of the Cuban navy on radar, they still made good time.

When Manning and Juarez arrived at Morro it was dark. Juarez hopped out and tied off the boat while Manning cut the engines and looked around to see if they were going to have a reception committee. With no sign of interest from anyone, Manning took out the hand-drawn map Vargas had given them and laid it out on a small work table on the bridge. Juarez stepped back onto the yacht and walked over to look at the map with Manning.

Judging by the bright, colorful lights and the sound of music and laughter from above, it was clear the evening festivities for the tourists were in full swing. During the day, the old castle hosted those interested in a pleasant outing in an historic setting, but at night, Morro took on the aspects of a trendy nightclub, with dining, drinking, music, and laughter for those wanting to experience a beautiful sunset and the lights of the Malecon, followed by opulence and excess.

Manning and Juarez were dressed in jeans, cotton pullovers, and light jackets that covered their shoulder holsters. In Manning's holster was a Sig-Sauer .357, while Juarez carried a Colt .45. Each man had three extra clips of ammo in the pocket of his jacket.

They started up the path that led to the fortress and merged with the tourists, crossing the moat as part of the group of sightseers. Morro was crowded with tourists and couples out for an evening of fun. There was a beehive of activity near the courtyard, where a brigade of Cubans, dressed in nineteenth-century garb like those who had fought for independence against the Spanish, were involved in some type of ceremony. As they watched, Manning and Juarez overheard a tourist telling his friends that each evening this brigade followed the same routine, ending with the firing of a cannon into the sea and a salute to Cuba Libre. Manning nodded for Juarez to follow, and they slowly made their way toward the stairs leading to where Vargas had indicated Tony was being held. There were several security men around the courtyard watching the crowds as well as the stairway leading to the lower levels.

"We need a diversion," Juarez said.

Manning looked back at the formally dressed brigade and nodded.

"I think our local friends will provide that for us," Manning responded.

Juarez glanced at the brigade, who were now marching toward a battery of cannons along the fortress wall, and nodded in understanding.

"Everyone will be watching the ceremony. When the cannon fires, that will be our cue," Manning said.

"I'll meet you at the bottom," Juarez said.

A three-quarters moon had risen in the night sky and was hanging directly over Castillo del Morro, bathing the harbor in a beautiful silvery glow. Those who weren't watching the ceremony were gazing at the colorful sights of the harbor and enjoying the cool evening breeze.

The silence of the night was broken by the thunderous crack of cannon fire, followed by loud cheers, whistles, and applause. Manning and Juarez quickly slipped down the four flights of stairs, stopping behind a wall only a few feet from the two men guarding the corridor.

Manning turned to Juarez and whispered, "I'll go out alone. You follow my lead. We need to take them out without gunfire."

Manning stepped out, wearing a wide grin, and clumsily walked toward the guards.

"*Hola, amigos….* This castle is amazing. Do you guys allow private parties here?" Manning asked, pretending to be an inebriated Australian.

The two guards, wearing fatigues and standing at ease, snapped to attention and pulled their weapons off their shoulders.

"This area is off limits. You must leave here immediately," one of the guards said in broken English.

Manning staggered past the guards to draw their attention away from where Juarez was hiding, and bent over with his hands on his knees.

"Oh, no…I think I'm going to be sick."

"*Hombre baboso que anda pedo*…stupid drunkard," the other guard said.

Both guards laughed and dropped their rifles to their sides.

With his Colt drawn, Juarez left his spot behind the wall and quickly slipped behind the closest guard. Using the butt of his pistol, Juarez swung the gun down in a quick blow to the back of the guard's head. The guard slumped to the ground and dropped his rifle.

Simultaneously, Manning came out of his crouch, and like a linebacker at the Super Bowl, charged at the other guard. He threw his shoulder into the guard's chest, then reached down and grabbed him behind the thighs and lifted him off the ground. He continued in perfect tackling form and drove the guard into the wall. The guard's head snapped back and thumped loudly against the concrete; his head slumped down and he went limp. When Manning released his grip, the rifle, which had been wedged between Manning and the guard, dropped at an awkward angle. The butt of the weapon hit the concrete floor, fell on its side, and landed on the trigger guard, causing the rifle to discharge. The bullet ricocheted, striking Juarez in the shoulder. Juarez slumped to his knees and rolled onto his back, with blood oozing from the wound.

Manning rushed over to his friend to check the wound.

"I thought you were a running back. Where did you learn to tackle like that?" Juarez asked.

"The damn Longhorns.... You get tackled like that enough times and you learn quickly. It doesn't look too bad, Mikey. I've got to get the bleeding stopped and find you some help."

Juarez looked past Manning and closed his eyes before responding.

"Maybe those guys are here to help."

Manning turned and looked back toward the stairway. Six security guards were standing at the base of the stairs with their weapons aimed at him.

CHAPTER
31

*I*t was late afternoon when Tripp returned to the Hotel on Rivington. A doorman opened the heavy brass door, and Tripp entered the opulent lobby. The concierge desk, made of a dark, lustrous oak, was opposite the front desk and staffed by a neatly dressed man, somewhere in his early thirties, who looked as though he had just stepped out of a Brooks Brothers catalog. Tripp walked up to him, gave the man his room number, his suit size, and a hundred-dollar bill, and asked if he could have a tuxedo delivered and charged to his room within the hour. The man assured Tripp it would be there.

Tripp stepped into an elevator and pushed the button for the sixteenth floor. He let himself into the suite and called out for Carmen. When he failed to get a response, an icy wave of apprehension coursed down his spine. He began to look around and found a note on the table saying that she had gone down to the training room to get in some exercise. Tripp's face strained into a frown; he wished she had remained in the room. He made his way to the second-floor training room, a state-of-the-art workout facility enclosed by floor-to-ceiling glass walls. As Tripp approached, he looked in and saw Carmen on a treadmill near the rear of the room. On the wall directly in front of her was a forty-two-inch flat-screen television that displayed a beach scene.

To the person jogging, it would be easy to imagine actually running along the beach. Tripp paused a moment and watched Carmen run. Her toned body moved effortlessly over the treadmill. Her hair was pulled back in a ponytail, bouncing like the tail of a wild mustang at full gallop, and a light sheen of perspiration covered her shapely frame.

He entered the training room, walked up to her, and said, "I thought you were going to stay in your room."

Carmen slowed to a walk, used a towel to wipe her face, and said, "I was feeling anxious. I like to run when I'm feeling that way. Besides, I never promised to stay in the room."

She set the towel down, took a sip from a bottle of water, and continued, "It's okay, Sean, I never left the hotel. I did, however, visit one of their boutiques and found a perfect dress for our dinner date tonight."

Even in her disheveled state, Carmen carried herself with a graceful beauty. Once again Tripp found himself drawn to her.

"I'm looking forward to seeing it," Tripp said.

Carmen took another sip of water and asked, "Did you find out anything about Tony?"

"A rescue is in the works as we speak. If all goes well, you could be reunited tomorrow."

A pensive expression crossed Carmen's face as she stepped off the machine and asked, "When will we know?"

"They're going to call me as soon as they hear anything."

Carmen's lips curled up into a soft smile and she said, "I need to shower. Will you escort me back to the suite, Mr. Tripp?"

Carmen and Tripp made their way back to the room, where Carmen excused herself and went to the bedroom. Tripp heard the shower begin and walked over to the wet bar. As he began to mix a drink there was a knock at the door.

Tripp set the glass down, walked to the door, and said, "Who is it?'

"It's the concierge, Mr. Tripp. I have your tuxedo."

Tripp checked the peephole, then opened the door. He took the tux, tipped the man, then closed and locked the door. He finished mixing his drink, walked out onto the terrace, and looked out over Manhattan. The sun was setting and the lights of New York City were beginning to color the early evening. The snow had stopped, replaced with a soft evening breeze that brought a chill to the air. Tripp took a long pull from his drink and thought about his friend Manning. He had all the faith in the world that Manning could do the job, but he wished he could be there with him. On more than one occasion they had saved each other's lives, and as Tripp looked out over the sky-line he had an uneasy feeling he should be with him now. He took another drink and listened to the sounds of the Manhattan evening. After a few minutes he heard the water turn off as Carmen finished her shower. He walked back inside, closed and locked the door, and took his turn in the shower.

Twenty minutes later Tripp finished his shower, dressed, and walked back to the wet bar. As he began to mix another drink, the bedroom door opened and Carmen stepped out wearing an elegant black one-shoulder Bianca Nero evening gown. Her long black hair softly fell off her bare left shoulder, and the outfit was accented with a string of white pearls around her neck. Stunned by her exquisiteness, Tripp stood speechless for several seconds.

Carmen looked up at him with her green-brown eyes and held his gaze with a warm and sensual smile. "What do you think?" she finally said as she spun around.

"Absolutely beautiful," he said, then continued, "Can I make you a drink?"

"How about some white wine?"

Tripp turned, opened a bottle of sauvignon blanc, and poured a small flute. He then set the bottle down, turned, and handed the flute to her.

"So where are we having dinner?" Tripp asked.

"I made reservations at the Water Club," Carmen said as she took a sip.

"Wonderful choice! And what time do we need to be there?"

Carmen set her drink down and reached up to adjust Tripp's bow tie. She looked into his green eyes, smiled warmly, and said, "As a matter of fact, we need to get going now."

Tripp put on his shoulder holster and coat, then helped Carmen with her coat. They rode the elevator to the lobby, walked outside, and waved down a taxi.

The taxi pulled onto Rivington, turned right on Allen, and took First Avenue. Ten minutes later the cab pulled up to the front of the Water Club restaurant at its prestigious waterside location. Tripp paid the driver and they stepped out of the cab. The Water Club restaurant had added a touch of the holidays to its classic décor. A fresh poinsettia centerpiece was placed in the center of a linen tablecloth, and the fine china had a delicate green and gold pattern. The dining room's floor-to-ceiling windows provided extraordinary views of the East River from every table. A silver-haired crooner played piano near an open fireplace next to the bar.

Tripp and Carmen entered the romantic ambiance and were shown directly to a table next to one of the windows. Tripp pulled the chair out for Carmen and seated himself next to her.

The waiter arrived moments later, gave them each a menu, and took their drink order. Carmen asked for a pinot grigio white wine, and Tripp said he would have the same. It was a gorgeous evening. The sky was clear, and the lights of the city, colorfully decorated for the season, sparkled against the inky black canvas of the December night.

"This is very nice. You have great taste," Tripp said.

"Thank you. This is one of my favorite spots, although I've only been here a couple of times."

Tripp wondered how those dates had ended.

As Carmen and Tripp studied their menus, Carmen glanced over at a Christmas tree, brilliantly lit with blue lights, and said, "The tree is beautiful. Christmas is my favorite time of year."

"Yes, it is nice. Everything is perfect," Tripp answered. "How will you be spending Christmas this year?"

"I usually spend a very traditional Christmas at my parents' house in Syracuse." Carmen smiled softly and continued, "My mother and I will spend most of the time in the kitchen cooking, or in the living room trimming the tree, while my dad fidgets with his electric trains. We usually exchange gifts on Christmas Eve, but I still haven't done my shopping. I had planned to do that today."

The sommelier arrived with their wine. He offered Tripp the cork and a tasting. Tripp nodded his approval, and the steward poured the wine and put the bottle in the ice canister. A few minutes later a waiter in a crisp white shirt and black bow tie arrived to take their order. Carmen ordered a shrimp cocktail for an appetizer, and for the main course, the pan-roasted giant shrimp. Tripp ordered the classic lobster bisque as his appetizer and Maine lobster for the main course. The waiter retrieved the menus and left.

"And what about you, Sean? How will you spend Christmas?"

"On my boat. Most of the boat owners around the marina get together to share some eggnog and enjoy the fellowship."

"And your family?"

"My mom's in Dallas. We usually get together for a few days to exchange gifts and eat turkey until we're miserable."

As Tripp poured more wine, Carmen looked over toward the grand piano in the corner as the pianist sang Nat King Cole's "More." She hummed the words to herself, *"More than the greatest love the world has known."*

Finally she turned back to Tripp and said, "What are you wishing for for Christmas, Sean?"

Tripp's eyes held Carmen's as he said, "I'm having dinner tonight at a great restaurant with a fantastic view, and sharing it with a beautiful lady.... I can't think of a better wish than this."

Carmen smiled warmly and said, "Thank you, Sean."

"And what's on your wish list?" Tripp asked.

Carmen paused a moment; her eyes became moist and reflective. She said, "The only thing I want is to find my brother."

Tripp reached across the table, took her hand, and said, "I'm not Santa, but I will do everything I can to make that happen."

The waiter arrived with their appetizers. They ate slowly and enjoyed the music. A few minutes later their main courses were served. The conversation throughout dinner was convivial and continued into a playful banter over dessert.

"It must be exciting...being an FBI agent, I mean," Carmen said. She sipped her wine.

"Some parts are. It can be hard on your personal life, however."

"Really? I thought you secret agents were constantly being dragged to bed."

"That's what I thought. I joined the spy game only to be disappointed by reality."

"Well, there are always the online personals," Carmen said, her face deadpan. She then continued, "So. Were you ever married?"

"Yes. She was also with the bureau, but she was killed on an assignment."

"I'm sorry, Sean."

"So how did you get into the airline business?" Tripp said quickly, to change the subject.

"My dad used to tell me I should travel and see the world while I was young. I decided to take his advice, so when I graduated from college I got a job where I could work and travel at the same time."

"It sounds exciting," Tripp said.

"Yes, I love it, and I've already been fortunate enough to see most of Europe."

Tripp was about to respond when his cell phone vibrated in his pocket. He answered it on the second ring. Carmen watched as the expression on Tripp's face turned solemn.

"I understand. I will be there as soon as possible," was all Tripp said before he clicked off and put his phone away. His face was blank and his eyes were fixed as though he was far away.

"What was that about, Tony?" Carmen asked as she held her breath.

Tripp's eyes refocused and his expression changed to one of resolve.

He looked at Carmen and said, "The team that was sent to rescue Tony is overdue and has not been heard from. It's assumed they've been captured."

Tripp could read Carmen's eyes and knew she was thinking she'd lost her brother a second time.

"Listen to me, Carmen. The man in charge of that rescue team is my best friend. I know him well, and there is no one I trust more for this mission. Wherever he is, I can assure you he is helping Tony."

Tripp paused a few moments before continuing, "I will go find him and Tony and get them back, I promise."

Carmen sat quietly for several seconds. Then her face too changed to one of resolve. "No," she said firmly, "*we* will get them back."

CHAPTER
32

*T*ony sat slumped on the edge of the soiled mattress, despondent. His left eye was swollen shut and his hair was matted with dried blood from a laceration on his scalp. This was the second day he'd spent locked away, and he was scared and hungry. The only food they had given him was a chunk of hard bread and a bowl of what was supposed to be soup, with something that looked like a piece of chicken at the bottom. He found the soup intolerably nauseating, so all he could eat was the bread, which he could only chew on the right side of his mouth because two of his teeth on the left side were loose.

It was dark all the time, but he could tell when it was evening because he could hear the faint sound of music from down the long corridor. The first night he had slept very little, and he didn't look forward to another night on the filthy, scant mattress. Tony tried to focus his mind on his "real" life; he thought about his mother and father in Monterey and how worried they must be. Then he heard the sound of scuffling coming from somewhere down the corridor. His mind was jolted back to the present, and he stood to walk toward the sound. He was trying to make out what was happening when the sound of a gunshot broke through the blackness. The loud report reverberated down the corridor and hit Tony like a clap of thunder. His heart raced as he stumbled back, trying to hide somewhere deep in the blackness of his cell. The voices were growing louder now, and he could hear footsteps moving toward his cell. A few moments later the footsteps halted outside his cell.

One of the guards kicked the door with a loud clang that reverberated through the cell and yelled, "Wake up in there, you've got company."

A dim bank of lights came on and the guards all laughed at seeing Tony cowering behind the filthy bunk. The titular leader of this mangy group was an overweight man in army fatigues; his main goal seemed to be chewing his cigar down to nothing. The man fumbled with some keys, turned the lock, and the rusty door began to creak open. They shoved two men inside, one of whom had blood caked down the front of his shirt.

"My friend has lost a lot of blood and needs a doctor," Tony heard the other man say in precise English.

The lead guard shoved the keys back into his pocket and responded in a blend of broken English and Spanish, "His wound doesn't look too bad. Someone may be in tomorrow to check on him. That is, if he is still alive."

Once again the guards laughed heartily, then slammed the rusty door shut and headed back down the corridor. Tony watched as the man helped his friend onto another bunk and began to dress the wound with strips of cloth he tore from his shirt. After several minutes the man finished with his friend and turned and sat on the edge of the bunk facing Tony. Tony studied the man, who appeared to be an American. The man had sandy-blond hair, blue eyes, and was built like a tank.

Finally the corner of the man's mouth curled into a thin smile and he said, "You, my young friend, must be Tony."

Tony stared in amazement before finally speaking. "Yes, I am. Who are you, and how do you know my name?"

"My name is Neil Manning, and I'm here to rescue you."

"I see…. And your plan to rescue me was to get locked in here with me?"

"Hey," Manning said with a skewed grin. "I'll do the jokes; you be the straight man."

Tony didn't know this man, but he could feel his confidence. Until now he didn't think anyone knew where he was, but somehow, though they were both locked up in an underground hell, he felt a huge sense of relief.

"How do you know me, and how did you find me?"

"A concerned friend of yours, Stony Barker, asked a friend of mine, Sean Tripp, whom I believe you know, to look for you. Tripp, who used to be my partner, asked me to help him. We followed your trail, and here we are."

"Where is Mr. Tripp?"

"I suspect he will be along shortly. He was on a rescue mission of his own."

Manning paused a moment, leaned over, looked Tony in the eyes, and said, "You see, I came here to get you. Tripp went to get your sister."

Tony stared back at Manning in stunned silence for several moments, trying to comprehend what he had said. "My sister?"

Manning held his eyes, smiled, and said, "Yes, your sister."

"She really is alive?"

"The last time I spoke with Tripp, he was with her and she was doing fine," Manning said with a grin.

"And my mother and father? Do you know anything about them?"

"Your father is being held in a prison not far from here. I'm afraid I don't know anything about your mother."

"Why did they bring me here?"

"Our guess is they want information from your father, and they're hoping to use you to get him to talk. By the look of your eye and the blood in your hair, it appears they've already been in to question you."

As Tony was considering all he had heard, the lights flipped off and plunged the group back into darkness.

"And I was just about to call for room service," Manning quipped.

"It's dark like this most of the time," Tony said.

"Probably a good idea to get some rest anyway," Manning said.

He checked on Juarez; other than being thirsty, he was doing okay. Then, using his jacket as a makeshift pillow, Manning stretched out on the floor and was asleep within seconds.

They had dozed for only a couple of hours when the lights flicked on and footsteps once again could be heard approaching the cell. Tony looked up to see Rogelio Cruz and Igor Petroff.

"Good evening, Mr. Favela. It is time for us to have another visit. I'm sure you remember my associate, Comrade Petroff. He will be joining us again."

Petroff unlocked the cell and Cruz stepped inside. Cruz looked down at Tony for a moment before turning his gaze toward Manning and Juarez.

"I heard Tony had visitors earlier this evening. My name is Rogelio Cruz. You two must be Tony's rescue team."

Cruz twisted his mouth into a sadistic grin and continued, "Foolish Americans. As usual, you fail when trying to compete with Cuba."

Manning stared back, but said nothing.

"You have nothing to say? Never mind. I'm sure we will cause you to be more talkative when it's your turn to join us down the hall."

Cruz turned back to face Tony and said, "Let's go. It stinks in here, and I have work to do."

When Tony didn't move, Cruz nodded at Petroff. Petroff grabbed Tony by the hair, lifted him to his feet, and shoved him toward the cell door.

"The boy is an American citizen. I suggest you remember that, because there are others who know he is here," Manning said.

Cruz followed Igor and Tony outside the cell, slammed the door shut, and looked back at Manning.

"If the two of you are examples of what America has to send, I think I have little cause to worry."

The two men escorted Tony down the corridor to the same cell they had been in earlier that morning. The video camera was still attached to the tripod, and Cruz inserted a new cassette. Once again Tony found himself behind hot lights, but this time there was a short, narrow table in front of him.

Cruz nodded at Igor, and Igor set the camera to record.

"You came a long way to see your father, Tony; you must have been very close to him."

"I love my father, if that's what you want to know," Tony responded.

"And you would do anything to have him back in your life?"

"Of course I would, but I don't know what it is you want from me."

"When your father left Cuba with us and your family, he took some things that belong to El Presidente Castro. El

Presidente wants his property back, and I have assured him I will get it for him."

"What did he take?"

"Let's just say it was a sizable part of the Cuban treasury."

"I know nothing of this. I was only four years old. Besides, I don't know where it is, so I can't help you."

"Well, Tony Favela, we believe you're going to be able to help us tremendously. You see, your father knows where it is, and we're going to let you convince him to return what he took from us."

Cruz turned off the camera and pushed a sheet of paper and a ballpoint pen toward Tony. "I want you to write a statement. You are to say that your father, Manuel Favela, left Cuba with money and treasure that belonged to Cuba, and that you urge your father to tell us where it is."

When Tony made no effort to pick up the pen, Cruz leaned near the table and said, "If you do not pick up the pen and write, I will not be responsible for what follows."

Tony looked at the paper and thought about his father. Then he thought about his sister, and although he was afraid, the knowledge that she was safe gave him courage. He looked up at Cruz, but still made no effort to pick up the pen. Cruz leaned back, turned the camera back on, and nodded at Igor.

The thick underground walls did nothing to absorb Tony's screams. As Manning listened to the screams from down the corridor, he could feel his anger building. The tortured wails echoing through the corridor sounded as if they came from an adjacent cell. Juarez was awake and conscious now, sitting on the side of the bunk. They had endured the howls and shrieks for almost an hour.

"We've got to find a way out of here, or they're going to kill the boy," Juarez said.

"I've searched every square inch of this place, and it's not encouraging," Manning said.

Tony was lying on the floor, blood coming from his mouth, nose, and ears, when the Russian finally paused.

Cruz looked at Tony and said, "Your father has asked to see you, Tony. Of course, that is not possible until we have the information we need. Nevertheless, I've decided to indulge him a bit by sending him a small part of you."

Using his foot, Cruz shoved a large canvas bag toward Igor. The Russian leaned down, unzipped the bag, pulled out a set of heavy-duty bolt cutters, and walked over to Tony.

Tony's eyes were swollen shut, but he strained to look. When Cruz gave the nod, the Russian knelt down, put his knee on Tony's arm, and guided the cutter blades around the little finger on Tony's left hand.

CHAPTER
33

*T*ripp watched Carmen as she crossed the carpeted floor in her bare feet. The way her hair swayed and the light glistened off the strands reminded him of the way the ocean looked from his houseboat when the first lights of morning danced across the surface of the water. Several times he caught himself fighting back inappropriate thoughts related to lingerie and satin bedsheets. He was considering how close he had grown to Carmen in such a short time when his cell phone chirped. He pushed the answer key before the first ring had finished. The voice on the line was Henry Powell's.

"We've checked the latest satellite images. Juarez and Manning's boat is still docked at Morro. Since we still haven't heard from them, we must assume they've been caught. They're probably locked up at the same place Tony is."

"I can be down there within three hours," Tripp said.

"You might as well get some sleep, Sean, and fly out in the morning. We've got some bad weather coming in. It looks like a freak tropical depression over the Atlantic, and we need to get more satellite shots. Also, we've got to think this thing through. We can't just go charging in there and risk losing more men."

"Okay. I'll leave in the morning, but I want you to find me a boat. And if there's a depression out there, make sure the boat is fast and seaworthy."

"Will do. Call me when you're in the air."

The line went dead and Tripp thought about Manning. He was angry with himself for not being with him, but he also had confidence that his friend could hold things together until he got there. He clicked his cell phone off and watched as Carmen moved silently over and sat next to him.

"What did they say?" Carmen asked.

"Neil Manning, my ex-partner, and Michael Juarez, another agent, went into Cuba to retrieve Tony. Their boat is still there, but they haven't been heard from for several hours. They may have been caught. I'm going to fly down in the morning and go get them, and Tony."

"I've already told you that you should be saying *we*, because I am going with you."

"Carmen, the men we're dealing with are ruthless. They wouldn't hesitate to kill us both. It's just too dangerous. I don't want anything to happen to you."

Carmen stood up, her body rigid and tense, and stared directly into Sean's eyes. "Listen to me, Sean Tripp. Tony is *my* brother. I was there when they began shooting at him. I was there when he was taken away. I was there when our lives were destroyed, and I am going to be there to bring Tony back."

Seeing the determined jut to Carmen's jaw and her eyes burning into his, Tripp knew that no argument he could offer would change her mind. He decided he would try a different tactic later.

"If we're both going, we need to get some rest. I'll take the couch here," he finally said.

Tripp woke early the following morning and made his way to the kitchenette to start some coffee. A few minutes later he poured himself a cup and walked over to the terrace window. It was still dark, and the lights of New York City were still bright. Once again a light snow was falling, and Tripp took another long sip of coffee. The cobwebs were beginning to clear as the coffee started working its magic. He walked back to the kitchenette, refilled his cup, and picked up his cell phone. He dialed JFK to have his Bonanza fueled and readied, then filed a flight plan. After clicking off, he quietly walked in to check on Carmen. His initial plan had been to slip out the door before she awoke, but she had given a convincing argument, and he knew she was a strong, determined woman.

The first blush of dawn was beginning to fill the room with a warm, delicate pink glow. Carmen was lying on her side, her ebony black hair fanned out across the pillow. Her lips were slightly parted and seemed to form a smile. For a brief moment Tripp anxiously wondered if she knew he was there watching her.

Finally he stepped closer, sat on the edge of the bed, and whispered, "Good morning. It's your wake-up call."

Carmen opened her eyes, grinned, and said, "I was wondering how long you were going to stand there and watch me."

Tripp grinned back sheepishly and said, "We've got to get going. We have people waiting on us."

He stood and walked toward the door, then turned back and said, "Breakfast will be waiting."

Ten minutes later Carmen stepped out of the bedroom and said, "I couldn't wait to see what you prepared for breakfast."

On the table were sliced fruit Tripp had taken from the guest basket, grapefruit juice from the bar, and coffee. The two ate quickly, and thirty minutes later they were at the front desk checking out.

After retrieving the rental car, they pulled out and headed west on Rivington Street. They took the Williamsburg Bridge to Brooklyn and through Queens, then went right onto the Long Island Expressway, and finally turned onto the Van Wyck Expressway into Kennedy Airport, where Tripp returned the rental.

The Bonanza G36 was fueled and waiting. The sun was climbing higher, erasing the last vestiges of night, and the snow had stopped, leaving behind a cool, overcast morning.

Carmen watched as Tripp walked around the Bonanza doing his familiar preflight inspection. After he completed the visual and felt assured all was well, he helped Carmen into the cockpit, walked around, and climbed in. They buckled themselves in and Tripp began the systems check. With all systems go, he switched the engine tab to ON and cranked the engine. The engine coughed once, then roared to life. He feathered the props, and with the release of energy the rumble in the cockpit dropped to a smooth hum.

Tripp followed the taxi instructions and fell in line behind other planes waiting for takeoff. He watched as the engine temperature slowly climbed to optimal range. Twenty minutes later they were cleared for takeoff. He eased the plane around, pointed the nose squarely down the center stripe, and applied the brakes. He did one final check, adjusted the flaps, pushed the throttle forward, and released the brakes. The Bonanza shot down the runway, softly lifted off, and began to climb. Tripp reached over, flipped a switch, and retracted the landing gear.

The morning sun was up but still low in the sky, and had begun to bathe the cockpit in shades of yellow and orange. Tripp glanced at Carmen and smiled as he watched the way the delicate warm glow illuminated her face.

"Next stop Miami," he said.

Carmen smiled back and said, "And the best part is that I don't have to serve drinks on this flight."

"Speaking of flights, have you told the airline you may be gone for a while?"

"I talked to them yesterday and told them I was mugged. They told me to take as much time as I needed."

They climbed to ten thousand feet and leveled off. Tripp entered the Miami airport's identifier code into the GPS and pressed the direct button. The horizontal indicator arrow swung around to point the way and Tripp adjusted his heading. He then activated the autopilot, took out his cell phone, and punched in the number for Henry Powell. They spoke for a few minutes; before clicking off, Tripp told him they should be there in a couple of hours.

"Is there any news?" Carmen asked as Tripp returned the phone to his pocket.

"Satellite photos show the boat Manning and Juarez took is docked in the same spot, and there still hasn't been any contact. He also said the local meteorologists are concerned that the freak tropical depression they've been watching in the Atlantic could turn into a hurricane."

"A hurricane in December?" Carmen asked in a bewildered tone.

"They are rare, but hybrid winter hurricanes are not unheard of."

Carmen sat quietly for several moments, her face stoic, then said, "Are you saying we may not be able to go after Tony?"

Tripp stared straight ahead, his face equally stoic, and said, "We'll get him back."

An hour into the flight Tripp turned the autopilot off to work his way around a towering bank of dark clouds that reached well over ten thousand feet. While working their way around the dark mass, the aircraft was buffeted by turbulence, making the plane pitch and yaw. Tripp had been watching a lightning storm off the port wing, but felt sure he was far enough away.

Suddenly, the plane was slammed by a series of wind gusts and Tripp had to fight to keep control. As the wind hammered the plane, a sudden electrical burst bit through the sky, and the plane reverberated with a thunderous bang. The plane began rolling to the right and fell into a spin. Tripp immediately loosened his grip and stood hard on the left rudder. When the plane stopped spinning, he pulled back to gain altitude. The nose slowly began to rise and the plane finally leveled out.

"Perhaps we should move farther away," Carmen calmly suggested.

"Your wish is my command. I only wish you had commanded a little earlier."

He pointed the nose away from the cloud bank, went to full throttle, and slowly climbed back to ten thousand feet.

"Tell me, Carmen, do you know anything about this money, or treasure, your father was supposed to have taken when your family left Cuba?"

"No. Before you mentioned it, I knew nothing about it. All I know is that he was a wonderful and loving father to Tony and me."

With the dark clouds behind them, Tripp once again engaged the autopilot.

"Tell me about him," Tripp said as he stretched his shoulders back to release some stress.

"I was his princess. He would take me to museums, movies, soccer games, and shopping. Basically, he spoiled me."

"Sounds like you were very close," Tripp said with a warm smile.

"Yes, we were. You know, looking back, he must have known we would be coming to the United States. Every day he would spend hours teaching me English."

Carmen turned to face Tripp, her eyes lit up bright with excitement, and she continued, "I remember how the two of us would play name games."

"You mentioned that once before. Tell me about it."

"We would take people's names and match them with an animal in English, as close as we could, anyway. Sometimes we would have to scramble or creatively edit the name. It was so much fun, and I never got tired of it."

"Give me an example," Tripp said.

Carmen leaned her head back on the headrest and starred out at the clouds."

"Okay, for example, we called Castro 'The Beaver.'"

"The Beaver?" Tripp questioned.

"Beaver is actually *castor*, but it's close."

"Give me another," Tripp said.

"Let's see...Aguilar we called 'Eagle.' Eagle is actually *aguila*."

"I got it. Sounds like a creative way to learn English."

"How about this one? Picasso was 'Woodpecker.'"

"And woodpecker in Spanish is?" Tripp asked.

"*Picaposte*," Carmen answered.

Tripp stared at her, his face masked in doubt.

"Sometimes you have to be very creative," Carmen said with a grin.

A short time later, as they closed in on Miami, the Bonanza G36 began to descend.

CHAPTER
34

anuel Favela sat in his cell, watching the shadows move slowly across the floor. The rat he had watched for the last hour had left at the first light of dawn. Manuel tried to make sense out of the message smuggled to him during the night from his friend Grouper. From what he could make out of the somewhat cryptic message, his daughter Carmen was safe, and a mission was currently underway to rescue Tony. The message urged him to stay strong and keep faith that Tony and Carmen would very soon be together and safe. He looked at the message one last time, then put the paper in his mouth and ate it.

Manuel sat back and thought about his son and what Castro's men would do to get what they wanted. He had spent many of the last fifteen years thinking about his wife and his children and what he had done to his family. He had also spent many of his waking hours reading; he especially liked the classics. He was given access to a fairly large library of material and would read throughout the day. It was not possible to read at night because there was no light in the cell. Now, as he reflected, what came to his mind was King Priam in the epic poem "The Illiad," by Homer. Priam knew that Troy's destruction was imminent, and he did not want to sacrifice his son, Hector. Hector was killed, however, his body abused and dragged through the city. Now, Tony had come for his own father, whose life, as Manuel saw it, was as good as destroyed. Manuel could not let Tony find the same fate as Hector. In the poem, Priam was not evil, but his decisions were so fraught with contradictions that complete destruction was the only possible outcome. Similarly, Manuel did not think of himself as evil, but his mistakes had led to his family's destruction. He had to save Tony, but the dilemma he faced was just what he should do. If he gave them what they wanted, he and Tony would probably both be killed, but if he didn't, he could be sacrificing his son. As Manuel contemplated what he should do, his thoughts were interrupted by the clang of steel against steel and the approach of footsteps. He looked up just as the cell block chief stopped to unlock his cell.

"The warden wants to see you, Manuel," the man said gruffly in Spanish. He opened the door and continued, "Let's not keep him waiting."

He escorted Manuel down the corridor and through the heavy steel door separating the cell block, then down another hallway that led to the warden's office. The cell block chief knocked lightly and opened the office door.

Just as before, the warden was sitting behind his desk and Cruz was standing to the left. The small table with the television and video cassette player were once again waiting in the center of the dreary office.

Without being asked this time, Manuel entered the office and sat in the wooden chair facing the warden. The warden removed a fat Cohiba cigar from his mouth and spoke.

"Manuel, I have known you for many years. You have been cooperative here at Guayabo, and you do not cause trouble."

He stood, walked around the desk, and sat on the edge. He stared down at Manuel and continued, "Because of this, I would like to help you now."

Manuel was staring at the floor, his face staid and his eyes fixed. Slowly, his eyes moved up to face the warden.

"I share a filthy cell with rats, I sleep on a dirty thin mattress that hasn't been changed in years, and I'm given food that is intolerable, but now you say you want to help me?"

"Perhaps your condition could be improved if you were to cooperate with Agent Cruz, but what I wish to do now is save you pain. Give Agent Cruz what he wants and save your son."

Manuel's eyes slowly dropped back to the floor, but he said nothing.

The warden stood, walked back behind his desk, sat down, returned the Cohiba to his mouth, and looked over at Cruz.

Rogelio Cruz walked past a picture of Castro that hung on the wall, stopped next to a window, and peered out at the prison yard.

"Not far from here your son sits waiting to see you," Cruz began.

He turned toward Manuel, leaned back against the windowpane, and in a cold, steely voice, continued, "Once before I gave you the opportunity to see him, but you refused to give me the information I want. I also told you I would visit with your son again."

He paused a few moments, watching Manuel. Cruz was concerned that Manuel seemed to show complete indifference to Tony. He wondered if he had misjudged Manuel and his relationship with his son.

"Perhaps you would like to know how my visit with Tony went. Why don't we take a look?"

Cruz pulled the remote from his pocket, pushed a button to turn the television and video player on, then pushed play.

The screen lit up with a full-screen shot of Tony facing the camera. He heard the voice of Cruz somewhere behind the camera, saying, "You must have been very close to him." Tony responded, "I love my father, if that's what you want to know."

Cruz pushed pause with Tony's face still in focus and said, "You may not wish to admit to a relationship with your son, Mr. Favela, but as you can see, your son loves you."

Manuel tried not to show any sign of emotion. He knew Cruz only needed the slightest sign to push even harder. He tried to focus his mind on something else. The first thing that came to mind was the epic poem "Paradise Lost," by John Milton, which he had read many times. Paradise was, of course, the Garden of Eden. As Manuel understood Milton, and believed himself, it was man's willful disobedience, not God's will, that brought about the loss of paradise. Sin and death, who were in empathy with Satan, built a bridge over Chaos to make their appearance on Earth. Adam and Eve were bitterly grieving over their fate, but in Heaven, God envisioned the day when there would be a final victory over sin and death. God sent the angel Michael to escort Adam and Eve out of Eden. Michael took Adam to a high hill and told him how the transmission of his seed would eventually lead to Jesus Christ. Eventually, Adam and Eve were consoled by the paradox that their fall would bring about a greater bliss, when all mankind would be redeemed by their offspring, Jesus.

Manuel turned to Cruz and said, "It is my actions that have put me here. It is what I deserve, but Tony is innocent. He does not deserve this fate." Even as the words were leaving his mouth, he thought about the innocent offspring of Adam and Eve who were for all time banished from Paradise. He thought about the line from John Milton's poem: "Paradise is now guarded by cherubim and a fiery sword, forbidding all to enter."

"It is you who chooses this fate for Tony Favela. You only have to tell me where the money is, and it will all be over."

Manuel thought about those words, "It will all be over," and knew it was true. If he gave Cruz the information he demanded, he and Tony would both be killed. Manuel's eyes returned to the floor, and he said nothing.

"Let's continue watching, shall we?"

Cruz pushed play on the remote, and for a good part of an hour Manuel watched and listened to the howls and shrieks as the Russian he knew as Petroff beat his son. Somehow he mustered the courage and determination to sit stoic through it all. The screams finally stopped, and once again he heard Cruz speaking to Tony.

"Your father has asked to see you, Tony Favela. Of course, that is not possible until we have the information we need. Nevertheless, I've decided to indulge him a bit." Manuel watched as the Russian picked up some bolt cutters and moved toward Tony. But when Petroff moved the cutter blades toward Tony's finger, Manuel could not watch. He shielded his eyes and turned away.

Cruz watched Manuel shield his eyes, and for the first time he could almost feel the money in his hands. He pulled a small matchbox from his pocket, walked over, and dumped Tony's finger on the table in front of Manuel.

"You wanted to see your son? This is as much as I could fit in this box."

Manuel's chest tightened and he couldn't breathe as he looked at the bloody appendage lying before him. Cruz paused for several moments before he continued.

"But if you still refuse to tell me where the money is, I'm sure I can find a bigger box for my next visit."

Manuel turned and looked at Cruz. He had never seen such cold malignity in a man's face before. He shifted his eyes to look out the window and thought about the last message Grouper had sent him: "Carmen is safe and a mission is currently underway to rescue Tony. Very soon, Carmen and Tony will be together and safe."

Manuel turned back to Cruz, stared into his eyes, and with a firm resolve said, "My son is always with me and I will always be with him. Nothing you do can take that away."

CHAPTER
35

*H*enry Powell sat alone in the operations room at FBI headquarters in Miami, reading intelligence reports and studying a stack of the most recent satellite photos. Tripp and Carmen had landed safely and were en route. Reports out of Cuba were sketchy, but they reinforced the satellite photos showing that only a small contingent of guards was currently stationed at Castillo del Morro. That was the good news. The bad news was that the tropical storm, looming some 150 miles out, was growing in intensity. Powell took a sip of coffee and leaned back in his chair. He picked up a tight shot of the fortress at Morro and counted six guards. He knew Manning and Juarez understood the situation they were in, and over the years he had grown somewhat inured to the hardships incumbent in this line of work, but he still took the loss of one of his own very hard. He believed Tripp could get his men out, but what he wasn't sure of was whether his men were still alive. His eyes moved up to a map of Cuba and the Florida Straits, and he considered the fact that they had heard absolutely nothing out of Havana. He hoped that was good news.

As Powell reached for the current weather report for the Florida Straits, the phone buzzed to inform him that Tripp and Carmen had arrived. Powell pushed the intercom button and asked that they be sent back. He stood and met them at the door.

"Sean, it's good to see you back. How was your flight?" Powell asked.

"Other than an interesting incident with some lightning, all went well." Tripp shifted his attention toward Carmen and continued, "Henry, I'd like to introduce Carmen Tully. Carmen, this is Henry Powell."

"Carmen, it's great to meet you. Sean told me about you, but he didn't tell me how beautiful you are."

"Thank you, Mr. Powell."

"Please call me Henry. I hope Sean's piloting skills haven't sworn you off flying for good."

"Well, I must say I'm giving serious thought to changing professions now," Carmen said with a wry smile.

"I get you two together for five minutes, and you're already turning on me," Tripp responded.

"Come on in. Let me get you two some coffee,"   Powell said.

He poured them each a cup, and they sat at a table covered with satellite images.

"So what's the current status?" Tripp asked as he took a sip of coffee.

"There still has been no word from Manning or Juarez, and the boat is still docked at the same place. Our guess is they're probably sharing a cell with Tony."

"Have you heard anything official out of Havana?" Tripp asked.

"No, but that's good. That means they're probably still alive."

"Any intelligence out of Morro?"

"We know, of course, Tony is there, and we know they're holding him. That was given to us by Enemencio Vargas. He also provided us with a map of the fortress and the location of the cell they're holding him in."

"Have you heard anything about Tony?" Carmen asked.

"No, I'm afraid not."

"What about security?" Tripp asked.

Powell picked up a satellite photo of Morro with a zoomed and enlarged image so clear the soldiers' fatigues could be seen. He handed it to Tripp.

"We counted six men—three along the perimeter, one at the top of the stairs, and two below. The two below are guarding the entrance to the corridor where Tony is being held. The image confirms the intelligence we got of a relatively small unit assigned to Morro."

Carmen set her coffee down and leaned close to Tripp to see the photo. Her eyes focused on the two guards at the bottom of the stairs and the opening to the corridor. She thought about the brother she had lost fifteen years ago, the brother she had thought was dead, and felt an almost tangible connection.

"He is there. I can feel him," Carmen said, just above a whisper.

Tripp handed the photo to Carmen and turned to Powell.

"Did you find us a boat?"

Powell hesitated a moment, his dark eyes flashing at Carmen, then turned back to Tripp.

"Yes, I did. A very nice one, actually, compliments of a drug bust we did not long ago. It's a solid boat, structurally sound, and fast, which you will need."

Powell handed Tripp a satellite image showing the current position of the tropical storm.

"That storm is about 150 miles out. It's growing in intensity and moving this way."

Tripp studied the image briefly and handed it to Carmen.

"There's something I'd like to show you in my office, Sean. Will you excuse us for a few minutes, Carmen? We won't be long."

Powell and Tripp stepped through a door into an adjacent office. The bookshelves and desks were filled with photos and memorabilia from around the world. Powell sat in a high-backed leather chair, swiveled around to a computer, punched a few keys, and hit enter. On the monitor was a color image of the tropical storm showing barometric pressures, wind speeds, and temperatures. Powell swiveled back around to face Tripp.

"This storm could easily turn into a hurricane. A category one hurricane has wind speeds of seventy-five miles per hour. While that's not a monster, it would be very dangerous."

Powell paused for a moment, then continued, "But the real danger is the gang of cutthroats guarding Morro. I guess you know I won't be able to help much if you get caught. Are you sure you want to put Carmen in that kind of danger?"

Tripp, who had been looking at the monitor, turned his eyes to Powell and said, "No, I don't want that, but I can tell you we would have to physically tie her down to keep her from boarding that boat. I've explained the situation to her, but she is adamant."

He paused a moment and continued, "I've been giving this some thought, and I think she could actually be helpful. She is Cuban, she knows Spanish, and she is attractive. She could very well be an asset."

Powell punched the computer off and said, "In that case, why don't we drive down and take a look at the boat."

CHAPTER 36

*M*anning had briefly nodded off, but the sound of Tony groaning woke him. He opened his eyes and looked over at the boy. Bloodstains covered his shirt and the sheet he was lying on.

Several hours earlier, Cruz and his goons had returned Tony to the cell and roughly deposited him on a bunk. They stationed a guard outside the cell, not in the interest of Tony's welfare, but because of the threats Manning and Juarez had made to make Cruz pay. The two men had made crude bandages out of torn sheets to try to stay the bleeding. Eventually Tony's cries died down and he fell asleep.

Manning swung his legs over the edge of the bunk and sat up. Tony was lying in the fetal position. His eyes were closed and he was shivering. Manning stood, walked over to Tony, knelt down, and touched his forehead.

"He is warm. He may have a fever."

"I'll find something to cover him," Juarez said.

Ever so slowly, Manning began to unwrap the bandage on Tony's hand. He examined the finger. The stub of Tony's little finger was still oozing, but had begun to scab over. Juarez covered Tony with several sheets from the other bunks.

"How's he doing?" Juarez asked.

"The wound is scabbing over. If there's no infection, he should be all right, but I don't like that shivering. If he has a fever, it very well could mean infection."

Tony opened his eyes and looked at Manning and Juarez.

"Is it bad?" Tony asked softly.

"You won't be playing handball anytime soon," Manning said, "but you'll be okay."

"I'm thirsty," Tony said.

Manning turned and looked at the guard who was sitting in a wooden straight-backed chair outside the cell. The guard was a large, rotund man in his mid-forties. He had short salt-and-pepper hair and dark eyes, and he looked out of place in his uniform. Manning figured they probably didn't have fatigues large enough to fit him. The guard had his rifle leaning against the wall beside him and he was eating a sandwich.

"The boy needs a doctor and something to drink," Manning said to the guard.

The guard mumbled something in Spanish and returned to his sandwich.

"Did you catch any of that?" Manning asked, looking at Juarez.

"I think he said he doesn't know what you're saying," Juarez said.

"Great. Now we've got Sergeant Schultz here watching us," Manning said dryly.

Juarez smiled at Tony, nodded toward Manning, and said, "Guess that means he's Hogan and we're the heroes."

Tony smiled weakly and said, "Hogan could always talk Schultz into anything." He had seen the old television standard many times on the TV Land cable station.

"That's true," Juarez said. He turned to Manning and continued, "Hogan, it's up to you to do some smooth-talking."

"The problem is, you Jolly Jokers, I don't have the Cockroach LeBeau here to bake me a chocolate éclair to bribe Schultz with. Come to think of it, I don't have Hilda, either. You know, I'm not sure I care to be Hogan, now that I think about it," Manning said with his best deadpan expression.

"I remember Schultz once told Hogan that if he should ever escape, he wanted Hogan to take him along," Tony whispered.

Manning thought about that for several minutes, his expression suddenly serious. He then turned to Juarez and said, "My Spanish is not too great; you might have to help me some here."

Manning once again faced the guard, who was still eating, and said in Spanish, "The boy may have an infection, and we need you to call for a doctor."

"No, I cannot leave my post," the guard answered.

"The boy needs something to drink," Manning said, again in his best Spanish.

"And I would like a cold beer," the guard responded between bites of sandwich.

Manning was quiet for several moments before he spoke again.

"I don't blame you. There's nothing quite like a cold beer, if it's brewed right." Then, as if it were an afterthought, Manning added, "I can personally assure you of that because my father owns one of the largest breweries in the states."

The guard gave a big grin, his mouth full of sandwich, and said, "You're a lucky man!"

Manning again waited several moments and said, "You know, my father is always trying to find men who really know their beer to help out at the brewery."

"Is that so?" the guard said, turning his attention from the sandwich to Manning.

"Yes, and the job pays well for men who really know beer. A man like that could get very rich."

The guard stopped chewing completely, stared at Manning, and said, "Rich, you say?"

"Yes, very rich. America is a rich country and the beer business is huge."

The guard again continued chewing, but very slowly now.

"What is your name?" Manning asked.

"My name is Juan Calderon," the guard answered enthusiastically.

"When I get back to America, I will remember your name. I'm sure my father would like to meet you some day, especially if conditions in Cuba should change."

The guard stood, walked over to the cell, looked at Tony, and said, "You say the boy is thirsty?"

"Yes, some juice or water would be good," Manning answered.

Calderon yelled at the men guarding the entrance to the corridor and told them to see about getting the prisoners' rations delivered. He ordered them to bring him some juice to wash down his sandwich.

The prisoners' meals consisted of table scraps left over from the dinners of the restaurant above. The scraps were all dumped into a big pot.

Twenty minutes later one of the girls from the kitchen delivered the slop and a bucket of water for the prisoners. She also brought a jug of orange juice and a cream danish for Calderon.

After she left, Calderon gave Manning the juice and said, "Remember to tell your father this juice is from Juan Calderon."

CHAPTER
37

Tripp leaned over the pier railing and looked at *La Princessa Delfin*, the boat Powell had procured for him. The vessel was a sleek metallic-gray Pershing 90 Mega-yacht. At ninety feet long with a beam width of twenty feet, the yacht was built for comfort on the open sea.

"She's a beauty," Tripp said.

"Wait till you see the inside," Powell said. "She has three staterooms, a full bath, and a dedicated home theater with a large-screen television."

"We'll take it," Carmen said with a grin.

Powell continued, "She's fast, too. There are twin twenty-four-hundred horsepower MTU diesels that can power her up to forty-four knots per hour or better—something you may need before you get back."

"What's her draft?" Tripp asked.

"Just over five feet. She basically skips across the water. You'll find she has all the latest technology, including a Maptech GPS/radar. Come, I'll show you around."

Tripp and Carmen collected what luggage they had and followed Powell toward the gangway. Ten minutes later they were standing near the sun pad on the aft deck. They made their way into the aft seating area, a flying bridge, complete with a bar and chaise lounges.

"Apparently our drug-running friends enjoyed movies during their cruises," Powell said as he pushed a button near the bar. A forty-two-inch plasma TV rose along the port bulkhead.

"It really is a beautiful boat," Carmen said.

They made their way belowdeck. The steps led into a galley covered in black marble and stainless steel, fitted out with more appliances than the average home. It spilled into a dining area with a table that looked as if it could hold eight diners. Next was the media room, where there was a large-screen television, an entertainment center with a DVD player, a wide selection of movies, and a plush sofa. On the walls were paintings by Monet, and everything was covered in teak and leather.

"It looks like a luxury hotel suite," Carmen said.

Next to the media room was an office with a large oak desk that held a computer, a fax, a radio, and an array of electronic equipment. They then followed the hallway to the forward stateroom. The VIP stateroom was circular and spacious, with a plush king-sized bed, a walk-in closet, three vertical windows, a wet bar, and a writing desk. Behind a translucent partition was an in-suite bathroom, complete with Jacuzzi.

"There are two more staterooms near the stern. They're a bit smaller, but still comfortable."

"Let's have a look at the bridge," Tripp said.

The group retraced their steps and climbed back up to the bridge. The yacht was equipped with a full-color monitor on the control panel and a navigational plotter, which was a shipboard computer loaded with marine charts linked to the boat's GPS. Tripp sat in the pilot's seat and studied the control panel.

"We will be in direct contact and will monitor you the whole time. Hopefully you will be back before the storm hits, but if not, as I said earlier, she is a sturdy vessel. She also has the required EPIRB—Emergency Position Indicating Radio Beacon—which is water activated, so if something should happen, we will find you."

"Is she fueled?" Tripp asked.

"Yes, fueled and ready, and the galley is fully stocked."

Powell pulled some papers from his inside coat pocket.

"These are the maps Vargas drew for us. They show the layout of Morro, the place they're holding Tony, and the best place to dock the yacht."

He handed the maps to Tripp and checked his watch. "It's almost noon; I've got to get back to headquarters. What time do you plan to leave?"

"We need to pick up a few things and get a bite to eat. I'd also like some time in the pilot's seat to get the feel of her." Tripp checked his watch and continued, "We should be able to shove off by four."

"I will be in contact. I wish both of you good luck." Powell shook their hands and left the ship.

Tripp turned to Carmen and asked, "What are you hungry for?"

"Seafood sounds good, but I'd like to clean up a bit first."

"You take the forward stateroom. I'll find one in the back. How about we meet back here in ten minutes," Tripp said.

"I'll see you here," Carmen said.

They picked up the luggage they had left in the aft seating area and made their way to their rooms. Twenty minutes later Tripp pulled the car out of the parking lot and began looking for a Red Lobster restaurant they had passed on the way over.

The afternoon was relatively calm, considering there was a tropical storm some 150 miles out. The skies were partly cloudy, but still had plenty of sun breaking through, and only a slight breeze. Ten minutes later they pulled into the Red Lobster parking lot.

Carmen ordered blackened sea bass with black beans, rice, and iced tea. Tripp had the same.

After the waitress left, Carmen said, "So, have you got a plan yet?"

"We're going to go in as a Canadian couple on a honeymoon cruise through the Caribbean. We'll go in, have some dinner, maybe some dancing, and then some sightseeing. I want to get my bearings and learn the guards' routine. After that, we're going to play it by ear."

When Carmen didn't say anything, Tripp asked, "Are you sure you want to do this, Carmen?"

"Absolutely I'm sure. I will do whatever it takes to get Tony back."

"There are a couple things I need to pick up after we finish lunch," Tripp said.

"I need a few things too, especially if we're on our honeymoon," Carmen said playfully.

The waitress arrived with their food and said she would be back to check on them.

After she left, Carmen said, "Actually, I need several things. We left my apartment rather abruptly. I didn't get to pack all that much."

They finished their meal, paid the check, and left. A few minutes later they found a mall, parked the car, and went in. Tripp left Carmen at a clothing store and walked a few doors down to an electronics shop. One of the sales clerks, a pimply faced young man who appeared to have attended one too many heavy metal concerts, approached and asked if he could help.

"I'm looking for a boom box that will give me plenty of volume."

"A boom box?" the kid asked with a grin. "They stopped making those about a decade ago. How about an MP3 player and a small speaker dock? They're small but can pump out the volume. You can turn it on and off from anywhere in the room with a remote."

"Sounds like that might work. Have you got something like that?"

"Yeah, man, this unit here is nice. It won't blow the doors off, but it can keep your neighbors awake."

The slim player and fold-up speaker dock could easily slip into a jacket pocket undetected.

"I'll take it," Sean said. "It's a gift for my son; I want to introduce him to some of my favorite tunes. You got any ZZ Top CDs?"

"I can show you how to download it directly to your device," the sales clerk offered.

When Tripp returned to the clothing store, Carmen had completed her selections. Tripp whipped out his credit card and handed it to the clerk before Carmen could dig hers out of her purse. She tried to protest, but he insisted it was a business expense, and they left for the car.

"What did you buy?" Carmen asked.

"Let's just say I thought Neil and Tony might enjoy some music."

By the time Tripp and Carmen returned to the yacht, it was after three. Tripp went to his cabin and changed into blue jeans and a white pullover. He left his Glock and shoulder holster in the cabin, but kept the small Kel-Tec on his ankle, and made his way to the bridge.

The wind had picked up, and it was now partly sunny. The waters were relatively calm, with only a few small whitecaps made mostly by the wake from other passing vessels. Tripp cranked the diesel engines and they hummed to life. He let them idle while he made himself more familiar with the control panel and the ship's systems. Finally he flipped the communications system on and radioed Powell that they were about to shove off.

A few minutes later Carmen joined Tripp on the bridge and climbed into the copilot's pedestal chair. Her hair was tied back with a white scarf, and she was wearing a blue turtleneck sweater with matching pants. Tripp glanced over at her. Her attractive external appearance could not mask the pensive emotions hiding beneath the surface.

"Are you ready to go get your brother?"

Carmen looked through the windscreen, her mind's eye focused on a vision from fifteen years earlier, and said in a somber but steely tone, "Yes, let's do it."

It was a little past four when they began to make their way toward open sea. Noisy seagulls flocked around the yacht as if pleading for their last meal. A flight of pelicans swept by off the starboard bow, their outspread wings floating on the wind.

The radar was on and the tropical storm clearly registered along the outer edge of the dashboard monitor. Tripp flicked a switch and entered Morro's coordinates into the navigational plotter. Thirty minutes later they had cleared the bay and entered the Intracoastal Waterway. Tripp looked out over the long, wide bow with his turquoise-green eyes. Beyond the bow rail, a dark-green sea filled with white-capped rollers stretched as

far as he could see. The afternoon was growing late, and a cold
wind had picked up. There was still another hour of sunlight
left when Carmen looked back to see the last vestiges of land
slip quietly into the sea. Tripp ran *La Princessa Delfin* at forty
knots. The yacht seemed to love it; she sliced through the rolling
sea.

Within an hour, they had entered the Gulf Stream and the
sea had turned an opaline blue. The waves, stirred by a cross-
wind, had grown short and choppy and were filled with white-
capped rollers, bringing with them the scent of kelp and seaweed. The sun was beginning to set; it looked like a disk of
mango-orange slowly gliding down into Mexico.

"Can I get you anything, Sean?"

"A bottle of water would be good."

Carmen retreated to the galley and returned a short time
later with two bottles of water, one of which she handed to Tripp.
The sky was turning to ink, and somewhere in the distance a fog-
horn moaned. Carmen and Tripp focused their eyes east toward
the haunting sound. The line of demarcation between sea and
sky could no longer be discerned, but far off in the distance the
lights of a small ship flickered like a lightning bug on a summer
evening. Carmen thought about another night when lights had
approached in these same waters. She and Tripp both watched
as the ship disappeared into the night, leaving only darkness
and the deep vibrato of their own engines rising up through the
decks.

"Listen, Carmen," Tripp said as he took a sip of water. "In a
little while we will be entering Cuban waters. We could encoun-
ter a Cuban coast guard ship. If we do, I want you to go below
and stay there."

"What will you do?"

"We're a couple on our honeymoon. My mind was on other things. I wasn't aware we were in Cuban waters, and I apologize. They will check my passport—the FBI fabricated one for me—and let us be on our way," he said, hoping she would believe him.

Carmen didn't say anything. Her mind had returned once again to another time when her family had been stopped by Cuban authorities.

Two hours later, lights from the island nation of Cuba were visible. Tripp slowed the yacht, checked the navigation plotter, and adjusted their course. They passed several fishing boats, wooden vessels with a single mast. There were only one or two men in each boat, and they were busy rigging trot lines and pre-paring nets. Tripp watched them closely, but they didn't appear to be a threat. Tripp brought the engine to idle and picked up the radio handset. Within seconds he was talking with Henry Powell.

"We're approaching Morro and should be docking soon. Have you heard anything from your sources?"

"Everything is quiet on the island, but the tropical storm is growing in intensity and moving fast. You need to go in, get the men, and get out."

Tripp signed off and turned to Carmen.

"It's time to get ready. Let's change into some dinner attire and meet back here."

They returned to their staterooms. Not wanting to be away from the bridge for long, Tripp changed quickly. He wore a white button-down oxford, khaki pants, and a blue blazer. Underneath the blazer he wore his shoulder holster and Glock, along with three extra magazines. He then picked up the MP3 player, checked the batteries the kid had installed earlier, inserted the device into the speakers, and slipped it into his pocket. The slight impression looked like a wallet, not a fully functional stereo system. He returned to the bridge to meet Carmen.

Carmen returned a short time later decked out in a revealing red flower-print blouse that hung open in front, jet black pants, and a fringed white cotton wrap pulled over her shoulders. Her ebony black hair fell loosely over the wrap and down her back. She wore the same string of white pearls she had worn at the restaurant; they formed a bridge across her ample cleavage.

"So what do you think?" Carmen asked as she climbed back into the copilot's chair.

"I think you look beautiful."

"Thank you. You're quite handsome, too."

"Are you ready to go?"

"Yes, I'm very ready."

Once again Tripp accelerated *La Princessa Delfín*, guiding her through the swells toward the channel that led to the harbor protecting Castillo del Morro. The evening was dark, and they couldn't see the channel until they were almost on top of it. Tripp eased back on the throttle and slowly worked *La Princessa Delfín* through. Rising two hundred feet above the cliffs on the right stood the old colonial fortress. As they made their way into the harbor, Carmen looked left, taking in the sights and sounds of Havana. She thought about the life she had once known there, the friends she had left behind, and the family that was no more.

She turned her eyes away, looked back to the right at Morro, and whispered to herself, "It won't be long now, Tony. We'll be together again soon."

Tripp pulled back on the throttle again, and almost at a coast eased the yacht into a berth. He shut down the engines and tied her off.

Lively salsa music could be heard coming from above. The wooden pier creaked and moaned like an old man trying to climb a set of stairs. Tripp could smell the scent of cigar smoke and looked around. At the far end of the pier a man was sitting on a wooden crate, smoking a cigar and holding a fishing pole with a line that disappeared into the water.

Tripp held out his arm and said, "May I escort you to dinner, Mrs. Tripp?"

Carmen gave him an indulgent smile, locked her arm around his, and said, "Yes, Mr. Tripp, I would like that."

In a low voice Tripp said, "Keep close to me and stay calm and loose. Remember, we're honeymooners without a care in the world."

They made their way up the path and followed another group toward the drawbridge. The atmosphere was lively and festive, with couples and tourist groups enjoying the sights and sounds. Tripp mentally noted how incongruous the jocund environment was with what he knew lay not far below them.

Carmen and Tripp strolled along toward the restaurant, their eyes dancing, smiling as though their faces had been stretched by one too many facelifts. They found a table on the terrace facing the courtyard. A few minutes later a waiter arrived and took their order. Tripp ordered *arroz con pollo*, or chicken and rice, and Carmen had the *ensalada del Morro*, or Morro salad. They both ordered spiced tea to drink.

As they dined, they watched the courtyard closely, focusing on a stairway that led to a lower level. There was one guard at the top of the stairs and three others spread at various distances around the perimeter. They had been dining only a few minutes when a young girl wearing a white apron appeared from somewhere near the rear of the restaurant and walked toward the stairway carrying a large pail in each hand and a jug of liquid under her arm. They watched her until she descended the stairway and disappeared from view. Ten minutes later, she reappeared on the stairs and returned to the rear of the restaurant empty-handed.

"I think they just delivered dinner to your brother and my friends."

A few minutes later the waiter approached their table.

"Are you enjoying your dinner?" the waiter asked in Spanish.

"Yes, everything is wonderful," Carmen answered in perfect Spanish.

"You are happy then?" the waiter asked, hopefully paving the way for a substantial tip.

"We are very happy." Carmen reached over and took Tripp's hands in hers and continued, "My husband and I are on our honeymoon."

"Congratulations!" the waiter responded in broken English.

"Thank you," Tripp said.

"Your wife is quite beautiful, señor."

"Yes, she is. I'm very lucky."

"It is very romantic here at Castillo del Morro, and in a few minutes you will get to see the firing of the cannon. It is a ceremony they do each evening to honor those who fought for independence from Spain. They fire the cannon into the sea and finish by saluting Cuba Libre. There will also be fireworks. Perhaps we will say it's a salute to the two of you for a long and happy marriage."

Tripp casually pointed at the stairway and said, "Tell me, where do those stairs lead to?"

"It was a garrison many years ago. I'm afraid it's off limits to visitors now for safety reasons."

Carmen smiled warmly at the waiter and said, "A few minutes ago I saw a young girl go down there."

"She was probably one of our kitchen staff delivering food to the guards."

"Oh, I see."

"And now, I must see to our other guests. Please let me know if there is anything more I can do for you."

The waiter left the check on the edge of the table and retreated. They dined for a good part of an hour, chatting and watching the courtyard. Tripp noted to Carmen that every twenty minutes the guards rotated and shifted positions.

Finally he checked his watch and said, "It's time for us to wander around and check out the romantic views."

He paid the check in American dollars—accepted everywhere, even in Cuba—and left a generous tip. As they lazily walked around the courtyard checking out the views, Tripp kept his arm around Carmen and smiled freely. A group of men dressed in nineteenth-century garb had begun to gather at the opposite end of the yard. A few minutes later, Tripp and Carmen stopped at a recessed stone area not far from the top of the stairs. A display had been set up there for visitors, and Tripp and Carmen stood studying the display. Tripp looked around to see if anyone was paying undue attention to them, but saw nothing of concern. Tripp knew what had to be done. He was no neophyte, yet he had been out of this type of action for a while, and he wondered if his training would come through for him. Carmen looked at him questioningly and Tripp snapped out of it.

"Okay, the guards will be rotating in five minutes. Every time they start a rotation, they leave the stairwell vulnerable for a couple of seconds. As soon as the guard at the top of the stairs begins to rotate, I'm going to create a diversion. When I do, stay close; we've got to get down the stairs."

He pulled the MP3 player and speakers from his pocket. He set it behind some papers and booklets left out for the tourists, and they waited.

Four minutes later, the guard at the top of the stairs nodded at one of the other guards, lifted his weapon, and began to loop the strap over his shoulder.

Tripp stepped back and pressed the slim remote. As the guard began to walk toward the next station, Tripp and Carmen stepped away from the display and furtively began to make their way toward the stairs.

The kid at the electronics store had been right. The MP3 player did indeed have enough volume to keep the neighbors awake. Tripp and Carmen were less than five feet from the stairway when ZZ Top's "La Grange" began to blare, breaking the stillness of the evening, blasting the words, *"Rumor spreadin' a-round, in that Texas town, 'bout the shack outside La Grange."*

Everyone in the courtyard and restaurant terrace began looking toward the display. The guards, who were also looking toward the display, were caught off guard and weren't sure if they should complete their rotation.

Within that first minute, while everyone was trying to find where the loud music was coming from, Tripp and Carmen began their move downstairs. The music continued: *"Just let me know, if you wanna go, to that home out on the range."*

After a few seconds of indecision, the guards regained their composure and sent a guard back to the stairs while the rest searched for the source of the music. By the time the instrumental rift cranked up, Carmen and Tripp were hiding behind a wall at the bottom of the stairs.

CHAPTER 38

*M*anning checked Tony's bandage. His color was better, and he no longer felt warm to the touch. Manning walked to the rear of the cell and sat on an empty crate next to Juarez, who was sitting on the floor with his back against the wall and his knees pointing to the ceiling.

"The bleeding has stopped and he doesn't seem to have fever. How does your shoulder feel?" Manning asked.

"Not too bad; it's mostly down to a dull throb."

Juarez paused a moment then continued, "I'm more concerned about the boy."

They looked toward Tony. He had stopped shivering and was lying quietly with his back to them.

Juarez continued, "Look, I know someone will eventually come for us, but we don't know how long that might be, and I'm not sure he could handle another visit from Señor Let's-Cause-It-To-Happen."

"I've been thinking the same thing. We'll have to come up with a plan to overpower them when they open the cell. The problem is, even if we're able to get through Cruz and his Russian comrade, they usually have two guards who are armed," Manning said.

"Yes, but one of them will be Sergeant Schultz over there, and he's already having visions of beer baths and bulging bank accounts. It might not take too much more to get him to turn."

They sat quietly, considering their options, when they heard Tony weeping. Manning stood, walked over to Tony, and sat on the edge of his bed.

"Are you hurting, Tony?"

"No, it's not that. I'm angry with myself. I have failed my father. He always said he would be there for me. He said he would always be in my corner. He wanted a better life for me and made sure I made it safely to America. Now, when he needs me, I have failed him."

He began weeping harder and Manning tried to think of words to help.

"You did not fail him, Tony. I think your father would be very proud of you. You came all this way for him, and you had no way of knowing what kind of men you were dealing with."

"I hate these men. I hate them. I want to kill them."

Juarez stood and walked over beside the bed.

"Listen to the words you used, Tony. Anger and hate. That's what's really eating at you. Anger and hate. Those feelings will destroy you. You've got to let it go," Juarez said. He paused a moment and continued, "And Neil is right, your father would be proud of you, just like we all are. I believe your father *is* in your corner, and always will be."

"And we're in your corner too," Manning said.

Tony was silent for a long time. He thought carefully over what the two men had said. Finally the silence was broken by the sound of approaching footsteps.

Schultz stood, his rifle still leaning against the wall, and said, "Finally, you have brought our dinner."

A Cuban girl wearing a white apron appeared carrying two pails and set them on the floor next to Schultz. She handed him the container of juice. She was escorted by a guard, who peered in at the prisoners.

"Did you bring me anything special?" Schultz asked in a beseeching tone.

The girl reached under her apron and brought out a long chunk of cinnamon bread that looked like a flattened football.

"This is all I could sneak out," she said.

"Thank you, it looks wonderful."

Schultz sat back down and looked at the bread the way most men look at their wives on their wedding night. The other guard unlocked the cell door and held the prisoners at gunpoint as the girl set the pails inside the cell.

"Dinner in a bucket. It's bound to be some good eatin'," Manning said dryly.

After the girl left, the guard locked the cell door and sat down beside Schultz.

"Shouldn't you be getting back out to your post?" Schultz asked, his tone annoyed and abrupt.

"There's another guard at the entrance. I think I have time to accept some of your cinnamon cake," the guard said in an austere tone.

Begrudgingly, Schultz shared his prize.

Manning and Juarez knew they had to eat to keep their strength up. They tried to get Tony to eat, but he refused. The two men ate in silence, listening to Schultz and the other guard throw jabs at each other in Spanish.

A half hour had passed when the relative quiet was broken by a sound Manning knew well. Coming from above was the unmistakable sound of ZZ Top playing "La Grange."

Manning looked at Juarez, a wide grin spreading across his face, and said, "The cavalry is here."

CHAPTER 39

*T*ripp looked up from the bottom of the stairs toward the blaring music above and saw that a curtain of clouds had moved in, obscuring the blanket of stars. A cool wind had picked up and rushed down the three-story walls, whipping up small clouds of dust along the columns Tripp and Carmen were hiding behind.

Tripp peeked around the corner at the entrance to the corridor. A guard in field fatigues leaned casually against the wall near the entrance, peering up toward the loud music with a blank expression, as though he were missing out on a good time. Slung over his shoulder was an assault rifle. Tripp pulled back and knelt next to Carmen.

"There's only one guard," he whispered. "He can be easily disposed of, but I'm worried about the support he may have inside the corridor should he scream out. I need a distraction."

Carmen removed the white cotton wrap from around her shoulders and laid it on the ground.

"I think I can handle that assignment," she said.

She stood and casually sauntered around the wall and past the guard, as though she were strolling through Central Park.

The guard pulled his rifle from his shoulder and barked in Spanish, "Stop, you are not allowed down here."

Carmen turned to face him. Her silky black hair, green-brown eyes, and olive brown skin, highlighted by the red blouse, were dazzling.

"I'm sorry, I was just looking around. It's been a long time since I've had the chance to get out and enjoy myself," Carmen said in Spanish with an almost perfect Cuban accent.

"You must leave immediately."

Carmen flashed a sensuous smile and tilted just a bit, allowing her blouse to fall open at the top.

"I've had such a good time this evening, but I think I may have drank too much."

She put her hand against the wall and leaned toward him slightly, revealing more skin and cleavage. She continued, "I'm sorry; I didn't mean to cause any trouble."

The guard eased his rifle down and let his eyes drop to Carmen's chest. His expression resembled that of a teenage boy who had just found a *Playboy* magazine under his brother's mattress. He opened his mouth to speak, but never got a word out.

In a split second, Tripp rushed from behind the wall, came up behind the guard, and with the butt of his Glock, came down on the back of the guard's head. There was a dull thud, and the guard's knees buckled. Tripp caught him under the arms and dragged him behind a column. He picked up the guard's rifle, removed the clip, and laid the rifle next to the unconscious guard.

"Nice job. Now I know why I brought you along," Tripp said.

"Glad I was able to help."

"You were great," he said admiringly.

Carmen smiled and pulled her blouse up tight around her neck.

Tripp stuck the clip in his rear pocket. "We've got to get moving. You stay behind me," he said in a hushed, serious tone.

Carmen swiftly went to the wall where she had left her white cotton wrap and returned.

"No, I've got an idea. It came to me when I saw the girl carrying dinner down here." She took the wrap, folded it corner-to-corner, and tied it around her waist to resemble an apron. "You follow me," Carmen said.

Tripp nodded, removed his blazer and shoulder holster, and tossed them, along with the clip from the guard's gun, behind a wall. He stuck the Glock under his belt in the back, pulled his shirttail out to cover it, and entered the corridor. As they moved deeper into the dimly lit corridor the air became stagnant and filled with an overpowering odor of mold and decay. The cells had iron bars and grates that were wet with condensation and covered with layers of rust. They paused at each one to peer inside.

Tripp and Carmen had taken only a few more paces when Tripp abruptly pulled Carmen against the wall and pointed down the corridor. Through the dim light, Carmen saw two guards far down the corridor.

"If the apron doesn't fool them, I'll have to fire on them, so be ready to hit the ground," Tripp whispered.

They were about to make their move when ZZ Top abruptly stopped playing and the corridor fell silent.

"We may not have much more time. Let's do it," Tripp whispered.

They turned and casually began walking toward the guards. Schultz first spotted the apron.

"You're back to collect the pails?" Schultz said in Spanish.

When the guards saw Tripp, both men stood and brought their weapons up.

"Who are you?" the other guard asked in Spanish.

"We're from the kitchen. We're here to collect the pails," Carmen responded.

"You are not Maria. Where is she?" Schultz asked.

"She wasn't feeling well and had to go home. They asked me to come down," Carmen said.

"And who are you?" the other guard asked, looking at Tripp.

"He is one of the cooks. I have never been down here, so I asked him to come with me," Carmen replied.

"How did you get in here?"

"The guard at the entrance knows me. He told me to come on back."

The guard seemed to relax some, but was still wary of Tripp.

"I don't suppose you brought me anything special?" Schultz asked hopefully.

"No, I'm sorry, but I didn't," Carmen responded.

"Come over here closer, I want to see you better," the other guard said.

Carmen and Tripp slowly moved toward the guards until they were within ten feet. They could see inside the cell, but Tripp kept his eyes on the guards. Carmen peeked in the cell and saw two men sitting near the rear and someone lying on a bunk with his back to them.

The guard stared at Tripp, and in broken English said, "You appear to be American. Do you speak English?"

"Only little English. I am Chekov from Soviet Union," Tripp said with the best Russian accent he could muster.

After several moments of indecision, the guard unlocked the cell, but kept his rifle trained on Tripp.

"You get the pails," he said to Tripp, nodding toward the cell.

Tripp entered the cell and moved toward the pails that were resting on a crate near Manning and Juarez.

"So you're the one sending this stuff down to us?" Manning said, looking at Tripp.

"I am cook," Tripp said.

"And what do you call this slop?"

"It Soviet dish I call T tight-36 Rip," Tripp said, looking at Manning.

"I think you need a new recipe."

Tripp picked up the pails and turned his back to Manning so that he was blocking the guard's view of him. He paused a moment, then started for the cell door. Before Tripp reached the door, strained shouts could be heard from outside the corridor. The guard aimed his rifle at Tripp and began to squeeze the trigger. In an instant, Tripp dove for the floor and a shot rang out. The shot, however, had come from inside the cell, and the guard slumped to the floor. Manning turned the Glock on Schultz, but he didn't have to fire. Schultz had already dropped his weapon and stood with his hands up. Carmen had covered her ears from the loud report, and when the guard fell at her feet, she looked up at Manning.

"Where did you get the gun?" she asked.

"T tight-36 Rip. The only time I ever got to run the ball," Manning said with a smile.

"It was a play where I would hide the ball behind my back and Manning would take it. Luckily he remembered the play and found the Glock," Tripp said.

"You act like you expected us," Carmen said.

"I knew you were here as soon as I heard 'La Grange' playing," Manning said.

"A song told you that?"

"Manning spent a good share of his time in La Grange during our college years. Just my way of letting him know I was here to take him home," Tripp said with a crooked grin.

"How did you get past the guard at the entrance?" Manning asked.

"Carmen handled that. It seems the guard was very interested in what one might call excessive cleavage."

"Excessive cleavage? Isn't that what one might call an oxymoron?" Manning asked.

"Sometimes I feel like I should wear a condom when I talk to you," Tripp responded.

Tony, whose back had been turned during the whole episode, finally turned over and made eye contact with Carmen for the first time in fifteen years.

CHAPTER
40

The Pentagon in Arlington, Virginia, was relatively quiet on this December evening only days before Christmas. The famous building, consisting of five concentric rings and six and one-half million square feet of floor area, housed twenty-five thousand employees, most of whom were home with their families. One of the exceptions was an agent of the Defense Intelligence Agency, or DIA, who sat at her computer in a dimly lit office.

Anita Montoya checked the clock on her computer for the third time in the past five minutes. It was almost eight, and the call she was waiting on should happen shortly. Anita was a tall, attractive woman in her mid-forties, with brown eyes and brown hair that was already streaked with gray. She carried herself with the polished manner of a successful corporate executive. She paused, leaned back in her chair, and looked at a photo of her husband and their two children. More family photos filled the walls, along with two shots taken of her standing next to two different U.S. presidents.

During her long career with the Defense Intelligence Agency, basically the military counterpart of the CIA, Anita had worked her way to the top, and with that ascension came a high-level intelligence clearance. She and her colleagues were tasked with collecting details on foreign militaries and assessing their capabilities. Her job, specifically, was to collect data on Cuban insurgents and find out what they were doing.

Her work had taken her all over the world, but what Anita was most proud of was the work she had done to bring hope to the people of Cuba. Since her humble beginnings in a small village in Cuba, where her father labored long hours each day in a sugar cane field to support the family, Anita had devoted her life to working for a better future for her native people. Once again she looked at the photos of her daughters; she hoped that one day she might be able to take them to Cuba to see her family and the home she had grown up in.

Anita often worked closely with Ben Hagle, who ran the Cuba desk at the CIA, and they had developed a close relationship. Hagle was getting regular updates from Henry Powell in Miami about the situation at Morro, and he in turn would update Anita. He was expecting an update at eight and had agreed to call her. It was five after eight when Anita's phone rang.

"The operation is on. Sean Tripp is at Morro now, so we should know something within the hour," Hagle said.

"Is everything going smoothly?" Anita asked.

"All is well so far. We're concerned about the storm. It's now a category one hurricane and moving fast toward Cuba."

"Thank you, Ben."

"May I ask you why you've taken such an interest in this particular case?"

"I guess it's because the girl reminds me of myself," Anita said, hoping Hagle would leave it at that.

"I'll let you know when I hear more."

Anita returned the phone to the cradle. Years ago she had been clandestinely contacted by a man who had once been a high-ranking general in Castro's forces but had escaped and was now working to help the insurgents. The man went by the name Grouper, and she regularly fed him information to help the cause. This, in and of itself, would be enough to destroy her career, but she believed strongly in that same cause and accepted the risk. The dark secret that haunted her now, about the Favela matter, was that several weeks back she had received a message from someone unknown, someone who knew what she had been doing, and who requested a meeting. They met in Arlington National Cemetery one afternoon, where the man, who spoke with a Russian accent, demanded she give him the identities and locations of the Favela children, or he would not be responsible for what might happen to her own children. She knew she should have reported it, but she feared for her children. It wasn't until after she had given him the information he wanted that she discovered his identity. The man was Yuri Petroff, a leader in the Red Mafia who worked out of Little Odessa.

Anita sighed, logged off her computer, grabbed her briefcase, and snapped the light off on her way out. Twenty minutes later she pulled out of the parking lot and turned for home.

CHAPTER
41

*C*armen's eyes met Tony's, and everything seemed to go silent. She saw his shirt and the bedsheets, stained and caked with blood, and felt a cold chill. Finally the corners of his mouth turned up in a smile.

"Hi, sis," Tony said weakly.

Carmen ran over and knelt by his bed. The emotions welling inside her were numbing. For so many years she had wondered if he was alive and if she would ever see him again, and now, here he was.

"It really is you," Carmen whispered with tears running down her face.

The sound of men yelling was growing louder. They now seemed to be coming from inside the corridor.

Tony reached out with his good hand, touched Carmen's face, and wiped away a tear.

"It's really me. I had just about given up hope of ever seeing you or anyone else again."

"You may not get to see her for long if we don't get out of here," Tripp said.

He reached down and pulled the Kel-Tec from his ankle, trained it on Schultz, and turned to Juarez.

"Tell him we're going to need his rifle. Looks like we're going to have to shoot our way out, and I only brought two pistols."

"We're going to need that rifle, my friend, if we're going to get you to that beer bath," Juarez said in Spanish as he stepped toward Schultz.

"You'll never make it out. They have many men and more will be coming," Schultz said, his Spanish coming out quick and strained.

"We'll have to take our chances."

Juarez walked outside the cell and Schultz handed him the rifle and the juice.

"I know another way out of here, but we'll have to hurry," Schultz said.

Juarez passed the juice to Tony; he gulped it down, its sugar making him feel stronger immediately. The shouts were even louder now, and they could hear the rumble of feet echoing off the thick stone walls.

"He says he knows another way out," Juarez said to Tripp and Manning.

"We've got to go now," Tripp said. "Can you walk, Tony?"

"I think so." Tony stood. Although his legs felt weak, he said, "Yes, I can make it."

Carmen took his hand and said, "This time we leave together."

"Follow me," Schultz said as he began to move ponderously down the corridor.

With Manning bringing up the rear, they hurried down the corridor. The group had passed several cells when they came to the one where Tony had been tortured. Tony looked in and saw the tall light stands and the tripod. On the floor he saw where a pool of blood had dried into a sickening black mass. They continued on, making several turns, and as they moved deeper into the corridor the voices behind them grew weaker, as did the lights. The last corridor they followed was short and led to a stairway where the lights played out completely. They followed the steps up to a pitch-black corridor and continued in the dark. Finally it ended at a thick iron door. Schultz turned the handle and shoved at the door with his shoulder, but it moved only an inch before it abruptly stopped. A chain with a heavy padlock snaked around the handle and held the door fast. The door led to the outside, allowing a small bit of light to filter in.

"We'll have to shoot it," Manning said.

"If you shoot, they'll hear it and find us," Carmen said.

"Eventually they'll find us anyway. We can't afford to wait and lose what lead we have," Tripp said.

"I'd suggest we move farther back up the corridor. I've already experienced a ricochet on this adventure, and it's not pleasant," Juarez said.

The group moved well back into the corridor, and Tripp raised the Kel-Tec. The report was deafening, reverberating throughout the corridors. The lock exploded and the chain fell to the floor. Tripp shoved the door with his foot, and it swung open into the night. They made their way out the door into fresh air and found themselves on a rock ledge overlooking the harbor. The sky was overcast, and the only light was what filtered down from the festivities above and from the Cuban mainland. They could hear the sound of the Rumba Cubana All-Stars playing "La Rumba Soy Yo." The wind had picked up and was blowing steady from the east. To the left was the channel they had taken into the harbor, and to the right were the lights of the Malecon.

"The boat will be moored to our right. We'll have to move quickly. Stay close and watch your step," Tripp said.

They worked their way along the ledge and steadily made their way down. Within minutes they saw the drawbridge beyond a flat outcropping. When the group reached the outcropping, they stopped and looked back. It had begun to rain, making visibility low, but so far everything looked clear. No one was behind them, and they couldn't see anyone at the door they had just exited. The drawbridge that led to the dock was only a short climb.

"When we reach the bridge, I'll help each of you up. As soon as you're on the bridge, make your way to the boat as fast as you can. Don't stop and don't look back," Tripp said.

Five minutes later they reached the base of the bridge. The ground was covered with rocks and small boulders, and there was a six-foot wall leading to the top. They gathered near the wall, with Manning still guarding the rear. Tripp stepped onto a flat boulder and turned to Juarez.

"You're first, Michael, then I'll send up Carmen and Tony. Once they're up, make sure you get them to the boat."

As Juarez stepped onto the boulder, Tripp bent down and cupped his hands together. Juarez slipped a foot into Tripp's hands and steadied himself with one hand on the wall and the other on Tripp's shoulder. Tripp lifted him several feet until Juarez got a handhold and pulled himself up. Then he leaned back over the side, nodded, and helped Carmen and Tony up. The three left for the boat.

"Okay, you're next, Neil, then your friend Schultz and me."

Manning stepped onto the boulder, slipped his foot into Tripp's hands and climbed up. Schultz stepped up and followed suit, but because of his size, he couldn't pull himself up. Manning reached down, grabbed his hand, and began to pull, but still could not get him up.

"Tell your full-figured friend here to step on my shoulders," Tripp yelled to Manning.

Manning relayed the message to Schultz in Spanish and Schultz moved his right foot onto Tripp's left shoulder. Then he pulled up some and got his other foot on. Tripp slowly stood up while Manning pulled from above. Finally Schultz leaned onto the bridge with his upper body resting on top. As he began to pull his legs up and roll over, they heard shouts coming from behind them where the guards had found their way to the big steel door.

Tripp handed the rifle to Schultz and started to climb up. Manning reached down, took Tripp's hand, and pulled him up. As they turned for the boat, two guards stepped behind them with their rifles drawn. Tripp glanced up at the heavens, hoping for a company of special-ops forces to land, but all he saw was rain falling in giant drops, as if someone held a water hose above them.

"Take your weapons out by the barrel, drop them, and lie down on the ground," the first guard said in Spanish.

"He requests that we toss our weapons and lie down for him," Manning said, looking at Tripp.

"We just met the man and he's asking us to lie down?" Tripp said.

"I'm picturing him unlatching his belt and loosening his trousers, and it's making me a bit uncomfortable. I mean, he could at least buy us a couple of drinks first," Manning said.

"Throw down your weapons, and don't go near the trigger," the guard barked again.

"He says he would really like us to toss our weapons, and he insists we don't touch the trigger," Manning said.

Manning reached for the Glock, carefully lifting it by the barrel, and Tripp did the same with the Kel-Tec.

"You know, I once knew a guy that could bean a man with a boomerang hard enough to punch his lights out," Manning said.

"Why are you looking at me when you say that?"

"Hey, you were the quarterback."

At that instant the second guard stepped forward, raising his rifle. Schultz immediately dropped his rifle and for a brief moment the guards looked toward Schultz. Tripp's movement was lightning quick, and the guards were too startled to react. They were standing less than six feet away, and in less than a second, the Kel-Tec smashed into the temple of the first guard, knocking him to the ground. The other guard instinctively turned his rifle on Tripp, but Manning was faster. He dove at the second guard, knocking the rifle to the side, and fell into him with his full weight.

They fell hard, but the guard was strong. He threw an elbow into Manning's jaw and rolled on top, throwing punches into his ribcage. Manning kicked a knee at the guard's groin, but the guard pulled up, avoiding a direct blow. The guard's fists were lighting quick, pounding Manning's ribs and stomach like a jackhammer. Manning reached up and grabbed the guard by the ears and smashed his forehead into the guard's nose. He heard a loud crunch as the cartilage gave way and blood squirted out, but it only slowed the guard for a moment.

The guard threw a hard jab, connecting with Manning's jaw. Manning countered with a left to the guard's temple, and the force of the blow caused the guard to roll enough for Manning to get out from under him. The guard stood and pulled a knife from the side of his pant leg and swung it in a crossing motion. Manning jerked his arm up and blocked the guard at the wrist.

The guard's arm glanced off as the knife cut through the air. Manning charged the guard, keeping his body in tight, and once again they hit the ground hard. They rolled several times, with the guard ending on top. The guard started to bring the knife up, but Manning whipped his left arm forward and knocked the guard to the side. The guard kicked a knee into Manning's groin and connected. Manning winced in pain and began to suck in air. The guard lifted the knife above his head and started to bring it down. The tip of the blade was only inches from Manning's throat when a shot rang out and the guard's lifeless body fell to the side.

"What the hell were you waiting on?" Manning yelled. "For him to die of old age?"

"You looked like you were handling yourself pretty well," Tripp responded.

"I felt like I was wrestling an octopus here, while you just watched."

"I was hoping I wouldn't have to fire and bring him reinforcements, but it's too late now."

They could hear the sound of men yelling and footsteps running toward them.

"If there are more like him, we might ought to be on our way," Manning said.

They picked up their weapons and began sprinting toward the dock, with Schultz bringing up the rear. Shots started to ring out, and bits of rock and dirt began to splatter as the bullets hit the ground around them. The men left the drawbridge and sprinted down the path. As they rounded a point halfway to the boat, Manning stopped and yelled for Tripp to start the engines and be ready to leave. Tripp continued to sprint, with Schultz lagging behind. Manning pulled the Glock out and waited for the pursuers. Several seconds later he saw two guards sprint off the drawbridge and turn toward him. He squeezed off a shot and hit one in the leg. The guard fell to the ground, clutching his leg, while the other dove for cover behind some rocks. Manning spun around and sprinted for the boat. It wasn't long before he passed Schultz, and seconds later he hopped onto the yacht.

The yacht was untied, with engines running and the bow pointed into the bay. Manning looked up at the bridge to see Tripp at the helm, waiting to throttle up. He spun around to help Schultz aboard as the guard rounded a point some forty yards up the trail. A shot rang out, and Schultz crumpled to the ground only feet from the yacht. Manning fired in the direction of the guard, but the guard had ducked for cover. Manning jumped off the yacht and ran out to Schultz, who was lying on his back with his eyes open and blood running from the corners of his mouth.

"Come on, my friend, I'll help you," Manning said.

"No, I can't," Schultz said.

Manning grabbed his hand and looked in his eyes.

"Go, my friend. Drink a cold beer for me," Schultz wheezed.

Manning started to object when Schultz's eyes closed and he was gone.

"I will remember you, my friend, and I will drink one for you."

Manning spun around and ran for the yacht. Just as he was about to board, the guard appeared with his rifle aimed at Manning's back. Tripp reached for his Kel-Tec, but he knew there wouldn't be time. He started to yell out to Manning when a shot rang out. Fearing that his friend was hit, Tripp stepped out onto the bridge wing, but what he saw was the guard on his knees with a crimson bullet hole in the center of his chest.

Tripp looked around to see where the shot had come from. At the far end of the dock stood the fisherman he had seen when they arrived, the cigar still in his mouth. The man gave Tripp the thumbs-up sign, shoved his pistol in his pocket, and dove into the bay.

Again they heard men yelling from above, and Manning jumped on board. Tripp shoved the throttle forward and the yacht shot out into the bay. More shots rang out, but the rain was heavy and it was dark, so the bullets found only air. Seconds later, *La Princessa Delfin* entered the channel and headed toward open waters.

CHAPTER
42

Grouper sat in a cable car as it leisurely made its way to the top of Sugarloaf Mountain. The sun had already settled in for the night, and the breeze off the Atlantic, along with the extreme height of the famous landmark, made for a cool evening. The base of Pao de Acucar, or Sugarloaf Mountain, is the exact place of Rio's foundation, but for defense purposes, it was moved to the top of a hill, which eventually became known as Morro de Castelo, or Castle Hill. Grouper pulled the collar of his jacket up and looked back toward the city.

The "high season," which runs from December to March, was in full swing with Christmas only days away and New Year's a week later. The incredible panoramic view of Rio and Guanabara Bay never failed to inspire Grouper. The bright lights of the city, along with the colorful lights of Christmas, were dazzling. He looked up at Cristo Redentor, the giant statue of Christ, and paused a moment as he thought of his friend Manuel Favela and his children. He had promised to watch over them, and he had done so for fifteen years, but now they were both on Castillo del Morro, clearly in reach of Castro.

Grouper allowed his gaze to fall to his left, where he saw the festive hotel-lined beaches of Ipanema and Copacabana. In little more than a week, he mused, this neighborhood would be filled with over a million people as they gathered to celebrate the New Year and watch the spectacular fireworks display.

He panned to his right, past Corcovado Mountain and the statue of Christ, and focused on the brightly lit Sombodromo, or Samba Drome, the stadium of samba. The stadium was built for the samba parade, a fiercely competitive event between the Rio samba schools that is unique to Brazil. Practice begins in December for Carnival, an annual celebration held forty days before Easter to mark the beginning of Lent. Each school reserved the Sombodromo for an evening of practice, and tonight was no exception.

The cable car continued to climb. As it neared the summit, Grouper looked out over the Atlantic. His eyes grew small as a distant memory flashed through his mind. He saw his wife, and unable to do anything to help, he saw her die. His eyes grew moist as he tried to count how many times he had cursed himself over the years for failing her, but it was useless. Again he thought about Manuel, Carmen, and Tony.

His eyes narrowed as he whispered to the empty car, "I failed my wife, but I will not fail you, my friend. Somehow I will find a way to free you and unite you with your children."

The cable car came to a sudden stop, jerking him back to the present. As he climbed out of the car, his cell phone chimed. He slowly lifted the phone to his ear, pushed the green talk button, and listened.

"A rescue team has been sent to rescue Tony," came the voice of Anita Montoya. She then continued, "Please do what you can to help him and Carmen. It's my fault they found the children."

Once again Grouper considered how he had been unable to protect his wife.

"You were protecting your own children," he said. "Do not feel you betrayed me. I already have a man on the island. He's a good man, and he will do what he can to help in the rescue."

CHAPTER
43

La Princessa Delfín was running at full throttle through the channel. Tripp was at the helm, while Manning and Carmen were belowdeck seeing to Tony and Michael. Heavy rains continued to beat down, and the wind had picked up, causing higher than normal waves along the channel. The yacht was more than up to the task, and cut through the water with ease. Tripp continued to monitor the radio, but so far was getting nothing but static.

Manning made his way up the stairs and stepped onto the bridge. Tripp stood at the wheel, his faced tinted an eerie green from the glow of the radar and sonar displays. Manning looked at the screen. He saw the outline of the channel and the open sea that were provided by the GPS system, which was laid out on the radar screen. He also saw four red blips converging on the channel.

"Looks like we're about to have some company," Manning said.

"We've got to clear this channel before they seal us off. If they get to the mouth first and set up a blockade, we won't have a chance."

"Have you been able to reach anyone on the radio?" Manning asked.

"Nothing but static."

The wind had picked up even more, blowing steadily at forty knots, with wind gusts of sixty. Manning looked back at the radar. Across from the red dots, the entire right side of the screen was covered with the storm cell.

"Looks like the gunboats aren't all we're going to be fighting."

"The way the barometer's dropping, it appears our storm has grown into a hurricane," Tripp replied.

The mouth of the channel was less than a mile away. They both watched as the red blips moved closer. What they also saw was a line of six more red dots closing in like a swinging gate less than a mile behind the first line of dots.

"It's going to be close," Tripp said.

Tripp and Manning peered out through the windscreen. It was dark and pouring rain as *La Princessa Delfin* slipped through the choppy water at almost fifty knots. They were less than a half-mile from the mouth when they spotted the lights from the first line of gunboats closing off their port bow.

When they reached the mouth, the gunboats were almost on top of them. Tripp cranked the wheel to starboard and gunned the engines. He aimed for a small passage between the rocks and the oncoming boats. *La Princessa Delfin's* bow surged and rose up, shooting white water away from the slicing bow. They were doing over fifty knots when they shot into open water. Tripp adjusted the trim and pointed the bow into the heavier chop, and the yacht smoothed out.

There were now four gunboats behind them and six ahead and to port, and they were all closing fast. The only way out was to starboard, directly into the mouth of what was now a category one hurricane. Tripp checked the radar screen again and then looked at Manning with a sardonic smile.

"Looks like we're going to find out how well this princess is built."

"You think they'll follow us into that?" Manning asked as he looked at the solid line of disturbance on the screen.

"Would you?"

"Not a chance."

Tripp turned the wheel to starboard, away from the gunboats, and pointed the bow east, directly into the meteorological hell.

The swells were growing each minute, and Tripp had to ease back on the throttle. The gunboats were still following, so he had to monitor his back, too. The temperature had dropped by ten degrees in the last ten minutes, and the barometer had gone into a free fall. Wind gusts slammed against the ship, causing the windows to rattle; lightning pierced the darkness.

La Princessa Delfin began to ride rougher as she cut across steeper waves. They had yet to reach the storm wall, yet the percolating mix of wind, rain, lightning, and the sea had now caused the Cubans to back off. They hadn't given up the chase yet, but were holding back to see if the Americans were really going into the maelstrom.

Belowdeck, Carmen's stomach had begun to churn from the tossing of the ship. With soap and hot water she had cleaned the wound on Juarez's shoulder and bandaged him with items she found in a first-aid kit. She then went to the next cabin to look after Tony. His hand had begun to bleed again, and a crimson ring was forming on the sheets around it. When Carmen entered the room, he tried to sit up.

"Hi, sis. What's happening out there?"

"Lie down, Tony. We've got a bit of a storm, but everything is going to be fine."

Carmen sat on the edge of the bed and touched his forehead. Tony had a fever, and she guessed he was probably fighting an infection.

"I need to clean your hand."

Tony lay back and watched as his sister began to unwrap the bandage. Carmen did what she could with his hand. She rinsed it out with alcohol, applied antibiotic ointment from the first-aid kit, and bandaged it back. Outside the walls of the ship's cabin, the storm was growing more intense. The boat was rocking and heaving, and they could hear the wind pounding against the thick wall of the cabin.

"I'm going to go up to the bridge to see if they need anything, but I will be back and see if I can find you something to eat," Carmen said with a warm smile.

Tony reached out and touched Carmen's face; a small tear formed at the corner of his eye.

"I can't believe it's really you; it's been so long."

Carmen put her hand over his, but said nothing.

"The last time I saw you was just before you fell into the sea. I thought you were gone forever."

"Dad pulled me out and put me onto another boat. It was horrible, leaving Mom and Dad behind. As we left, I watched them until it got too dark to see anymore."

"Those men said that Dad is alive and being held not far from here," Tony said.

"I know, Sean told me. It's been so long, it's just hard to believe."

"They also said our dad took some of Castro's money."

"That's why they wanted you, Tony. Sean said they were using you to get him to talk."

"Do you think we will ever see him again?"

"I don't know; I hope so. But right now we need to get you back safe. Then we'll talk about that. I'll be back in a few minutes."

Carmen left the cabin and made her way up the stairs. When she reached the bridge, she looked out through the windscreen. The rain was sweeping across the field of vision in giant silver sheets. She stepped between Tripp and Manning, and the three stood watching the sea whirl itself into a rage. The wind whipped against the windscreen and howled like a pack of wild dogs. In addition to the powerful winds and piercing rains, the waves had grown to ten feet. They looked like rolling hills as they hammered against the hull. Each time the hull smashed through a wave, the boat would shudder and two sheets of white spray would arch off the bow; flashes of lightning only added to the spectacle. Carmen glanced down at the radar screen and watched the bright green radar beam sweep across the dark background. She saw the incoming hurricane that formed a solid green wall across the screen.

"Are we going into that?" Carmen asked warily.

"It's the only way." Manning pointed to the radar screen and continued, "Those ten red dots are Cuban gunboats about a quarter mile behind us. They're just waiting for us to turn back."

Carmen looked at the screen and saw a semicircle of red blips behind them. She turned around and looked past the stern. Through the rain and waves she could see faint lights flickering in the distance.

"How long until we hit the wall?" she asked.

"Maybe an hour at the most. How are Tony and Michael doing?" Tripp asked.

"Tony has a fever; I think he's fighting an infection. Michael is fine, just hungry."

"You might want to get him something to eat before we hit that wall," Tripp said. "Also, I want you to get life jackets on yourself and the men below, and tell them to be prepared."

"I will. Let me know if you need anything," Carmen said.

Carmen turned, climbed below, and stopped at the galley. She searched the pantry, found some cream of chicken soup, and put it in the microwave to warm. She saw some coffee, and figuring it was going to be a long night, started a pot. A few moments later the microwave pinged. She poured the soup into a big mug and carried it to Juarez. After setting the mug beside the bed, she looked in a closet and found a life jacket.

"Before you eat, you're going to have to put this on."

"Things must be looking bad up there," Juarez said.

"A hurricane is coming, but we can't go around it because there are gunboats behind us."

Carmen helped Juarez with his life jacket and handed him the mug.

"We've got maybe an hour before things really get rough. Sean said to tell you to be prepared."

Juarez could read the tension in her face.

"Listen, Carmen, if I have to go into a hurricane, I can't think of anyone I'd rather have at the helm than Tripp. He'll get us through," Juarez said reassuringly.

Carmen smiled weakly.

"I'll be back in a bit," she said as she left the cabin.

She returned to the galley, poured another mug of soup, and went to Tony's cabin. Tony was looking out a porthole, but he turned when he heard Carmen enter.

"I've been watching the lightning. It looks pretty bad," Tony said.

"Yes, it is bad, and it's going to get worse. I need to get a life jacket on you."

Tony didn't respond, and turned his head back to the porthole. Carmen set the mug down and pulled a jacket from the closet. She helped him into it, then sat beside him on the edge of the bed. She reached for the mug and began to spoon-feed him the soup.

"Tony, we're about to enter a hurricane. I know we'll get through it, but if something happens, you'll have to be prepared."

Once again, Tony didn't respond. Carmen fed him another spoon of soup.

"If something happens and we have to abandon ship, the life jacket will keep you afloat, but you'll have to get out of the ship quick. I'll stay close and make sure you get out."

"These waters haven't been very lucky for us," Tony said.

Neither spoke for several moments as they looked at each other. Finally, Tony broke the silence. "I'll get out all right. You just be sure you do too. I don't plan to lose you again."

Outside the walls of the cabin, the storm was growing more intense. The yacht had begun to rock and pitch, and the wind was howling and gusting against the walls. Suddenly, the entire cabin lit up with a blinding light so intense it made them freeze. A fraction of a second later, a peal of thunder exploded so loudly it rattled the doors.

"I think I better get one of those life jackets on too," Carmen said.

Up on the bridge, Tripp and Manning saw and felt the sharp crack of lightning that arced from one side of the sky to the other. It lit up the sky as bright as midday. The peal of thunder was so loud the men felt as though they had been hit with a body blow. The yacht and sea around them lit up from the lightning flash, then disappeared in the darkness again, but in that moment, they both saw the front ahead of them. It looked like a solid black wall that extended straight up to the heavens. Within minutes, the squall closed in around them in a wall of driving rain and devastating winds. The hurricane was in full force around them. The rain blew horizontally, and waves crashed over the bow. Inside the wall, the lightning intensified; it looked like flickering white lights. Tripp and Manning clung to the ship as it tossed wildly.

Tripp had learned to ride heavy seas standing up, keeping his knees flexed and his arms and shoulders tight. He expertly guided the yacht through the maelstrom, fighting to keep the bow to the waves. The ship pitched and wallowed as it was pounded by waves up to twenty feet. He could feel the mountainous swells that rolled under the keel, one after the other, as if on a conveyor belt; they were beginning to come in shorter periods. This was not good, because the shorter the period, the steeper the waves, and the closer they were to breaking. A nonbreaking wave wasn't as dangerous because he could climb the swell, but a breaking wave could flip the boat over. He backed off on the throttle and turned more to starboard, trying to increase the angle and take the rollers at a forty-five-degree angle. The maneuver made it easier to climb the crests and slide down the troughs. One wave after another, the yacht rose up a slick black wall of water, crested, and slid down the back side. Visibility had dropped to almost nothing, but at one crest there was a tremendous flash of lightning that lit up the night. In that brief moment, Tripp and Manning looked out and saw wave after wave after wave as far as they could see.

"Is it too late to get a refund for this cruise?" Manning yelled.

"If these waves start breaking, we're going to be in for the fight of our lives. We better get our life jackets on," Tripp yelled back.

Manning strapped his jacket on and helped Tripp into his.

Belowdeck, Carmen sat with Tony looking through the porthole. The chaos outside was terrifying. Waves were either crashing against the window, blocking everything out, or the rain was hitting the window like pellets. The wind hitting the ship sounded like fists slamming against the wall. Every time the ship slid down a trough, they felt their stomachs drop from the force of the plunge, and the yacht would begin the climb again. Then the cycle would start all over. Sometimes when they came off a crest, the bottom would seem to just drop from under them, and the ship would slam straight down. At one point, the whole cabin lurched to the right, tossing Carmen off the bed and across the room. The ship pitched and rocked, and then began the climb back up. The lights flickered, but came back on, and Carmen returned to Tony's side.

The storm continued to grow in intensity. Surface winds raged higher and higher, with gusts of over a hundred miles per hour. As the wind and sea continued to buffet the yacht, Tripp kept the bow at three-quarters on. The barometric pressure continued to drop and the lightning flashed like a strobe light. A rogue wave blindsided them at one point, crashing over the ship and tossing it like a toy in a pool, threatening to broach the vessel. The wave knocked out their antennae, effectively making the GPS system useless and destroying any chance for radio contact.

"Another one like that and we may be paying a visit to Davy Jones," Manning yelled.

"I just wanted to see if you were paying attention."

The pressure from the waves and wind pounded the ship unmercifully, but like a true champ, she took the blows and kept going. The sturdy vessel was determined to fight her way through.

After several hours, the wind began to ease and the rain died out. It was early morning, and the sun had yet to rise, but the skies had opened up to reveal a blanket of stars overhead. They were in the eye of the hurricane, and as they looked through the windscreen, they saw a comforting sight: calm waters, clear skies, and only a soft, cool breeze. The air was dense and had a rotten, moldy smell from the deep ocean water that had been driven to the surface. Tripp looked behind them and saw the rim of the storm as it receded. It was almost a solid line of dark purple clouds climbing into the sky.

"I'm going to think twice the next time you offer to take me for a boat ride," Manning said.

"Hey, look around; it's kind of beautiful here."

"Yeah, if you're Rod Serling."

"Look out there. The sea is as still as glass, there's a nice cool breeze, and the sky is filled with stars."

"I'm just hoping you didn't bring me here to the twilight zone for the submarine races."

Tripp didn't respond, and Manning noticed an almost melancholy expression cross his friend's face.

"Do you feel how peaceful it is? It reminds me of the times Katie and I would sneak down to Catalina. I can still remember the way the ocean breeze blew her hair and the way her eyes sparkled when she laughed. It was times like that when the rest of the world disappeared."

"It really is beautiful, my friend," Manning finally said.

Tripp looked over at Manning and smiled. "Unfortunately, this is only a brief reprieve. We're in the eye, and when we hit the next wall, we'll be right back in it. She's just catching her breath, and next time, the winds will be coming at us from the port side," Tripp said.

"At least we know the boat can hold her own. This gives us a chance to catch our breath, too."

"Can you take the wheel a while? I'm going below to check on our passengers, maybe see if I can find some coffee," Tripp said.

In the cabin below, everything was calm and quiet. Tony sat up and looked around. Amazingly, he had slept off and on, and his fever had broken. Although he felt cool, beads of sweat had formed on his skin. He looked down at his hand and saw strips of cotton, stained red with blood, wrapped around the stub of his finger. Carmen stood up and walked beside him.

"Lie back, Tony; I'm here."

"Are we out of the storm?"

"We're in the eye. How are you feeling?"

Tony lay back and closed his eyes. There were waves of pain shooting up his arm, but he opened his eyes and smiled. "I'm fine, sis, but I could use something to drink."

"As you wish, sir. I'll be right back."

As Tripp had found his way to the galley, he was met with the rich scent of black coffee. He pulled his life jacket off and poured himself a cup. As he took a sip, Carmen walked up beside him.

"I had planned to bring you a cup, but I wasn't sure I could make it up the stairs," Carmen said.

"No, you probably wouldn't have made it. How are the guys doing?"

"Tony's fever has broken, and he's asking for something to drink, so that's a good sign. I haven't checked on Michael yet."

Just at that moment, Juarez walked up. "That coffee smells good," he said.

"Better than Starbucks. We aim to keep our passengers happy here," Tripp responded. He handed Juarez a mug. "How is the shoulder?"

"A little tight, but it's okay. Are we clear of the storm?"

"It's only halftime; we're in a lull. We'll hit the other side of the storm in a bit, and we'll be right back in it, only the winds will be from the opposite direction."

Juarez took a long sip and asked, "Have you been able to contact anyone?"

"Our radio is useless, and no luck with the cell phones either."

"I think I'll go topside and take a cup of this to Manning," Juarez said.

Carmen found a can of Sprite and said, "I need to take this to Tony. Why don't you come on back?"

Tripp followed her to Tony's cabin. Tony was sitting up and beginning to get some of his color back.

"How are you feeling, Tony?" Tripp asked.

"I've been better, but I'll make it."

Carmen opened the Sprite, handed it to Tony, and sat next to him.

"I want to thank you for rescuing us," Tony said to Tripp.

"You're welcome, but we're not completely out of it yet."

"Carmen said we're in the eye."

"Yes, but we'll make it. At least we know what we're doing now," Tripp said with a grin.

Juarez stepped onto the bridge and filled his lungs with fresh air. He looked around at the shiny glass surface of the sea, then walked over to Manning and handed him the mug of coffee.

"Thank you," Manning said as he took a long sip.

"You guys did a good job up here. From where I was, it looked pretty bad."

"Thanks, but it was mostly Tripp. I more or less just kept him company."

"It's a beautiful boat. How did she handle?"

"She pitches quite a bit because she's narrow, but she did great. What helps is she's low and heavy, so she takes the wind well, and the two strong engines helped."

Tripp and Carmen stepped onto the deck and walked toward the stern. They stopped next to the taffrail and peered out over the sea.

"Tony was right. We all have a lot to thank you for. Three days ago I had no brother, and now he is back with me in the same waters where I lost him."

"There are a lot of people who have helped."

"Tony and I talked about our father earlier." Carmen paused a couple of seconds, then turned and faced Tripp. "Didn't you tell me you know where my father is?"

"Yes, he's in a prison called El Guayabo."

"Do you think we'll ever get to see him?"

"Not as long as he's a guest in one of Castro's cells."

For a few moments neither spoke. Carmen turned, leaned against the taffrail, and looked back at the sea.

"I wish there was a way to get him out," she said.

"Actually, I've been thinking about that, and I think I know someone who may be able to help us."

Carmen turned and looked into Tripp's eyes. She was about to question him when the wind suddenly picked up and the rain returned.

Carmen and Juarez returned belowdeck, and Tripp went below for his life jacket. Once again the ocean began to swell around them, and the yacht began the familiar rocking motion. By the time Tripp returned to the bridge, the rain was sheeting sideways across the deck; the pellets stung his skin as they hit.

They had left the eye, and once again the wind began to shriek and howl. The lightning had returned as well, and jagged bolts of fire arched overhead, followed soon after by booming concussions of thunder. Occasionally, the lightning would streak down into the sea around them, ending in a thunderous hiss as the water sizzled in anger.

The wind was driving sideways across the water, bringing with it the familiar rollers that had again grown to some twenty feet. When they reached the crest of a wave, the sky would light up, displaying an endless range of mountainous waves as far as they could see. Then came total darkness as they slid back down. Manning was now at the wheel as the devastating mix of wind and sea raged around them. Like Tripp, he kept the bow pointed into the waves at three-quarters on. Hour after hour passed, but the yacht continued to fight her way through the hurricane.

Just after dawn, the winds slowly died down and the pelting rains ceased. The thrashing seas gradually began to lose power, and the heavy black clouds began to break apart. Shafts of early morning sunlight started to peek through, bringing with them a soft blue sky. A few minutes later, it was over. The sea was little more than a gentle, rolling current. Manning throttled back and let the boat ease to a stop.

CHAPTER
44

*R*eginald Beauregard Hollinsworth III sat in a lounge chair on the deck of his sixty-foot Jongert 17S sailing yacht, sipping orange juice and eating a hearty breakfast of sausage, eggs, biscuits with gravy, and a fruit salad with cantaloupe and honeydew. Hollinsworth was a large, jovial man in his mid-sixties, of medium height, with blue eyes, deeply tanned skin that was hard as leather, and a big, round head covered with thinning silver hair. He was wearing a short-sleeved floral shirt, blue jeans, sandals, and a captain's hat.

At one time, Hollinsworth had been a professor of biology at Princeton, before making his fortune with the development of an artificial heart valve. To call him eccentric would not be a stretch. He looked and acted a bit theatrical, and could easily pass as either a Wall Street tycoon or a gypsy bullfighter, but he was truly in his element at sea. Hollinsworth had just been through a hurricane, alone on the open sea on a sixty-foot vessel, but by all appearances, he seemed to be having a picnic on his terrace. His only companion was his cat, Caesar. Caesar, a striped Manx with a double coat and no tail, was somewhat eccentric himself. He pretty much ruled the ship that bore his name, *Caesar's Lair*. Caesar had his own plate at the table, and he stayed well fed. Between bites, Hollinsworth glanced out over the bow. Suddenly he spotted another ship far off on the horizon.

"I guess we weren't the only ones out in this mess," he said to Caesar.

* * *

Tripp, Manning, and Juarez were at the dining table having a breakfast of canned beef stew. Tony was up and moving around now, and he and Carmen had gone up on deck.

"Well, I don't think we'll have to worry about the Cubans anymore. My guess is they turned back before they hit the wall," Tripp said.

"Unfortunately, we have no way of contacting anyone, and we have no idea where we are," Juarez said.

"Hey, we're basically on a floating luxury hotel here. I say we just relax and enjoy ourselves. Eventually they'll pick us up on satellite and come get us," Manning said.

Tripp was about to respond when they heard Carmen rushing down the stairway.

"There's another boat out there," she said excitedly.

They made their way on deck and looked out over the long, narrow bow. Beyond the bow rail, the sea was dark green, with small rollers stretching to the horizon. They could just make out the ship out on the horizon.

"Let's go see if they had better luck with their radio," Tripp said as he turned for the bridge.

The engines rumbled to life and they were on their way. A few minutes later they could see the long, sleek sailing vessel. It had two masts and Tripp made her out to be about sixty feet long. Tripp pulled up to within a hundred feet, killed the engines, and began to look for signs of life.

"Ahoy there. Is anyone aboard?" Tripp yelled.

There was silence for a few moments, then they heard a man's voice, American, coming from the ship's loudspeaker.

"Avast, me hearties. Who be ye?"

"Avast, me hearties?" Manning said, looking at Tripp.

Tripp shrugged his shoulders and yelled, "We are *La Princessa Delfin*, out of Miami. We just limped through that hurricane, and our communications were knocked out. Do you have a radio we could use?"

"Smartly make ye way to your poop deck, so's me crew kin see how many ye be."

"Where's the poop deck?" Tony asked.

"I think he means the stern. Can anyone see him?" Tripp asked.

"No, but I'm watching for anyone with a hook and a parrot," Manning said.

"Look, we lost our radio, and we're hoping you could help us," Tripp yelled, his voice beginning to show an irritated edge.

"Arrrrg, then too, ye may be pirates here to plunder me booty."

"Did he just say 'arrrrg'?" Tripp asked.

"Listen, we're not pirates. There are only five of us, and we're regular people who got caught in a hurricane. I'm from New York, and I just want to get home," Carmen yelled in a strained voice.

After a moment of silence they heard a deep, strong, precise voice, one that would be right at home on a Broadway stage. "New York, you say. Home of the theatre. For many years I resided just across the river in New Jersey. How did you get caught in that hurricane?"

"Can we possibly come aboard so we don't have to yell?" Tripp said.

"Of course, my manners are most repugnant. Please come aboard."

Juarez stayed aboard to watch the ship while Carmen, Tony, Manning, and Tripp took a small dinghy over to *Caesar's Lair.*

Wary of company, Caesar had perched himself on a shelf, giving himself a safe distance to watch the invaders as they boarded the ship.

"Allow me to introduce myself. My name is Reginald Beauregard Hollinsworth III, but my closest friends just call me R."

"We appreciate your help, R. My name is Sean Tripp. This is Neil Manning, Tony Casteel, and the lady is Carmen Tuttle."

Hollinsworth shook hands with Tripp, Manning, and Tony, then bowed slightly and kissed Carmen's hand.

"And now that we're on a first-initial basis, please join me for some breakfast."

He led them to his table and excused himself to get place settings for his visitors. The table was filled with dishes of eggs, sausage, biscuits, gravy, fruit salad, and various other items that had yet to be touched. A few moments later, Hollinsworth returned with four place settings and poured four glasses of orange juice.

"Everything looks delicious, but we don't want to take food from your crew," Carmen said.

"I have no crew; this is all mine, and I wish to share it with you."

Manning looked at the ample supply of food on the table and said, "You have no crew?"

"Well, that is not entirely correct." Hollinsworth pointed to Caesar's plate and said, "I share the yacht with Caesar."

As if on cue, Caesar jumped from his perch and onto the table next to his plate.

"This, my friends, is Caesar, namesake of this yacht."

"You mean to say you came through that hurricane on this ship with just yourself and that cat?" Manning asked.

Hollinsworth shrugged off the question as though it were really nothing. His insouciant disregard for a storm of that magnitude at sea left Tripp and Manning speechless. Hollinsworth stared at them as though they were intellectually vapid.

Finally he said, "Please everyone, I wish to break bread with you. Don't be shy."

It was quiet for several minutes as everyone filled their plates.

"So tell me, what brought you out here on this glorious day?" Hollinsworth asked as he continued with his breakfast.

As they ate, Tripp, Manning, and Carmen revealed the whole story of how the Favela family had left Cuba fifteen years ago, how they went to Castillo del Morro to rescue Tony, and how they ended up in the hurricane.

"It's all my fault. I guess I was a fool to fall for their trick," Tony said.

"You, my young friend, are no fool, and I am loathe to explain how anyone could believe that. The words that come to mind as I consider your plight are *sensitive*, *virtuous*, *courageous*, *ardent*, and *loyal*," Hollinsworth said.

"Thank you, Mr. Hollinsworth, but I can't help but feel like a bit of a dunce."

"Please call me R, my young friend. And there may indeed be those of a pretentious bent who will espouse such dribble, but I would remind you of a quote from William Shakespeare: 'It is a tale, told by an idiot, full of sound and fury, signifying nothing.'"

Tony looked at Tripp and Manning, unsure of what to say. Tripp and Manning stared back, equally unsure of how to respond. Hollinsworth took a big bite of biscuits and gravy and continued.

"It brings to mind a colleague I once had who truly was most pretentious. I would often sit in on his lectures. He would face the class with a distant look and pontificate in a most hyperbolic idiom. His self-aggrandizing and imperious commentaries were, I'm sure, most appealing to himself and his egocentrism. However, his grandiose and haughty idiosyncrasies were lost on myself. To be fair, I'm sure there were some who may have appreciated his exalted, and if I may say, superficial words."

Hollinsworth paused and stared into space for several moments before snapping back. "He truly was a good friend and colleague, and I miss him," Hollinsworth said as he shoveled in another bite of biscuit.

Tripp put his fork down, took a sip of juice, and cleared his throat. "Listen, we appreciate your hospitality, but the time has come that I must ask to use your radio."

The tone of Tripp's voice caused the jowls of Hollinsworth's face to fold into a dejected frown. He too put his fork down and studied Tripp's face before speaking.

"You are right, my sagacious friend. I'm afraid I have been rambling. It is rare that Caesar and I have company. Come, I will show you to my communications console."

He walked Tripp to the bridge and gave him their current coordinates. Ten minutes later, Tripp returned to the table.

"Powell is sending a chopper to take us back to Miami. He will leave a crew here to bring the yacht back."

As they were about to leave *Caesar's Lair* for their return trip to *La Princessa Delfin*, Hollinsworth pulled Tripp aside.

"Listen, Mr. Tripp. I am a man of substantial means. The boy's and girl's story has touched me. Is there anything more I can do to help the children?"

"Thank you, R, but you have already been most helpful." Tripp shook Hollinsworth's hand and continued, "We appreciate what you've done for us."

As the dinghy pulled away, Hollinsworth stood near the rail holding Caesar.

"May the winds keep your sails taut," he said, before he turned and walked away.

Two hours later the chopper arrived to carry those aboard *La Princessa Delfin* back to Miami.

CHAPTER
45

*T*ony and Agent Juarez were flown directly to emergency facilities for medical attention; Juarez would need to be admitted to the hospital, but Tony could be released after treatment. Carmen stayed behind with Tony while Tripp and Manning left for a nearby Hilton where Henry Powell had reserved rooms for everyone. Ben Hagle flew down from Washington to assist Powell with the debriefing.

After the men settled in and cleaned up, Powell and Hagle met with each man separately, then brought them together in a luxury suite. The room was beautifully furnished in a Caribbean island décor, complete with potted tropical plants. The walls were a warm ivory, with expensive framed art and photography of beaches and sunsets. Room service had brought up sandwiches, and the men ate as Powell spoke.

"Gentlemen, it's good to have you safely back. As you can guess, we were on edge when we lost contact with you. Our satellites tracked you right up until you entered the hurricane, then nothing. I think I speak for everyone when I say job well done. And now, we have another matter we need to discuss. I think all of you know Ben Hagle. I'm going to let him brief you."

Powell sat down and Hagle stood.

"As you may expect, our government is very interested in Manuel Favela. We believe the information he might provide is invaluable in fighting the flow of drugs into the United States. He might also provide us with a wealth of information on Castro's inner circle and all they're involved in. And, of course, we would like to get him out."

He paused a few moments, watching for their reaction.

"I'm sure Tony and Carmen would like that too," Manning said between bites.

"The problem is not in getting him out, but in avoiding an international incident. A U.S. force going into Cuba is out of the question," Hagle said.

"So what you're looking for is a small group with a personal motive who could be disavowed by our government," Tripp said.

"That's pretty much it."

The room was quiet for several moments as the men thought about what they were being asked to do. Finally, Manning broke the silence.

"What type of support will you be able to give us?"

"We have men in Cuba, but your support will mainly be limited to intelligence."

"Fortunately for me, your man on the pier gave us more support than just intelligence. We may not have gotten away from Morro without him," Manning said.

"He was not one of our men," Hagle said.

Manning looked at Tripp questioningly.

"Actually, I've been giving some thought to that. If you remember, when we had Zavala released from prison through the witness protection program, he said he had a contact in Rio called Grouper, who was staying in contact with Favela. Zavala also said Grouper had been using him to help protect Carmen and Tony. I think the shooter who saved Manning on the pier that night was one of Grouper's men. This Grouper obviously has a strong network, and he has someone on the inside helping him. If so, I think this Grouper would be the man to see about arranging a rescue. My guess is that he would have the manpower and resources," Tripp said.

"We need to get you down there to visit with this Grouper."

"That may not be too easy. We don't know who he is, and Zavala was pretty adamant about not discussing him with us. All we got was that Grouper was a friend of Manuel's, that he promised to take care of the children, and that he was able to contact Manuel," Manning said.

"Can you make arrangements for us to see Zavala again?" Tripp asked.

"Yes, I will set things up and let you know the arrangements this evening," Hagle said.

A few minutes later the meeting broke up and the men returned to their rooms for some much-needed sleep. Tony had been released from the hospital, and he and Carmen also went to their rooms to sleep.

Tripp slept off and on. His mind kept going back to Zavala and Grouper. He was missing something, but he couldn't figure it out. Finally that evening he got up, slipped on a robe, mixed himself a drink of bourbon and Coke from the mini bar, and stepped out onto the balcony. The night was cool and quiet, with only a gentle breeze blowing off the Atlantic. The skies were crystal clear, leaving the balcony where he sipped his drink bathed in a snowy luminance from the bright moon and the blanket of stars.

He thought about Carmen and how close he had grown to her in such a short time. He thought about Katie and how her eyes had sparkled on nights like this when the moon was so bright. He never imagined he could ever meet anyone like her again, but now he wasn't so sure. Once again he thought about Carmen, replaying everything she had told him...and that's when it hit him. What had been puzzling him was the friend of Manuel's in Rio. He must be a man of substantial influence, someone close to Manuel, with high-ranking contacts—someone Manuel would call a close friend. Tripp opened the sliding glass door and took off his robe in almost the same motion, slipped on some jeans and a white cotton T-shirt, and left for Carmen's room. He knocked several times before her door finally opened a crack and Carmen peered through with sleep-blurred eyes.

"I need to talk to you. I've got an idea," Tripp said.

Carmen excused herself a moment, slipped on a white terrycloth robe provided by the hotel, and let Tripp in.

"What have you got?" she asked.

"You remember how you and your father played the name game as a child?"

"Of course I remember. Why do you ask?"

"I want to play the game with you."

"You woke me from a sound sleep to play the name game?"

Tripp stepped closer to her and said, "I want to give you an animal and I want you to tell me what name it might match."

Carmen saw in his eyes that he was serious and said, "Okay, what is the animal?"

"Grouper."

Carmen repeated the name, then paused in thought. "The name could be Cabrilla."

Tripp turned, running through the names, trying to get the piece to fit. Finally, he turned back and looked at her.

"Or maybe Cabrillo...as in Omar Cabrillo?"

Carmen sat on the edge of the bed, staring up at Tripp.

"Omar was my father's best friend. He was with us that night."

"He was also one of Castro's generals, just like your father, and he hasn't been heard from since that night. It was assumed he was killed."

CHAPTER
46

*J*osé and Raul Soto sat in a shabby apartment tucked away in a run-down neighborhood of Miami, a hundred square blocks of tattered bungalows, wood-frame shacks with faded paint, ratty decaying warehouses that had long ago gone under, and a host of noisy bars scattered throughout. The only hint that Christmas was near was a single string of lights haphazardly strung around the façade of one of the bars. The apartment smelled of stale cigar smoke and the floors creaked and groaned with each step, like an old man getting out of an easy chair.

It was nearing midnight, and the bars that lined the street near the apartment were packed with Latinos in guayabera shirts and linen pants. From a nearby bar, lively salsa music made its way to the apartment, urging the brothers to join the festivities, but they had been instructed to wait. And when Yuri Petroff asked you to wait, you waited.

Thirty-year-old Raul Soto had dark mocha skin and long hair, as shiny and black as an eight ball, which flowed down over his shoulders. His five-foot, eight-inch frame was muscled and trim, and his arms were laced with tattoos. Under dark, lifeless, uncaring eyes were a narrow nose and a razor-thin mustache. His brother

José was two years older and looked much like him, but had more tattoos, and his oily black hair was shorter and combed straight back.

Raul stepped into what represented a kitchen to get a beer when the flight of stairs outside the apartment began to protest the weight of three men who had begun their climb to the second floor. José pulled a gun from his waistband and stepped over to the window. With his back to the wall and the gun pointed down, José leaned over, pulled the curtain back a crack, and peered out. Raul set the beer down, picked up his gun from the counter, and walked over to the door. A few seconds later there was a knock at the door.

"It is Yuri. Let him in," José said.

Raul slipped the gun back in his waistband, unlocked the door, and pulled it open. Three men wearing Italian business suits faced Raul with cold, emotionless stares. Raul opened the door wider and let the men enter.

Yuri Petroff was almost eighty, but his body was still trim and fit. He was just under six feet tall, with gray hair, gray lifeless eyes that gave nothing away, thick bushy eyebrows that resembled furry caterpillars, and a pit bull face that was cold and hard. When he finally spoke, his deep, rich voice still carried a thick Russian accent.

"Gentlemen, I think you know my son Igor," Yuri said, indicating the man to his right.

Ignoring the man to his left, he continued, "Igor has just returned from Cuba, and we have a problem that I want fixed."

Yuri looked around the room, debating whether to sit down and risk soiling his suit. Finally, he walked over and sat at the table. His son Igor and the Soto brothers joined him, but Frank, the third man to enter the apartment, stood watching near the door, as though at attention.

"Twice we have had the Favela children, and twice they have escaped."

Yuri looked through heavy eyelids at the men sitting around the table.

"This is not acceptable. I want them found."

"*They* let the boy out of Cuba," Raul said, staring at Igor. "He could be anywhere."

Igor peered back with a stare as sharp as a razor.

"And *you* let the girl get away," he said.

Yuri quickly interrupted to break the tension. "We have all failed, gentlemen, but the game is not over. My sources tell me the Favela children are here in Miami. We will have another chance, and I do not need to tell you that this time we must not fail."

The room was silent for several moments as Yuri looked around the table.

Finally he continued, "This time you will all work together. I am leaving Igor here to go with you. You will find the children and bring them to me."

"Where are the children?" José asked.

"The men jailed at Morro with Tony Favela we know to be FBI agents. We have identified them as Michael Juarez and Neil Manning. Agent Juarez works out of Miami, and this is where they brought the children. It will be your job to find where they have them. We believe Manning's ex-partner, an agent by the name of Sean Tripp, was the one who helped them escape, and he will be with them also," Yuri said.

Raul turned to José, his razor-thin lips twisting into a grin, and said, "Sean Tripp. Seems like we've heard that name before."

José returned the malevolent grin.

"Guess we'll have a chance at another Agent Tripp," he said.

"We took out his wife. It seems only right we send him to be with her."

CHAPTER
47

*R*olando Zavala, now known as Davio Guerrero after receiving a new identity through the witness protection program, had been set up in a small apartment on the outskirts of Phoenix, Arizona, and given a job in the city's maintenance department.

Since Zavala was considered a high flight risk, he was monitored closely, and it didn't take long for a local FBI agent to pick him up. Zavala was put on a red-eye that evening and was in the Miami FBI offices the following morning for a meeting with Tripp and Manning. With his release from prison, Zavala's appearance had changed; he was dressed in a wrinkled blue shirt with charcoal pants, and his pale skin now held a touch of color. He was still lean and wiry with a shock of white hair, but he didn't seem as old.

Tripp walked over and met Zavala as he entered the room. "It's good to see you again. Thank you for coming."

Despite the change in appearance, his demeanor was the same.

"I didn't have much choice," Zavala responded in a less than exuberant tone. He looked at Tripp and then let his eyes trail over to Manning before continuing. "But you did get me out of prison, and you saved the children; for that I am grateful."

Tripp and Manning stared at Zavala with stunned amazement.

"You know that Carmen and Tony are safe?" Tripp finally asked.

Several moments passed before Zavala spoke. "They are safe for now, but Castro will never give up until he gets what he's looking for."

"Actually, that's sort of why we needed to speak with you," Manning said.

Zavala studied Tripp and Manning the way an alley cat eyes a plump mouse, but said nothing.

"When we visited with you before, you spoke of a man you called Grouper who asked you to watch over Carmen and Tony."

Zavala's eyes dropped. He spoke purposefully. "I did what I could to protect them."

"Is Grouper the one who informed you the children had been rescued?" Tripp asked.

"Grouper is my friend."

"You also said Grouper was able to contact Manuel Favela," Manning said.

"Yes, but Manuel already knows the children are safe."

"Grouper must have high-level friends in Cuba," Manning responded.

"Do you wish to send a message to Manuel?"

"We wish to meet with Grouper," Tripp said.

Zavala's eyes fell again. "That is not possible. I will not betray his trust."

"Perhaps you won't have to. The children say he is practically an uncle to them. He may wish to see the children," Tripp said.

Zavala looked up now, searching Tripp's eyes. "What do you mean?"

Tripp walked to a door opposite the one Zavala had entered and opened it. Tony and Carmen walked in, and Tripp closed the door behind them.

"Carmen, Tony, I would like to introduce Rolando Zavala, the man who has been watching out for you all these years."

As Carmen and Tony walked over, Zavala stood and greeted them. "I'm glad to see you're both safe," Zavala said in an avuncular tone.

"We're glad to be back, but we'll be happier when our father is back here with us," Carmen said, looking Zavala squarely in the eyes.

No one said anything for a moment, then Tripp said, "Why don't we all have a seat."

Zavala sat at the head of the table with Tony and Carmen on either side. Tripp sat next to Carmen and Manning sat next to Tony.

"You said you'll be happy when your father is back here?" Zavala said, looking at Carmen.

"That is why we need to meet with Grouper," Tripp said. "We plan to rescue Manuel from prison, and we believe Grouper can help."

Zavala stared at Tripp for several moments.

"What makes you think Grouper would be willing to risk his life and everything he's worked for to save Manuel?"

The room was silent for several moments. Carmen locked her green-brown eyes on Zavala; she held his gaze as she spoke in a strong and sincere voice. "I believe Omar would do anything he could to help us get Father out of Cuba."

Zavala stared back with a stunned expression. When he finally was able to break eye contact with Carmen, he shifted his eyes to Tony.

"Uncle Omar wanted us safe from Castro, and he would want my father out even more," Tony said, staring back at Zavala.

"Omar?" Zavala asked tentatively.

"Omar Cabrillo was with us that night when the gunboats came. He is the one who told you to separate us and watch over us. Omar Cabrillo is Grouper," Tony said.

"I know my father and I know Omar Cabrillo. He was doing what our father asked of him," Carmen said.

The room was quiet, and everyone sat still. Zavala stared at Carmen and Carmen stared back. Tripp watched Zavala and mused at Tony's and Carmen's acuity and the way they handled themselves with Zavala. Zavala held his hard stare, but Tripp noticed an almost imperceptible change as Zavala's cold exterior began to break, as if some long-dormant emotion at his center was working its way out. He remembered that Zavala's family had also been victims of Castro. Finally, Zavala's eyes shifted over to Tripp.

"Unless I'm mistaken, my guess is you would want to be first in line at the chance to free Manuel and get back at Castro," Tripp said.

Zavala moved his eyes back to Carmen and spoke. "I think Omar will be glad to see you." He turned to Tony and continued. "He will be glad to see you also."

CHAPTER
48

Rio de Janeiro, 2007

*T*he Antonio Carlos Jobim International Airport in Rio de Janeiro is named after one of Rio's most famous musicians. The modern facility is the main hub for air traffic in Brazil. Tripp, Manning, Carmen, and Tony arrived at the airport that evening and checked into the beachside Copacabana Palace Hotel, where they had booked two suites, each offering spectacular views of the Atlantic Ocean. Tony and Carmen had each contacted their parents to assure them they were safe and would be home soon. It promised to be a very special Christmas for their families.

After checking in and getting settled, the group met downstairs in the lobby. The men wore coats and ties, while Carmen wore a white silk jacket over a beige shell and black pants, with a white sash tied around her waist. They made their way to the upscale Hotel Cipriani Restaurant, where they were seated at a large oval table next to a picture window. Manning ordered the risotto di zucca profunato, Tripp and Tony ordered the smoked duck breast with a cherry and merlot wine sauce, and Carmen ordered the arugula salad with shiitake mushrooms and parmesan cheese. A few minutes later the waiter returned with their wine orders. After the waiter left, Tony turned to Tripp.

"Where are we supposed to meet Omar?"

"Zavala said we were to check into the Copacabana Palace and that Omar would contact us," Tripp answered.

"I've got to admit it, Cabrillo certainly has good tastes," Manning said.

"He certainly does. It's absolutely gorgeous here," Carmen said.

Sitting several tables over, on the other side of a grand piano, two men sipped on vodka martinis and watched the diners. On top of the piano was a small Christmas tree that partially obscured the men. Omar Cabrillo had watched the group enter, but his eyes were locked on Carmen and Tony. He thought back fifteen years to a time when the two young people he was watching were children, a time when he still had his wife. He took a long, slow drink of his martini and thought about his friend Manuel and the promise he had made to watch over the two children.

"The children have turned out good. The girl is a beauty, and the boy is strong and handsome," Cabrillo finally said. He took another long drink and continued, "Manuel would be very proud of them."

"They are healthy and safe because of you, Grouper," the other man said.

"I did what I could."

Omar watched as the waiter arrived at Carmen and Tony's table with the food. Omar waved a finger and a moment later his glass was replaced with another martini. As Carmen and Tony began to dine, Omar looked over at Tripp and Manning and studied their faces.

"Getting Manuel out will be very risky," Omar said as he started on his fresh drink.

For several moments neither man spoke. Finally the man sitting next to Omar broke the silence. "They are the same men who rescued Tony; they can be trusted."

Omar said nothing at first, but continued to watch Tripp and Manning. Finally he turned to the man sitting next to him.

"Are you certain they are the ones?"

"It is them. I remember their faces."

While Carmen and Tony were talking between themselves, Tripp casually glanced around the room, studying the other diners. One table over, between the window and a service bar, was a young couple, probably in their mid-thirties. The man was trim, lightly muscled, tanned a deep bronze, and wore a perfectly fitted tuxedo. The focus of his attention was the dark-haired, olive-complexioned lady sitting to his right, her cream-colored evening gown covering a thin, shapely figure. Two tables over, between another picture window and the grand piano, was another couple. The man was older, probably in his mid-fifties, with a ruddy complexion and light almond-colored hair. He wore a white shirt with a blue blazer and a matching tie. The lady next to him was young, probably in her early thirties, with dark hair, dark eyes, and perfect features. She wore a black evening gown with straps that fell over bare, porcelain-colored shoulders. And two tables behind them, partially blocked by the grand piano, were two men. Tripp continued to dine and joined the conversation at his table, but he also watched the two men. One of the men was older, with dark skin, salt-and-pepper hair, thin lips, a narrow nose, steady eyes, and a strong face. The other man, whom Tripp thought he recognized, was much younger and had dark skin and dark hair. The men seemed to be paying an inordinate amount of attention to Carmen and Tony. Twice Tripp caught the second man's eye before the man looked away.

Thirty minutes later, with the main course complete, Carmen and Tony began to argue over whether to have torta di cachi, persimmon cake, or the torta croccante al gelato, crunchy ice cream pie, for dessert. As Tripp listened, he glanced over and noticed the two men at the far table push away from their table and stand. As they prepared to leave, the older man looked directly at Tripp and gave a brief but direct nod. The men then turned to leave. Carmen had noticed Tripp and Manning staring toward the piano, and she followed their gaze in time to see the brief exchange.

"Could that be Omar?" she asked.

"I don't know," Tripp responded. He then turned and looked at Manning, who had also seen the exchange.

"Did you recognize either of those gentlemen?" Tripp asked.

Without taking his eyes off the men who were about to leave, Manning said, "I don't know the older man, but I believe I owe my life to the younger one."

"He was the man on the dock at Castillo del Morro?"

"It looks like him," Manning said.

Tripp and Manning excused themselves and followed after the two men. They reached the restaurant door in time to see the two men step into the Copacabana Piano Bar. They quickly made their way to the bar and stepped inside. The older man and his companion stood at the far end of the lounge, leaning against the bar.

The Copacabana Piano Bar was a rich and sophisticated lounge, with enough room to serve as an informal meeting place for small groups, but designed with a discreet charm for those seeking a cloister in which to withdraw from the crowd. Along the walls were plush sofas set behind small mahogany tables, and scattered throughout were smaller round tables with chairs that matched the design of the sofas. Large mirrors hung on the walls, surrounded by thick, elegant wall coverings and highlighted by intricately designed gold sconces that provided just enough light for the perfect atmosphere. In the back corner, beyond the bar, was a baby grand, where a tuxedo-clad man in his mid-fifties was playing softly.

Tripp and Manning made their way to the back and stepped up to the bar next to the man they believed to be Omar. A bartender quickly appeared to take their order.

"What can I serve you?" the bartender asked in English with a Portuguese accent.

"My friend and I will have a Chivas, straight up, and I'd like to buy another round of martinis for these two gentlemen," Tripp said, looking at Omar and his companion.

"Right away, sir," the bartender said as he retreated.

For several seconds, Omar scrutinized Tripp. His eyes shifted slowly to Manning before he spoke.

"Thank you for the drink," Omar said in English, still carrying the Cuban accent. "You are American?"

"Yes, my name is Sean Tripp, and this is Neil Manning," Tripp said as he extended his hand.

Omar shook Tripp's and Manning's hands and said, "What brings you gentlemen to Rio?"

"We're down here looking for someone, and a friend recommended we stay at Copacabana Palace," Tripp said, his eyes locked on Omar's.

The bartender returned with their drinks and set them on the bar. As Tripp and Manning picked up their drinks, Omar lifted his in a toast. "I wish you success in finding the one you're looking for."

The men all took a small drink, except for Manning, who downed his and motioned to the bartender for a refill.

"Your friend is quite thirsty," Omar said with a grin.

"He's always thirsty when I'm buying," Tripp said with a crooked smile.

"Why don't we move to a back table? The sofas are much more comfortable and we can talk with some privacy," Omar said.

Tripp sat across from the man he believed was Omar, and Manning sat across from Omar's companion.

"Tell me, who is this friend who recommended that you stay at the Copacabana Palace?"

"His name is Rolando Zavala," Tripp answered.

Tripp watched Omar's eyes for a reaction, but saw nothing. He glanced at Manning and could tell that he saw nothing either.

Tripp then said, "I don't believe we caught your names?"

"No, you didn't," Omar said.

At that moment a waiter appeared and asked if they needed anything. Tripp started to order when Manning interrupted.

"Please bring us all another round, and bring an extra Chivas for my friend here," he said, nodding at the companion across from him. "It is an excellent drink; I think you will like it."

The waiter turned and retreated.

Tripp looked at Manning with a quizzical expression.

"You're buying? Well, this is quite an occasion," he said.

"It's the least I can do for the man who saved my life," Manning said with a grin.

The man said nothing and looked over at Omar.

"Actually, he may have saved your life too, Sean. I mean, if it wasn't for him, I wouldn't have made it to the boat, then you probably would have come after me, and then you too may have bought it there at Castillo del Morro."

"What do you mean probably? You know I would have never left you behind," Tripp responded.

"Well, there were a lot of bullets flying around and there wasn't much time to get away."

Omar listened with amusement until Tripp and Manning were interrupted by the sound of Carmen's voice. "You guys leave us at the restaurant to pay the check, and then we find you..." Carmen's voice trailed off in midsentence when she looked at Omar. Her mind raced back fifteen years. There was no mistake; the man sitting only feet away was Omar Cabrillo.

"Uncle Omar? Is it really you?"

Omar looked at Carmen and Tony, then at Tripp and Manning, but said nothing. Finally, he stood and walked around the table and took Carmen's hand.

"Yes, Carmen, it's really me."

Carmen hugged Omar warmly and said, "I can't believe it. I thought you were dead. How can this be?"

"We have much to talk about, but yes, it is me."

Omar pulled back, looked again at Carmen, and said, "You have grown to be a beautiful young lady."

He then turned and looked at Tony, who had followed Carmen into the bar. "And you, Tony, you have grown into a fine young man."

He lifted Tony's left hand, looked at the stump of his finger, and said, "And you are a brave young man. I am very proud of you."

"How did you get away from the patrol boat that night?" Carmen asked.

"So many questions you all have. Please sit, and I will answer them."

As they found a place to sit, the waiter arrived with their drinks. Carmen sat at the end of the table between Tripp and Omar, and Tony sat at the other end between Manning and the second man. After the waiter left, Omar introduced his companion.

"My friend here, whom you recognized from Morro, is Tuco. He is a member of a small group of men I have put together to help the dissidents in Cuba. I sent Tuco to Morro to assist you should the need arise. And Tuco, I believe you know everyone here."

Tuco nodded at the group and said, "Yes, I know everyone, and I am glad to finally meet each of you face to face."

"How did you know we were planning to rescue Tony?" Manning asked, looking at Omar.

"Perhaps it is best that I start at the beginning. When we left Cuba that night fifteen years ago, we had only one bullet-proof vest. Manuel gave it to me and asked that I watch over his children should something happen to him. When the patrol boat began to fire on us, I fought back and provided cover so he could get Carmen and Tony away.

"After you left, there was only Manuel and myself left to fight. My wife and your mother had been hit, and Manuel's arm was covered with blood where he'd been wounded. We continued to fight, and then I was hit in the chest; the force of the impact knocked me into the water. The vest saved my life, but I lost my weapon. I knew at that point all was lost, but I thought they would spare Manuel and take him back to Cuba, so I stayed under the water and swam until I was out of sight. When I came up, the fighting had stopped, but it was dark, so they couldn't see me. I found some floating debris and held onto it to keep afloat. I watched as they took Manuel aboard and turned toward Cuba. I floated the rest of the night and most of the following day until I was finally picked up by a cargo ship headed for Rio."

"And our mother?" Tony asked.

"I'm sorry, Tony, but they took only your father aboard; the small boat your mother was in sank well before the gunboat left."

Tony's eyes dropped as the final hope that he might find his mother was dashed. Carmen's eyes began to water as she too felt the pain.

In an attempt to alleviate the emotional tension, Omar continued. "When I reached Rio, I called some contacts in Miami to see if Carmen and Tony had made it. The two of you left in different boats and arrived in separate locations. Thanks to a close-knit exile community in Miami, it didn't take long to find you had both arrived safely and were staying with different families on opposite sides of the city. Neither knew if the other had made it, so I decided for your safety it would be best to keep it that way. Then I used my contacts to have you placed with families on opposite sides of the country."

"So it was you who decided to separate us and let each of us believe the other was dead?" Carmen said in a truculent tone that shot through the lounge like a bolt of electricity.

"Regrettably, it was necessary, Carmen. I knew Castro would stop at nothing to find you. Castro has people in the United States, and they are not stupid. They would be looking for a boy and a girl together. It was your best chance to stay free, and it was the best chance for Manuel to stay alive."

Tears were streaming down Carmen's face as guttural sobs forced their way up from deep inside her. "Do you know what it's like to lose everyone you ever loved? It hurts like hell. Your heart is ripped out and you're left alone with nothing," Carmen cried.

"Yes, I do know what it's like, Carmen. I do."

Carmen looked into Omar's eyes and saw the pain he too was feeling. Tony reached out and took Carmen's hands. "We're together now, Carmen. Soon we will have our father and we will always be together," Tony said.

As Carmen began to compose herself, Omar continued, "I worked odd jobs around Rio and vowed to find a way to get back at Castro—and a way to free Manuel. One day I met a man who provided me with the financial resources to do that. I put together a group of men I trusted, and at every opportunity we helped the Cuban dissidents. I also sent one of my men to America to watch over the two of you."

"I assume that man would be Rolando Zavala," Tripp said. "But you must also have access to someone in the government who has access to intelligence. You seem to be well informed, and you're always a step ahead of us."

"Yes, I have a friend who works within your intelligence community. She is sympathetic to the Cuban plight and helps me when possible, but I cannot give you her name."

The waiter returned to see if drinks were needed, but Omar waved him off.

"How did Castro eventually find us?" Tony asked.

"It was the same contact I just spoke of. Somehow one of Castro's people discovered she had been helping me protect the two of you. They threatened her children if she refused to give them the information they wanted. My friend was scared and had no one to turn to, so she gave them your names. She never reported the incident because it would have destroyed her career and the people of Cuba she was trying to help. It wasn't until Tony went missing that she called and told me, but it was too late."

"Do you think you can help us get our father back?" Tony asked.

Omar didn't speak for a moment as he looked over at Tuco. When Tuco nodded, Omar's eyes shifted first to Manning, then to Tripp. "It will be a very risky operation," Omar finally said.

"Do you have the means to help us?" Tripp asked.

"Actually, the operation has already begun. We have been planning such an operation for a long time, but we were waiting for the right time. When I heard Tony had escaped from Castillo del Morro, I knew it was time. You see, it is now only a matter of time before they make Manuel pay with his life. Castro was keeping Manuel alive as long as there was a chance he would talk. Now that they no longer have Tony and Manuel didn't talk, Castro will not hesitate to finish him. Then, when I heard you were coming here to seek my help in saving Manuel, I gave the order."

"What is your plan?" Manning asked.

"I will go into detail later, but as we speak, my men are on a ship near the Batabano Gulf."

"You already have a ship near the Batabano Gulf?" Tripp asked incredulously.

"We have ships disguised as fishing trawlers that work out of Havana. We work with the dissidents who are funded by your United States government."

"Our government finances Cuban dissidents?" Carmen asked, unsure she had heard correctly.

"The funds are given to political opposition leaders, who pass them on to dissidents. Anyway, when I called and told them the operation was on, a ship was on its way within an hour."

"When are you planning the rescue?" Tripp asked.

"We will fly out tomorrow morning by sea plane to meet the ship. If all goes as planned, the rescue will take place tomorrow night. I've already sent Manuel the message. He will be expecting us."

Tripp looked at Manning, who flashed his famous "kick ass" grin and said, "I guess we better get a good night's sleep."

"But first, I have a question for you," Omar said. "The only name I have ever given anyone here is Grouper. How did you know it was me?"

"I guess I should answer that one," Carmen said. "You see, my father and I used to play the name game all the time. It would seem he played it with you as well."

CHAPTER
49

anuel lay on the soiled mattress in his dark cell, clutching what he knew would probably be the last message he would receive, and listened to the thunderstorm outside the prison walls. It was two in the morning as he watched the walls of his cell briefly light up from the lightning streaking across the sky. The cell was actually cool this evening as the wind and rain pounded against the ceiling and walls. The distant thunder sounded like cannon fire, causing the cell doors to rattle, and with each flash Manuel could see the water flooding through his cell, causing the rats to scurry for higher ground. Once again his mind went back to the message: "Tony is safe and has been reunited with his sister. Now it is your turn. The day has come."

Manuel knew his time was short now that Tony had been rescued. He knew Castro would be coming for him; he just didn't know when. He did not fear death. Death would almost be a welcome reprieve from the hell he had lived with for the last fifteen years. What he feared was not being able to see his children again. What angered him most was the utter helplessness to do anything about it.

A loud clap of thunder shook the wall next to him, followed by a bright flash. The lightning lit up the entire cell. The bright flash of light reminded him of that night on the open sea when the gunboats flicked their floodlights on. It brought to mind a recurring dream he had had over the years, in which he was floating on a calm sea with a starless sky above him. There were bodies floating all around him, but he couldn't see who they were because of the utter blackness around him. The water was warm and dense, like blood, making any movement slow and laborious. In the dream, there was complete silence. He could hear nothing, and even his own voice sounded as if it were coming from somewhere deep inside a well. But he could smell, and what he smelled was a repulsive stench, like that of rotting flesh. Suddenly, in the dream, floodlights snapped on from somewhere, illuminating the corpses of his family floating around him.

Manuel shut his eyes hard and slammed his fist against the wall, trying to block out the image. He sat up in a cold sweat and began to sob. Finally, he brought himself under control and lay back.

"At least my children are safe," Manuel whispered to himself. "I only hope my rescuers get here before Castro does."

CHAPTER
50

The Beriev BE-12 Chayka, or Seagull, is a Soviet twin-turboprop amphibious aircraft that began serving the Soviet navy in the 1960s. The Seagull that now approached Cuban waters had been converted from a machine of war to one that fought forest fires in Brazil. Removing nearly 3,500 pounds of torpedoes and bombs and enlarging the fuel reserves more than doubled the time the aircraft could fly and be of service. With an airspeed of almost 450 miles per hour and a strong tailwind, the trip had taken almost twelve hours, but finally the ship being sought was spotted.

The pilot turned into the wind, eased the stick down, and set the flaps. Their airspeed dropped and the glimmering surface of the sea quickly came up beneath them. The hull of the Seagull began to skim across the water, shooting plumes of white water out from the hull. The pilot cut the throttle, feathered the props, and let the craft ease to a crawl. As the water began to fan out around them, they felt the craft shift forward under its own weight. The Seagull began to coast smoothly over the water toward the waiting ship.

Once the group had boarded the ship, the Seagull left to refuel in Jamaica. It would wait for the signal to pick them up after the operation was complete. Cabrillo led the group belowdeck to a dining area next to the galley. Spread out on the table was a detailed map of El Guayabo Prison, and next to it, a detailed map of the island, showing the location of the prison. Cabrillo poured coffee for everyone and began the introductions.

"Gentlemen and Carmen, this is Captain Ramon Carasco, and to his left is his first officer, Baltazar Benitez. I have worked with these men for many years. They are excellent officers and trusted friends."

Captain Carasco, a rugged, clean-shaven man with thick dark hair and penetrating dark eyes, gave a quick nod.

"Captain, you know of course my assistant Tuco, and next to him I would like to introduce Mr. Sean Tripp and Mr. Neil Manning."

Tripp and Manning each saluted the captain.

"I welcome you aboard the *Isabella*, gentlemen. I have heard of the rescue operation at Castillo del Morro, and I welcome your input on our plan for Guayabo," Carasco said in near-perfect English.

Cabrillo then turned toward Carmen and Tony. "And our two young passengers here, whom I have known since they were very small, are the children of Manuel Favela. Allow me to introduce Carmen and Tony Favela."

"I also welcome you aboard," the captain said, "and I hope I can help bring your father back to you."

"And now, let us all be seated. We have a short time and much to prepare for," Cabrillo said.

As everyone found a place to sit, the first officer excused himself and returned to the wheelhouse.

Cabrillo continued, "In front of you is a map of El Guayabo. I have circled the cell where Manuel is being held. I have high-lighted a side entrance to the prison where the guards and visiting officials enter, and I have marked where the commandant's office is located. As you can see, the entrance is very near Manuel's cell, and it is at the opposite end of the building from the commandant's quarters."

"How do you plan to get through that entrance?" Manning asked.

"We have studied this plan for a very long time. The shift changes at 8:30, so we will go in shortly after that. The guards will be expecting a visit from a man by the name of Rogelio Cruz, one of Castro's enforcers. I believe Tony knows Mr. Cruz quite well."

"You mean Mr. Let's-Cause-It-To-Happen," Tony said, looking at Manning.

"Anyway, Cruz will be coming for Manuel, so we will lead them to understand we were sent by Cruz."

"Would they not expect Cruz himself to come?" Tripp asked.

"Perhaps, but we have acquired military uniforms that should pass, and we intend to be very persuasive," Cabrillo said flatly.

"How far is it to the prison from our docking spot?" Tripp asked.

Cabrillo pulled the second map over and pointed to where an "X" had been drawn.

"We will drop anchor just offshore from here and send a dinghy to the beach. From there it will be approximately five miles to the prison. We have arranged for a truck to be left for us. It is not unusual to see military personnel moving about the island."

"How many men are we taking in?" Manning asked.

"Along with Tuco, there will be five other men. These men are all part of my organization, and I assure you they are well trained. So, with the two of you, there are eight," Cabrillo said, looking at Tripp and Manning.

"No, there will be nine. I am going too," Tony said, his eyes burning into Cabrillo's.

"This operation will be very dangerous, and will require a surgical touch. I think it would be best if you waited here for your father."

Tony held up his left hand, showing the stub of his finger, and said, "I want to be there for my father. I believe I've earned that right."

No one spoke for several seconds. Tripp finally broke the silence.

"I think you're going to find you'll have to tie him down to keep him out of that dinghy."

Cabrillo studied Tony's eyes for several moments.

"Manuel is lucky to have such a brave son. I stand corrected. There will be nine men."

Tripp, Manning, and Tony studied the details of the prison map well into the evening. By eight that evening they felt as if they knew the prison well enough to enter blindfolded and go directly to Manuel's cell. Also, they had gone through the rescue plan enough times to recite each step perfectly. If Cabrillo's sources were correct, there were only fifteen guards in the whole prison, but only four at night, and only two of them would be in Manuel's wing. Once they gained entry, the plan was to disable the two guards if necessary and get out within minutes.

"Well, guys," Manning said. "It's getting close to that time."

They folded the maps, set them aside, and began to put on the uniforms Cabrillo had provided. Next, Tripp and Manning applied a dark shade of skin toner to their faces and necks in an attempt to pass as Cuban. Finally, they checked their weapons.

Cabrillo had given each man a .38 automatic equipped with a silencer.

"Are you ready?" Tripp asked, looking at Tony.

"Yes, I'm ready."

Carmen had been on deck, but she now made her way to the galley and stepped into the dining room.

"Uncle Omar asked me to tell you guys it's time," Carmen said.

She walked over and sat next to Tony.

"I'm very proud of you, Tony, but please be careful. I want you and Dad both back here."

Tony reached out and hugged Carmen. "I'll be back in a little while, and I'll bring Dad with me."

Carmen hugged him back. "I know you will. Just don't try to be a hero. Okay?"

Tony grinned at Carmen and said, "Okay, I promise."

Carmen then hugged Manning and Tripp and wished them well. Tripp held Carmen for an extra moment and whispered, "Don't worry, we'll watch out for him."

Carmen gave a weak smile and said, "And watch out for yourself. I'd kind of like to see you back here too."

As they started up the stairs, Manning stepped next to Tony and said, "Just stay close to me and you'll do fine."

At exactly 8:30, right on schedule, the dinghy, with nine men aboard, left the *Isabella*. Twenty minutes after that, the dinghy was tied off on the beach and the men were in the truck on their way to the prison. Tuco drove through the night at a slow pace, so as not to arouse suspicion from anyone who might be out. He checked his watch, which read 8:55. They should arrive at the prison gate at 9:00 p.m., exactly on schedule. There was no conversation from the men in the back of the truck as they concentrated on the job ahead of them. Manning, who rode in the cab with Tuco, continuously scanned the countryside and intersections for signs of anything that didn't look right. The road was dark and empty of traffic.

Finally Manning looked over at Tuco and said, "Tell me something, Tuco; you saved my life on Morro, so I feel we're close enough for me to ask. I know Clint Eastwood was the good, but I always get the other two confused. Were you the bad or the ugly?"

"You should pay better attention to your movies, my friend. Angel Eyes was the bad; I am the ugly. At least, that's what my wife keeps telling me."

The two laughed for a moment, appreciating the momentary break in tension. Five minutes later the truck approached the front gate of the prison.

Tuco stopped the truck twenty yards from the gate and left the engine running. They could see a single guard, his back to the window, reading a magazine. Tuco eased the truck up to the gate and killed the engine. A moment later, the guard, clearly irritated at being disturbed, ambled out to see who was causing the disturbance. When he saw Tuco's uniform and recognized the colonel's insignia, he stood erect and gave a sharp salute.

Tuco returned the salute and said in Spanish, "Rogelio Cruz with the Ministry of State Security has sent us to collect a prisoner. Open the gates."

The guard reached for his keys, but then hesitated.

"Sir, I will need to see your papers."

"Of course. That is the mark of a good soldier."

The guard's face lit up with pride at hearing those words from a colonel. Tuco turned toward Manning.

"Lieutenant, show the guard our papers."

Manning stepped from the cab and walked around the front of the truck. He pulled an envelope from his uniform and handed it to the guard.

The guard turned toward the booth and said, "Excuse me for a moment, Colonel."

Tuco stepped from the truck and said in a loud and threatening tone, "Do the guards at this prison not salute an officer when taking their leave?"

The guard quickly stepped up to face Tuco, gave a sharp salute, and held it there.

"Forgive me, Col—"

Before he could finish his sentence, Manning came down on the back of the guard's head with the butt of his gun, and the guard slumped to the ground.

Manning grabbed the envelope, stuffed it in his uniform, and with Tuco's help, dragged the guard into the booth. While Tuco began to tie the guard's hands behind his back, Manning pulled the keys from the guard's belt and opened the gate. Tuco then ordered two of his men to stay and guard the gate.

Back behind the wheel, Tuco drove the truck to the side entrance of the prison and parked. It was a clear night, and the grounds were empty and quiet. The moon and stars overhead served to light the night in a warm glow. Tuco and Manning climbed from the cab, walked to the rear of the truck, and pulled open the canvas. The team of men crawled out and formed a marching unit behind Tuco. He led them to the door and rang the bell.

A young sergeant on duty had fallen asleep and didn't wake up until the second ring. Finally he opened his eyes, stood, and stretched. He then slowly made his way to the door. When he saw the colonel's insignia on Tuco's uniform, he quickly unlocked and opened the door. He then stepped back and held a salute. Tuco saw the lines on the sergeant's face and understood he had been asleep. Finally Tuco gave a quick salute, as though put off with the sergeant.

"Why was I made to wait at this door, Sergeant?" Tuco said sternly, his eyes boring into the young officer's.

"I'm sorry, Colonel, I have not been on duty long, and I was not told to expect visitors."

"What is your name, Sergeant?"

"My name is Joaquin Balaguer, sir."

"Didn't the guard at the gate call you? Or were you asleep?"

"Colonel, I apologize. I did fall asleep for a moment. I guess I did not hear the radio."

Tuco turned to face Manning.

"Lieutenant, make a note of that."

Tuco then turned back to face the sergeant.

"Well, Sergeant, do you intend to make us stand out here all night?"

"No, sir. I apologize again, Colonel."

As the sergeant ushered them into the office, Tuco ordered two of his men to stand guard outside the door. The office was bleak and dreary, furnished with an old metal desk and two metal chairs. The floor was covered with worn and yellowed tile, and the walls were barren except for pictures of Fidel and Raul Castro hanging haphazardly behind the desk.

"Now, Colonel, how may I be of service to you?" the sergeant finally said, trying to repair his damaged first impression.

"I have been sent by Rogelio Cruz of the Ministry of State Security to collect Manuel Favela."

The sergeant hesitated, trying to decide how to ask for his papers, but before he could speak, Tuco stepped forward and stood within a foot of the sergeant.

"I hope, Sergeant Balaguer, you do not intend to delay me again."

"No, Colonel," the sergeant was finally able to force from his mouth. "But it is my duty to ask to see your papers."

Realizing his bluff had failed, Tuco stepped back.

"Lieutenant, give Sergeant Balaguer the papers," he finally said without dropping his eyes from the sergeant.

Manning once again reached into his uniform, fished out the envelope, and handed it to the guard.

A look of confusion blanketed the sergeant's face as he opened the envelope to find an old road map. When he looked back up at the colonel, he saw four pistols pointed at his chest. He looked back at Tuco, who was also brandishing his sidearm.

"Sergeant Balaguer, should you choose to yell out, you will be dead before anyone can hear you. And, should you make any movement to reach for an alarm, you will be dead before you reach it," Tuco said in a cold, hard voice. "Now, I want you to slowly sit in your chair. I have some questions for you. And, Sergeant Balaguer, if I do not get an answer, you will not be going home to your family after your shift. Do you understand?"

"Yes, I understand," the sergeant said as he slowly sat down.

Tripp and Manning quickly came around the desk and checked him for weapons, but found none. They found a set of keys attached to his belt, which they removed and tossed to

Tuco. They then began tying the sergeant to the chair with his arms behind his back.

"Sergeant Balaguer, I am going to begin my questions now. Please know that I expect correct answers."

Tuco paused as Tripp and Manning finished tying the man's arms and moved to his feet.

"Tell me, Sergeant Balaguer, which of these keys fits the steel gate that leads to the cells?"

"It is the long flat key with the slots on the sides."

Tuco found the key, removed it from the ring, and dropped it in his pocket.

"And which of these keys, Sergeant Balaguer, fits the cell doors?"

"It is the short round key."

Once again Tuco found the key, removed it from the ring, and dropped it in his pocket.

"Now, Sergeant Balaguer, where is the alarm you would set should there be a problem in your prison?"

"It is the orange button next to the telephone."

Tuco's last soldier, whom he kept with him for this very task, immediately went to work disabling the alarm and the communication system.

"And finally, Sergeant Balaguer, how many guards are there in this first cell wing?"

Balaguer hesitated a moment before answering. "There is only one guard in Cell Block A."

Tuco stepped over and lowered the gun until the silencer was touching Balaguer's head.

"Are you certain there is only one guard, Sergeant?"

Balaguer's eyes closed as sweat began to run down from his forehead and sting his eyes.

"There might be two guards."

Tuco pulled a small roll of duct tape from his leg pocket and tossed it to Tony.

"Please see that Sergeant Balaguer will be quiet until we have completed our task here."

Tony went behind the desk and began taping the sergeant's mouth shut while Manning retrieved the envelope and stuffed the map back inside.

With the office secure, the team was ready for the next phase. While Tuco's man stayed behind to watch the office, Tripp, Manning, and Tony followed Tuco down the dim passageway toward Cell Block A. Thanks to the maps they had studied, the men knew exactly where they were. The low ceilings and dim lighting gave them a feeling of claustrophobia, and the stench from the cells was already invading their nostrils. Within a minute they had reached the heavy steel gate. Tuco pulled the long flat key from his pocket, inserted it into the slot, and turned. The locking mechanism turned and the door cracked open.

"Okay, this will be the tricky part. Do not use your weapons unless absolutely necessary. Remember, we are from the Ministry of State Security, so look and act the part. Our orders come from no less than Castro himself. Check your uniforms to make sure they are neat and presentable, and follow my lead. Most of all, you must show no sign of concern for the prisoners," Tuco whispered.

Tuco turned, pushed the gate open, and stepped into the cell block. A guard who had been sitting at a desk stood and pulled his sidearm.

"Stop right there! Who are you, and why are you here?"

"I am Colonel Tuco Ramierez from State Security. We are here to collect a prisoner for Rogelio Cruz."

The guard stood silent for several moments and stared at the four men.

"Are the guards at this prison not required to salute their superiors?" Tuco said, raising his voice.

The guard gave a weak salute, but kept his weapon trained on the men. Tripp looked around the corridor for the other guard, but saw no one.

"Where is Sergeant Balaguer? Proper procedure is for him to accompany you inside the block," the guard said warily.

"The sergeant follows orders from his superior officers. I presented him the documents to show I have the authority to collect a prisoner and ordered him to stay in the office and watch the door. The sergeant is a good officer," Tuco said.

"I will need to call the commandant," the guard said as he reached for the telephone.

Manning stepped next to Tuco and said, "That may not be the best idea. We asked to speak with the commandant earlier, and Sergeant Balaguer told us the commandant was with a lady friend."

The guard said nothing for several moments, clearly undecided on what to do.

"If you would look at our documents you will see that we have the proper authorization," Tuco said. "And I suggest you put that weapon down and show me the proper respect."

The guard continued to hold his weapon on the men and said, "Let me see your papers."

"Lieutenant, toss the guard our papers."

Once again, Manning pulled the envelope from his uniform and tossed it toward the guard. The envelope fell short, and when the guard bent to retrieve the document, Manning quickly leaped at him, attempting to knock the gun from his hand. The guard fell back but held onto the weapon. He rolled over, aimed the gun at Manning, and began to pull the trigger. At that instant a soft pop, like the sound of an arrow punching through a plastic bottle, echoed down the corridor, and the guard fell back with blood seeping from his shoulder.

As Tripp shouldered his weapon, the guard began to scream out. Tuco quickly knelt down, covered the guard's mouth, pulled his own weapon, and pointed it at the guard's head.

"You will be quiet, or I will make it so you are permanently silent," Tuco said to the guard. He then turned to Tripp, tossed him the other key, and said, "Quickly, go and get Manuel. I will stay here with this guard."

Tripp, Manning, and Tony raced down the corridor toward Manuel's cell. The lighting was poor in the dungeon-like corridor, but thanks to the map they had studied, they knew exactly which cell to go to. As they ran along the corridor, rats scurried into various cells in search of cover. Finally they reached the cell. The putrid smell was almost overpowering as the men stepped up to Manuel's cell. There was almost no light, but they could see the figure of a man sitting on the side of his bunk.

"Excuse me, but did someone call for an exterminator?" Manning said in English.

The figure turned and looked toward the cell door, but said nothing.

"Are you Manuel Favela?" Tripp asked.

"I am Manuel Favela. Who are you?"

"We've come to take you out of here," Tripp replied.

Tripp inserted the key, turned the rusty chamber, and swung the door open. Manuel stood and watched the three men as they entered the noisome cell. The somewhat atrophied figure stood still, his eyes first studying Tripp, then Manning. Finally his eyes locked on Tony. His body froze; he wondered if his mind was playing tricks on him. Tony stepped forward and stood in front of the frail figure.

"Father, it is me, Tony."

Manuel began to sob in long, plaintive cries. Could this all be a dream? He reached out to touch Tony, to see if he was real, but he stopped short. He was afraid the vision would disappear.

"Are you real, my son?"

Tony reached out, took his father's hand, and said, "Yes, Father, it's really me, and I've come to take you home."

With tears streaming down his face and his body shaking uncontrollably, Manuel stepped forward and embraced his son. For several moments he held Tony close, afraid to let go.

"I'm sorry, my son. I'm so sorry for all I've done. All these years I prayed that one day I might be able to tell you this."

Tony held his father close and also began to cry.

"It's okay, Father. We are together again, but we must get out of here."

Manuel was afraid to let his son go. He was afraid Tony would disappear.

"I love you, Tony. I just wanted the chance to tell you."

"I love you too, Father, and so does Carmen. That is why we must go now. She is waiting to see you."

Manuel pulled back and searched Tony's eyes.

"Carmen is here?"

"No, but she is near, and she is waiting for you."

"I am afraid to let you go, Tony."

"Hold my hand, and we will go together."

The men started to leave, but suddenly, Manuel stopped short.

"Wait, I must get my book."

Manuel bent down, lifted the mattress, and retrieved a small, tattered journal that he had kept over the years.

"I am ready now," he said.

As the men stepped quietly out of the cell, a menacing voice from the opposite end of the corridor broke the silence.

"Stop right there," the voice barked in Spanish.

The men turned to see the second guard with a rifle pointed at them.

"Well, what have we here? Are you trying to escape, Manuel?" the guard said as he turned the rifle on Manuel.

Tony winced at the sight of the rifle on his father.

"He's not escaping. We are taking him to Rogelio Cruz," Tony said, his voice raised in panic.

The guard looked at Tony and said sarcastically, "So, is State Security hiring children now?" The guard turned the rifle on Tony and continued, "You know, son, you can be shot for aiding in an escape."

Manuel stepped in front of Tony, shielding him from the guard.

"Do not shoot the boy," Manuel said, staring into the guard's eyes.

The guard was quiet for a moment, studying the situation, when an irate voice broke the tension.

"No one will be shot here," Tuco said as he stepped toward the group.

The guard saw the colonel's insignia, pulled the rifle up, snapped to attention, and held a salute.

Tuco snapped off a quick salute and said, "Three times now I have presented proper documents to show I have authorization to collect this prisoner." He paused a moment, his eyes burning into the guard's, and continued, "Are you going to interfere with my duty here?"

"No, sir, Colonel, I thought a prisoner was trying to escape."

Tuco continued to stare the guard down. Finally he spoke in a controlled and intimidating tone.

"Don't you have other duties you should see to?"

"Yes, sir," the guard said as he snapped off a salute and quickly retreated into the blackness of the corridor.

"Lieutenant, continue on with your duties. Escort your prisoner out of here," Tuco said to Manning.

The men turned toward the cell block door, with Tony helping his father along. As they made their way down the corridor, several prisoners had stepped up to their cell doors to see who was being taken away. The gaunt faces of men who had become inured to prison life stared out with the eyes of corpses. The team knew they could not allow themselves to sympathize now. Their compassion was real, and it was a gut-wrenching situation, but they knew they would have to come to terms with it later.

A minute later they reached the heavy steel door and saw where Tuco had duct-taped the guard's arms and legs together and his mouth shut. After another minute they reached the office and passed Sergeant Balaguer, who was still tied to his chair. Tuco cracked the door open and peered out. All was quiet, and the two men Tuco had left to guard the door were still there. They hurried out of the prison, helped Manuel into the back of the truck, and headed for the gate. At the gate, Tuco stopped briefly to let his last two men crawl in, and they proceeded to the beach.

Knowing that a casually moving truck would be less likely to draw attention, Tuco fought the urge to speed. When they were five minutes from the beach, Manning radioed Omar aboard the *Isabella* and reported they were on schedule and should be back on board in thirty minutes. Five minutes later they parked the truck, untied the dinghy, and motored for the *Isabella*.

CHAPTER
51

*R*aul Soto slipped out the front door of the Hilton Hotel in Miami and stopped briefly to scan the parking lot. The rain that had fallen for most of the day was beginning to let up, and the rain-slick street reflected the multicolored Christmas lights from the front of the hotel. A cool breeze blew through the portico. Raul pulled his collar up before heading to the car, where José and Igor were waiting.

Behind the wheel, José saw Raul approaching and cranked the engine. A minute later Raul opened the passenger door and crawled inside.

"They were here," Raul said as he closed the door behind him.

The rain had stopped as José pulled out of the parking lot.

"When did they leave?" José asked.

"Two days ago. Our man will call us should they return."

They drove slowly past the colorful shops and nightclubs that lined the streets. It was almost midnight, and the nightlife was in full swing.

"So, what now?" José asked.

Igor finally spoke from the backseat. "Yuri tells me the children have not returned to California or New York, so we keep looking."

José lit a cigarette, took a long draw, and looked back at Igor through the rearview mirror. "They could be anywhere," José muttered with disgust.

"They may also have just changed hotels. Yuri wants us to keep looking."

There was silence for several moments as José continued to draw on his cigarette; his anger at wasting time on what he considered a futile effort was clearly visible.

"Perhaps you would like to call Yuri and discuss the matter?" Igor finally said.

As José started to respond, Igor's cell phone rang. He spoke for several moments before he punched off and closed the connection.

"That was Yuri. Manuel Favela has escaped from his Cuban prison cell. He believes Manuel will show up here to reunite with his children. He made it quite clear we must find them at all costs."

CHAPTER
52

*I*t was just before ten at night when the dinghy carrying Manuel Favela coasted up to the *Isabella*. The entire operation had gone flawlessly and had taken less than two hours. Carmen was waiting nervously on deck as the men began to climb aboard. When Manuel stepped onto the deck, the first person he saw was Carmen. When their eyes met it was as though time stood still. All the sights and sounds of the night vanished as Manuel focused on his daughter. Finally, Carmen rushed up and locked her arms around him. For several moments neither said a word. Finally, Manuel pulled back and looked at her again.

"I love you, Carmen. You don't know how many times I've said that over the years, hoping that somehow my words could find their way to you."

A cascade of tears began to flow down Carmen's face as she looked into her father's eyes. "I love you too, Father," she finally managed.

Manuel reached up, wiped the tears from her eyes, and kissed her cheek. He then glanced over her shoulder and saw Omar.

Omar stepped up and embraced Manuel.

"Welcome back, my friend," Omar said.

"Thank you, Omar. I don't think I could have made it without you. You kept me going during my darkest times, and I will never forget it."

At that moment Baltazar Benitez, the ship's first officer, stepped out of the wheelhouse and ran up to Captain Carasco.

"I hate to interrupt, Captain, but we have trouble coming," Benitez said.

"What is it?" Captain Carasco responded.

"I've been monitoring the radio and the Cuban military has gone on alert. They have discovered the prison break, and they're sending out gunboats."

"Have you radioed the Seagull for the pickup?"

"Yes, sir, but the Cuban Air Force has been scrambled too. Our pilot said the air force is ordering all aircraft to stay out of Cuban airspace. Any aircraft found in Cuban airspace will be shot down. He will not be able to make the pickup."

Tripp stepped forward. "Captain, where is the nearest landfall from here?"

"The closest port that could offer safety is the Cayman Islands, but that's at best four hours away."

"Captain, I suggest we get the passengers below and make for Cayman immediately," Tripp said.

With Carmen, Tony, and Manuel safely below, the *Isabella* made for Grand Cayman Island at full throttle. The night was cool and still, and the waters were calm as the bow of the *Isabella* hissed through the water. High above, the sky was dotted with a trillion stars, and a quarter moon lit the ocean with a silver glow. The *Isabella* was making good time, and with each mile, the crew grew more hopeful.

The *Isabella* was not an ordinary fishing boat. The hull lines were sleek and smooth, with a graceful rounded bow that cut through the water with ease. Similarly, the bridge was not the usual eyesore. Instead of having sharp, square edges, it was curved and smooth, and on the inside it was equipped with a global positioning system, sonar, radar, and a state-of-the-art communications system.

While the captain and first officer manned the helm, Tripp, Manning, and Omar monitored the radar and communications. What they saw was a blip on the screen about ten miles behind them.

"They've picked us up and are closing in," Tripp said.

"Can we get any more speed out of her?" Omar asked the captain.

"We're doing just over fifty knots and we're at full throttle," the captain answered.

"It looks like we're going to have some company. I estimate they'll overtake us in less than an hour," Manning said.

Belowdeck, Manuel was lying on a bunk, holding a mug of hot coffee. Carmen and Tony sat on each side of him. Manuel took a long sip of coffee and set the mug on a stand next to the bunk.

"I had forgotten how wonderful coffee could taste," Manuel said, looking at his two children.

Manuel's eyes were watering as he reached out and lifted Tony's left hand. "They brought your finger to me, Tony. I felt as though a thousand arrows had pierced my heart. I knew it was my fault, and there was nothing I could do. I'm sorry, my son."

Tony smiled and flexed his fingers. "I'm fine, Father. I rarely used that finger anyway."

"I had almost given up, but I had just received a message from Omar that a team was on their way to rescue you. All I could think of was that I wanted to be there for you."

"Somehow you were there, Father. It was as if I could feel you with me. And you were especially in my corner at the prison when the guard pointed his rifle at me and you stepped between us."

Manuel turned to Carmen. "And Carmen, my daughter, you've grown into a beautiful young lady. I'm sorry I was not there for you all those years."

"You're with me now, and we will have each other from now on."

No one spoke for several moments as Manuel held Carmen's and Tony's hands. Finally Carmen broke the silence. "Tell us, Father, what happened to mother?"

Once again Manuel's eyes filled with tears, and he closed his eyes as he thought of that night. Finally he opened his eyes and looked at his children.

"Your mother is dead. I can still remember that night as though it were yesterday. The two of you had safely left, and Omar had been knocked out of his boat. The shooting had stopped and my boat was sinking. I went to your mother and knelt beside her. She was covered in blood and still, but she seemed at peace as I held her in my arms."

As Manuel began to cry uncontrollably, Carmen and Tony leaned over and held their father.

A few moments later there was a light tap on the door, and Tripp and Manning stepped into the cabin.

"There is a gunboat approaching. The three of you must stay down here," Tripp said.

"It seems like we've been here before," Tony said.

"You will need help," Manuel said.

"No. Do not under any circumstance come up on deck. I have a plan, but they must not see you," Tripp said.

Carmen stood and walked over to Tripp.

"Please be careful," she said, reaching out to take his hand.

Tripp leaned over and kissed her lightly on the cheek.

"We will be fine. You just take care of your father," Tripp said, his green eyes smiling back.

Tony stood and walked over to Manning. "You know, you told me to stay close to you. Are you sure you don't need help?"

Manning reached out, put his hand on Tony's shoulder, and said, "Don't worry, Tripp's plan will work. We will all get out of this okay."

As Tripp and Manning closed the cabin door to return to the bridge, Manning turned to Tripp. "So you've got a plan. No doubt it's truly inspiring, tactically brilliant, and amazingly foolproof," he said with a smirk in his voice.

Tripp grinned back, but didn't say anything.

"You have no idea, do you?" Manning said.

"Nope."

"I didn't think so."

When they returned to the bridge, they checked the radar and found the gunboat had closed to within seven miles.

Tripp looked out over the rear deck, trying to come up with an idea, when he spotted two diving tanks strapped securely to the stern. He turned toward the helm.

"Captain Carasco," Tripp said, "do you have diving gear aboard?"

"Yes, there are two sets in the aft lockbox and two full tanks at the stern." He tossed Tripp the keys.

Tripp made a beeline for the lockbox, with Manning on his heels. In the lockbox were two neoprene diving suits, two regulators, two BCs, two sets of goggles, two diving belts with an assortment of weights, and two sets of fins. Together they pulled the equipment out, and Tripp continued to look through the box. He found a pair of dive lights, several underwater flares, and a long coil of rope. Under the rope he found a twenty-foot length of chain and a small toolbox. He removed the chain and dug around in the toolbox until he found a steel safety link used to attach a rope or chain together.

"I think this should work nicely," Tripp said.

"I'm guessing you've come up with a plan?" Manning said.

"I have."

A few minutes later, the fishing boat came to a stop and Tripp went over the plan with Manning, Omar, the captain, and his crew.

Shortly thereafter, with Tripp and Manning fitted out in full diving gear, the lights of the gunboat could be seen closing in. With the crew on the aft deck putting out nets, as though preparing to fish, Tripp and Manning checked their air supply and regulators.

Before slipping into the water, Tripp turned to the captain. "Remember, you've got to get them to kill their engines. Then wait for the diversion, and when they clear the bridge, you give it full throttle. Remember, don't look back, do not let anyone board your ship, and be sure your crew takes cover when you hit the throttle. They'll probably start shooting and a stray bullet could find someone."

"And the two of you will be back on board by then?" the captain asked.

"We will be back, but do not wait. When they clear the bridge, you hit the throttle."

The captain stared at Tripp for several moments before he spoke.

"I understand," he finally said.

Captain Carasco turned for the bridge, and Omar and Tuco stepped forward.

"I wish you each good luck, my friends," Omar said.

With the gunboat less than a mile away, Tripp and Manning adjusted their goggles, grabbed the chain, and slipped below the surface. They descended to twenty feet and adjusted their BCs for neutral buoyancy.

A few minutes later the sixty-foot twin diesel gunboat throttled down and stopped sixty feet from the *Isabella*. The crew of the fishing boat, with their nets out, stopped and stared at the gunboat. A second later, a searchlight snapped on, flooding the fishing boat with a blinding light. Twenty feet below, Tripp and Manning made their way toward the light. From a loudspeaker, somewhere near the top of the tower, came a Cuban voice. "This is Captain Ramon Villegas of the Cuban navy. Prepare to be boarded," the captain barked in Spanish.

Omar stood on the aft deck, and keeping his voice barely audible, pointed at the water and pretended to yell back.

"Speak up, old man," the loudspeaker boomed. "You are to be boarded immediately."

Again Omar pointed excitedly at the water, and keeping his voice low, pretended to yell back.

"Kill the engines," the captain said to his first officer. "I can't hear the old fool."

"What are you trying to say, old man?" came the voice, again from the loudspeaker.

"Of course you may board," Omar said. "But our fishing nets are out; we must bring them in."

"Be quick about it, old man. We haven't the time."

As Omar pretended to help with the nets, Tripp and Manning had reached the rear of the gunboat. Working quickly, they wrapped the chain around the two propellers and linked the chain tight. They then surfaced, dropped their tanks and fins, and quietly crawled up the stern and peered over the railing. As Tripp had hoped, the crew of the gunboat was on the forward deck watching the small fishing boat. Tripp looked around. On the port side he saw a stack of blankets tied against the wheelhouse frame, and on the starboard side were stacks of life jackets with two overstuffed duffel bags tied on top. Tripp and Manning quietly slipped over the railing and onto the deck. Tripp crawled up and ducked behind the blankets on the port side, while Manning ducked behind the duffel bags on the starboard side.

Without a word, each man reached into his wetsuit and pulled out a flare. Tripp stuffed the flare between the blankets, and Manning did the same with the duffel bags. At the same instant, they sparked the flares to life, dove into the sea, and began swimming furiously for the fishing boat. Because of the intense heat produced by the underwater flare, it took only seconds for the stern section of the ship to burst into flames. The men had swum only halfway to the *Isabella* when all hell broke loose on the gunboat.

It is said the most dangerous situation a crew can face on the open sea is fire. The men on the bow of the gunboat dropped their weapons and began yelling and screaming as they searched for anything to extinguish the flames. They stomped at the edges and slapped the flames with clothing and anything they could find, but their efforts were futile. A crewman found a fire extinguisher, forced his way through the chaos, and began to douse the flames. The captain dashed from the bridge, grabbed the extinguisher from the crewman, and ordered the men to return to their posts and open fire.

Tripp and Manning were almost to the stern of the *Isabella* when the first shots rang out. As bullets began to pepper the aft deck of the fishing boat, the crew of the *Isabella* dropped the nets and ran for cover. Tripp knew they would not be able to make it without being hit. He grabbed the fishing net tightly and yelled at Captain Carasco. "Go now! Get your ship out of here!"

Carasco hesitated only a moment, then hit the throttles. The ship lurched forward and began to accelerate, ripping a trail of white wake into the face of the ebony sea. When Manning heard the engines roar to life, he reached out and clamped onto the net. With shells spitting into the water around them, Tripp and Manning held tight as they were dragged behind the boat. The captain of the gunboat saw the *Isabella* throttle up and yelled for the first officer to follow them. The first officer immediately hit the ignition, but the chains held tight and nothing happened.

With Tripp and Manning in tow, the *Isabella* sped through the water for nearly a mile before Carasco throttled down. Omar and Tuco were the first to the stern when the boat finally coasted to a stop. Tripp and Manning released their grip on the net and floated freely on the surface.

"You know, this would work a lot better with skis," Manning said.

"I have a feeling my arms have stretched out a good three inches," Tripp responded.

As the two men crawled into the boat, the crew pulled in the rest of the net, and Captain Carasco continued on to Grand Cayman. Tripp removed the top of his diving suit and peeled down the top half of the overalls. He sat on a bench seat along the starboard rail and looked back. The lights on the gunboat could still be seen, along with a trail of smoke rising into the night sky.

"They won't stop looking for the *Isabella*," Tripp said to Omar.

"I've already radioed a friend who owns a dive operation on Seven Mile Beach. He's holding rooms for us, and his men will ferry the boat around West Bay to a secluded cove on the east side of the beach," Omar said.

Two hours later they docked at the Calypso Bay Dive Resort on the island of Grand Cayman.

CHAPTER
53

The first light of dawn began to bathe the room in a soft, warm glow as Manuel Favela opened his eyes to a new life of freedom. For the first time in fifteen years, he awoke in a real bed with clean sheets, a clean mattress, and a real pillow. He allowed his eyes to play across the room.

The room was simply furnished. The walls were soft beige accented with coral and turquoise and bordered with thick strands of rope. The pictures were scenes of divers sharing space with various sea creatures and seascapes, but what he noticed most was the smell and the sound. Gone were the pervasive stench and the sound of rats scurrying about. He glanced to his left, where Carmen and Tony were asleep in the adjacent bed.

Reaching under his mattress, he carefully pulled out the journal he had brought from El Guayabo. Manuel leafed through the journal, reading the countless names of men he had come to know over the years, men cruelly imprisoned for speaking out against the inhumane conditions in Cuba, including saying the wrong words at the wrong time and paying for it with a lifetime behind bars. He thought about how flimsy the wall between life and death was, between innocence and ugliness, and how it could take only a moment in time to destroy a life forever. Manuel closed the book and returned it to the mattress. He crawled out of bed, dressed, and slipped out of the room. He walked over to the next room and lightly rapped on the door. Omar had been awake for a while and was sitting on the patio drinking coffee he had brewed from the coffeemaker in his room. He set his coffee on the small round table, left the patio, and opened the door.

"Come in, my friend. Let me get you some coffee," he said warmly.

"Thank you, I would like that."

As Omar poured the coffee, Manuel stepped out onto the patio to a view that was absolutely stunning. The sky was a robin's-egg blue, the turquoise waters were calm and clear, the sand was sparkling white, and the early morning sun was warm and soft against his skin. A soft, cool breeze wafted through the patio, bringing with it the scent of pine. Omar stepped back onto the patio and handed Manuel the coffee.

"Sit down, my friend. It's good to have you back after so many years," Omar said.

Manuel took a sip of the coffee and sat. "It is beautiful here. I had forgotten there was such beauty in the world," Manuel said.

"I know it was hard, my friend, a life void of beauty and happiness. But you must put that behind you now."

Manuel took another sip of coffee and paused a moment, his mind far away.

"You don't think about beauty when you are starving. You don't worry about happiness when those around you, those who have become your friends and your family, are dying of starvation."

The two men sipped their coffee and stared out to sea in silence.

"What are your plans now?" Omar asked.

"I want to help them. I want to help my friends who are rotting away in that prison, and in all the prisons in Cuba."

Manuel continued to stare out to sea as he set his cup down. "I want to get the gold," he finally said.

Omar stared at Manuel and said, "That gold has brought us nothing but sadness. Let it go. You can build a new life and again know happiness, my friend."

Manuel turned and locked eyes with Omar. "It is not for me, Omar."

"If you wish to do something to help, why don't you come to Rio with me and join my group? We can work together."

"I have thought about this for a long time, Omar, and this is something I need to do. I believe I can make a real difference for those I left behind."

The words hung in the air as the two men studied each other.

"Will you help me, my friend?" Manuel asked.

Omar continued to stare, but said nothing.

"I know it will not be easy, but in time I believe we can find it," Manuel continued.

Omar turned and looked out to sea again. A couple of minutes passed before he spoke.

"Actually, I believe I know where it is."

Manuel stared at Omar in stunned silence.

"You were trying to find the gold?" Manuel finally said.

"No, I wanted to know the place where my wife was laid to rest."

"But how did you find it?"

"We used a side-scan sonar tow fish. We knew the general area where our boats went down, so we set up square grids that marked out ten square miles. Then we swept the grids in imaginary parallel lines, similar to walking the ticket lines at the ball park. When we finished one square, we went to the next, with each one overlapping. We were out there for weeks and were about to give up when we spotted two boats about thirty meters apart, each boat about twenty feet long."

"Are you sure they are our boats?"

"No, but I believe they are, and it gives me comfort. Each year I make a trip there to leave a wreath."

Omar paused momentarily before he continued. "The boats are located about a hundred kilometers from the keys, resting on a shelf some two hundred feet below the surface. Assuming they're our boats, I guess you could say we're lucky, because less than fifty meters to the south the shelf abruptly drops to a thousand feet."

"I want to find out if they're our boats. Will you help me, Omar?" Manuel asked.

For several moments Omar didn't speak as he continued looking out to sea. Finally, he shifted his eyes toward Manuel. "Yes, I will, but it could be dangerous. With you missing from Castro's prison, he will have patrol boats out. And we know from experience that it matters little that we won't be in Cuban waters."

"Perhaps the two Americans will help us?"

"They might. I have seen them work, and I would feel much safer if they joined us. We will talk to them over lunch today," Omar said.

Manuel left Omar and returned to his room. Quietly he slipped in and closed the door behind him. Carmen and Tony appeared to still be asleep. He crept over to their bed and looked at his children. An exuberant wave of felicity swept through him, and he smiled to himself. As he turned toward his bed, a pillow, tossed playfully, struck him in the back. When he turned around, Carmen and Tony again pretended to sleep, but with grins on their faces.

Manuel picked up the pillow and said, "How many times have I told you kids not to horseplay in bed?"

With that, he threw the pillow, smacking Carmen in the head. The next few minutes were a joyous blur, with all three rolling around on the bed tossing pillows, Tony hitting Carmen, Carmen hitting Manuel, and Manuel hitting Tony.

In the adjoining room, Tripp was awakened by the racket. Fearful of what was happening, he rushed to the adjoining door and flung it open, then stood there in the bottom half of his pajamas watching the scene. The three Favelas were rolling and spinning over the sheets, with pillows flailing and plopping against each other. Finally, Tony grabbed his father around the neck and kissed the top of his balding head. Carmen then put her arms around both men and kissed each of them. Both laughing and crying, the three collapsed onto the bed in exhaustion. Then they glanced up and noticed Tripp staring at them in amusement.

"I guess it's safe to say everyone's okay in here," Tripp said with a grin.

"Yes, we're very much okay. I apologize if we woke you," Carmen said.

"No problem. I'm just glad you're all safe."

"Mr. Tripp," Manuel said, "I would like it if you and your friend Mr. Manning would join my family and me for lunch today."

"You've got a date; we'll be there."

The restaurant at the Calypso Bay Dive Resort offered informal dining in a Cuban-style atmosphere. The group was seated on a palm-covered terrace, where the scent of pine and bougainvillea served to complement the atmosphere. The terrace offered a panoramic view of Seven Mile Beach and the turquoise waters of the Caribbean Sea. Beachside activities were in full swing, with guests swimming, snorkeling, and playing volleyball under a sky of pure blue.

Tripp and Omar ordered the Maine lobster wrap, Manning the mushroom-crusted rack of lamb, Carmen and Manuel the passion-fruit flan, and Tony a cheeseburger. As they waited for their lunch, the group watched the activities. One boat, pulling a young lady in a parasail, moved lazily across the water, while further out, several dive boats were off to the reefs, also called Sting Ray City.

When the food arrived, the small talk died down and they began to dine. After several minutes, Manuel set his fork down and looked across the table at Tripp and Manning.

"Mr. Tripp, Mr. Manning, I want you each to know how much I appreciate everything you've done for me, for Carmen, and for Tony," Manuel said. "I cannot find the words to describe how grateful I am, and I don't know if I will ever be able to repay you.

"We're just glad everything worked out and you're all together again," Tripp said.

"There is no need to repay us, Manuel. I guess you know, however, that there are some men from my government who are going to want to talk with you," Manning said.

"I understand," Manuel said. "I will certainly speak with your government, but there is something I must see to first."

"What is this thing you must see to, Father?" Carmen asked between bites.

Manuel's eyes shifted slowly from Manning to Tripp and then to Carmen and Tony before he spoke.

"I must retrieve a trunk from the boat that was shot from under us fifteen years ago."

The table fell as quiet as the inside of a coffin. Several seconds passed before Carmen found her voice. "Father, you can't be serious. Whatever is in that chest has almost destroyed our family and taken away fifteen years of your life. You don't need it. The three of us can start a new life in the states."

"I ask only that you trust me when I tell you I want the chest for unselfish reasons," Manuel said, looking at Carmen.

"A small boat buried beneath a vast area of sea will be very difficult to find. You could look for months and not find it," Tripp said.

Manuel's eyes shifted to Omar, who set down his fork.

"I already know where the boats are," Omar said. "We searched for several weeks before we spotted two small boats close together, almost two hundred feet down."

"But you will need a dive boat with proper equipment," Manning said.

"And at that depth your divers will need a mixture of gases to breathe safely," Tripp added.

"Oscar Burke, the owner of this dive resort, was one of the men I initially hired to help me with the search. I have already spoken with him, and he has agreed to lease a fast boat to me, along with all the necessary equipment," Omar said.

"You cannot do this by yourselves. Is Burke also going to provide the men?" Manning asked.

"Actually, we were hoping the two of you would help us," Manuel said.

"What about the *Isabella* and her crew?" Tripp asked.

"The *Isabella* no longer exists. She is now *La Virazon*. Castro would never stop searching for that fishing boat, so Captain

Carasco and his crew are busy repainting her and changing her registry," Omar said.

"What about security, in case one of Castro's boats should happen along?" Manning asked.

"The captain assures me *La Virazon* will be ready by tomorrow. They will follow us in case there should be any problems," Omar responded.

"You aren't really considering helping him, are you?" The words burst out of Carmen like steam from a kettle that had reached its boiling point.

Reading the tension in her face and voice, Tripp searched for words to assuage her anxiety. "It sounds as though your father is going to do this with or without us. It might be better if we tagged along for support."

Carmen stood and threw her napkin on the table. "That trunk has brought this family nothing but pain and misery. Now, when we're finally back together, you want to go after it again and put us all back in danger," Carmen cried as she turned and ran toward the beach.

Manuel stood to go after her, but Tripp reached out and grabbed his arm.

"Let me go talk to her," Tripp said.

Tripp made his way to the beach, found Carmen sitting in the sand a few yards from the shore, and sat beside her.

"Of course you're right to feel the way you do, Carmen. It's hard to watch someone you love put their life at risk," Tripp said as he watched the sea lap against the powdery white sand. "My wife's name was Katie. Many times I watched her leave for some covert operation, knowing she would be at risk, and it was never easy."

They both sat quiet for several moments before Tripp continued. "We were supposed to grow old together. Take long walks along the beach, share each other's triumphs and each other's failures. Sometimes I make it a whole month without thinking of her. Then I catch a quick glance of someone who reminds me of her, or I smell a perfume that she wore, and it all comes flooding back."

"But Father is being foolish. Our family is finally back together, and now he wants to risk it again for some sunken treasure. It would seem that treasure is more important than Tony or me," Carmen said.

"No, it's not more important, Carmen, and I don't believe your father feels that way. He says he wants whatever is down there for unselfish reasons. I think you must trust him. Your father sat in that cell for a long time. Pleasant memories of good times only last so long before they fade, but life's failures, like the death of a wife and the loss of your children, tend to stay with you. They tap you on the back during the day and haunt your sleep at night. He must have his reasons, Carmen. You need to trust that your father is doing this for the right reason."

CHAPTER
54

The first light of dawn was just breaking over the calm, rolling waters of the Caribbean Sea as the two boats left Grand Cayman Island. The softness of the honey-colored morning light and the beauty of the clear turquoise waters served to brighten their spirits and give them hope. The skies were clear and all reports indicated good weather ahead.

With near-perfect conditions and a favorable tail wind, the dive boat and her escort, *La Virazon*, arrived at the coordinates of the sunken vessels with daylight remaining. As the boats dropped anchor, Tripp and Manning began to slip into their neoprene diving suits. To keep the dissolved nitrogen in their blood to a minimum and prevent nitrogen narcosis, the air tanks were filled with Trimix, a mixture of helium, oxygen, and nitrogen, enabling the men to safely dive at two hundred feet. During their ascent, they would switch to the enriched air mixture Nitrox, and finally to pure oxygen as they neared the surface.

Carmen and Tony stood to the side, next to their father, looking into the sea. There was a grim aura about the setting, and the three held each other close. Carmen could feel her heart pounding inside her; she turned her eyes toward Tripp.

Reading her thoughts, Tripp said, "Everything will be fine. We'll be back in about ninety minutes, and that includes twenty minutes of bottom time and forty-five minutes for decompression stops as we surface."

"Please be careful," Carmen said.

With that, Tripp checked his air one last time, glanced at his watch, and pulled his mask down over his face. Sitting on the edge of the boat, he leaned backward and dropped into the turquoise waters just ahead of Manning. The men made their way to the anchor line, cleared their ears, and began their descent. At thirty feet they reached the thermocline, and Tripp rolled on his back and looked up. The water was clear and he watched as the bubbles from his regulator raced toward the surface, as if in a champagne commercial. The bottom of the dive boat seemed to hover above them like a dirigible. He turned, gave Manning the "OK" signal, cleared his ears again, and continued down the line that angled off into the depths. The water was much colder below the thermocline, but the thick neoprene suits held in their body heat, and it took only a moment for them to adjust to the change in temperature. As the men continued to descend into the eerie depths, the increasing pressure tightened around their bodies. Schools of multicolored fish darted here and there, stopping occasionally, as if curious to see who was entering their domain, before darting away. At one hundred feet Tripp stopped again and looked up. The two boats could still be seen, but they were indistinct. Tripp glanced a few degrees to his right. About sixty feet above him two manta rays, each at least fifteen feet across, glided lazily by like giant birds with wings stretched out on the wind. Hand over hand, the two men continued down the line, and the deeper they descended, the less natural light there was to work with.

When they reached the bottom, there was very little light. Each man switched on his dive light and began to make a slow, sweeping circle, the powerful beams lighting up the floor of the sea. They had almost made a complete three-sixty when an indistinct shape rose up in the murky distance. As Tripp and Manning began to swim closer, the clear outline of a boat began to take shape. The boat rested upright at a forty-five-degree angle to starboard and was covered in a thick layer of silt. Tripp swam over and hovered above the boat while Manning made his way to the bow. Slowly, so as not to create a blinding cloud of silt, Tripp settled onto the stern. The men slowly made their way toward one another, looking for a large trunk. They met at the center of the boat near the helm, but neither had found a trunk. Realizing the trunk must have fallen from the boat as it fell to its grave, the men played their lights along the seabed surrounding the boat, but still they found nothing. They began to guide their beams in expanding circles around the boat, and as the beams swept farther into the distance, the vague outline of the other boat came into view. The men swam over and hovered above the boat. The boat was lodged in a bed of rocks and rested almost perfectly upright. The men once again started at each end of the boat and slowly worked toward the center.

Tripp had moved only a short distance from the stern when he found something. It was coated in sediment, but in the beam of the dive light he could discern a trunk with bands of metal strapping around the sides. He flashed his light at Manning to get his attention and waved him over. As the men began to brush the sediment away with their hands, clouds of sand and silt began to bellow out in front of their masks. The swirl of sediment rendered the dive lights nearly useless as the particles reflected the light back.

With zero visibility, the men were forced to wait for the cloud to disperse in the current. When the cloud finally dissipated, the men looked down and what they saw sent shivers down their spines. Lying next to the trunk were the skeletal remains of one of the boat's passengers. The bones were dark brown and partially covered in sand.

Tripp and Manning paused and looked at each other in understanding. After a few moments, Tripp checked his watch and saw they had only eight minutes of bottom time left. He caught Manning's attention, held up eight fingers, and pointed toward the surface with his thumb. Manning removed the cord he had strapped to his weight belt, and together the men began to harness the trunk. With the harness secure on all four sides of the trunk, Tripp attached the inflatable buoy to the other end of the cord. Using air from his tank, he inflated the buoy and released it. The men shined their dive lights above them and watched as the buoy floated towards the surface.

As the buoy began to disappear into the distance, the men caught sight of something they did not care to see. Gliding fifty feet above them was a ten-foot bull shark. They held their beams on the shark, hoping it would continue on, but the shark turned in a circular pattern above them. Tripp checked his watch to find they were down to four minutes of bottom time. He signaled to Manning that they should make their way back to the anchor line. The men made their way to the first boat, where they stopped and checked the water above. The shark was still circling, and they continued on to the anchor line. The men grabbed the anchor line and looked up again. The shark was still there, and they were out of time.

They had now been on the bottom twenty-one minutes. Tripp and Manning both knew there was nothing they could do but wait. They knelt at the line and watched as the shark moved slowly through the beam, her gaping mouth open and her tail

sweeping slowly back and forth. Several minutes passed before
the shark finally turned from her pattern and slipped out of the
beams. The men waited another five minutes, and still there
was no sign of the shark. Both men understood they were well
over their bottom time limit and had to surface. They stared at
each other for a moment, then each gave the thumbs-up sign.
They looked at the sloping line disappearing into the dark and
began their ascent. Hand over hand, they climbed the line, all
the while expelling air from their lungs and watching for the
shark.

The decompression stops seemed to last an eternity, but
forty-five minutes later they finally broke the surface. Daylight
had given way to darkness, but the bright lights of the two boats
only yards away were a welcome sight. Tripp and Manning swam
over and were helped aboard.

"Remind me to never go in the water again," Manning said
as he began to remove his gear.

"It was just a little bull. She would have given you the
chance to test your rodeo skills," Tripp responded.

"I didn't see you testing your skills," Manning said.

As they finished removing the dive gear, Carmen brought
each man a towel and wrapped it around their shoulders. Tripp
thanked her and turned toward Manuel.

"We found only one trunk. The second boat was empty.
Somewhere around here is a buoy with your trunk tied to the
other end."

As the group began searching the waters for the buoy,
Manning noticed the lights of a third boat several hundred yards
away.

"Looks like we're not alone out here," Manning said.

Tripp followed Manning's gaze and saw the lights.

"Omar, how long have we had our company?" Tripp asked, nodding toward the lights.

"The boat appeared shortly after the two of you began your dive, while there was still daylight."

"Could you tell who they are?" Manning asked.

"No, they were too far away."

"Any radio contact?" Tripp asked as he watched the lights.

"Not a sound," Omar responded. "They stopped where they're at and haven't moved since."

"I think we need to retrieve the trunk and get out of here," Manning said.

They located the buoy, and using a winch, began to pull it toward the surface. Fifteen years after it had dropped below the water, the trunk broke the surface. Manuel and Omar watched closely as the trunk was winched up and onto the deck. No one spoke as the two old friends knelt and stared at the trunk. It was covered with silt and sediment, but the trunk had held up relatively well in the cold waters. They looked at each other and knew it was one of their trunks. Finally Omar put his arm around Manuel's shoulders and smiled.

"It is yours, my friend. I hope you use it well."

As the men began to open the chest, Carmen turned and made her way to the bow. She leaned against the rail near the hawsehole and looked into the water.

"I love you, Mother, and I miss you so much," she whispered into the quiet of the night.

After a few moments Tony noticed his sister was no longer beside him. He looked around and saw her standing at the far end of the boat. He too made his way to the bow and walked up behind her.

"Are you okay, Carmen?" Tony asked.

"Yes, Tony, I'm fine," she said, still looking into the water.

Tony stepped closer and put his arm around her.

"You know, before Morro, the last time I saw you was when you fell in the water. I guess it was just about here," Tony said.

Carmen held her brother close and said, "The last time we saw our mother was here, too."

"Mother loved us very much and would be very happy to know we're all together again."

"I know, Tony. It is very hard—being here, I mean, and knowing she lies down there below us."

"She's not down there. She's with us here, in our hearts, and always will be," Tony said.

Back on the stern, Manuel and Omar finally lifted the lid of the trunk and peered in at a chest filled with gold, silver, and cash.

"I really think we should be getting out of here. There are agents in Miami who are anxious to speak with you, Manuel," Manning said, with growing concern about the boat anchored in the distance.

"Yes, yes. We can go now," Manuel said.

Omar turned and faced Manuel. "I will not be going with you, Manuel. I still have work to do," Omar said. "And I suspect you now have work to do too."

Manuel embraced his friend and held him for several seconds.

"Thank you for everything, my friend," Manuel said as he released Omar.

"You are welcome. I wish you and your family all the best."

Omar then turned to face Tripp and Manning and said, "When we get to Key West to refuel, I will return on *La Virazon*. I will send a couple of my men with you to return the boat to Cayman."

Manuel looked around and noticed Carmen and Tony standing on the bow.

"Please, can you give me a few minutes with my children here?" Manuel said to Manning.

Manuel made his way to the bow and stood behind his children. "Carmen, Tony, I know this has been hard for the two of you. I want you to know I love both of you very much, and I loved your mother very much. This was something I had to do, and I know she would understand. I hope some day you will understand."

Carmen and Tony each took one of Manuel's arms, and the three of them looked toward the sea.

Twenty minutes later, Manning radioed Henry Powell that they were on their way, and the "package,"—Manuel Favela— was secure. He told Powell they should arrive at Key West in an hour. Powell said he would have a company plane waiting for them at the international airport.

What Manning didn't know was at that same moment, another radio message was being sent from the mysterious boat they had been watching. The short message, spoken in Spanish with a Cuban accent, said simply, "They are leaving, and heading for Key West."

CHAPTER
55

After refueling at Key West, Manuel bid his friend Omar farewell and watched until the lights of *La Virazon* had faded into the night. An hour later, Tripp, Manning, and the Favelas boarded the plane for Miami. Upon their arrival in Miami, Manning called Powell to let him know they had arrived safely. Powell informed Manning he had reserved two adjoining rooms for them at the Hilton and would be sending a car around in the morning to collect him and Manuel. Manning then checked out a vehicle from the motor pool and left for the Hilton. They checked into the hotel and were asleep by midnight.

The following morning Manning escorted Manuel down to the car that was waiting to take them to FBI headquarters. Carmen and Tony spent most of the day on the telephone, catching up with their adoptive parents. The Casteels, in California, were elated to hear that Tony was still safe and couldn't wait to have him home for Christmas. They were happy for Tony when he told them about his newfound father and sister, and welcomed them for Christmas, too.

The Tullys, in New York, were also excited that Carmen was safe and that the ordeal was finally over. They also invited her newfound family to share in Christmas celebrations. Carmen and Tony spent the rest of their day Christmas shopping and playing video games in their hotel room.

Manuel didn't have quite as joyous of a day. He spent twelve hours answering questions with FBI agents and Ben Hagle of the CIA about everything he knew relating to Fidel and Raul Castro, clandestine activities in the Cuban military, and drug smuggling. He provided valuable information regarding Castro's operations in South America and the United States. He also provided information on Castro's ties to the Soto brothers and their association with the Red Mafia. Because he cooperated unconditionally, the authorities agreed to set Manuel up with citizenship and a new identity, with the understanding that he would continue to work with the FBI and CIA.

The evening was growing late when Manuel and Manning returned to the hotel. Manning filled Tripp in on what Manuel had told them, specifically regarding the Soto brothers and their drug-smuggling operation. Tripp suggested they all go out for dinner, but Manuel was exhausted, and they decided to order in through room service. Tripp, Manning, and Manuel were watching the Dallas Cowboys and the Washington Redskins with the volume turned up, while Carmen and Tony had retreated to the adjoining room and closed the door to wrap presents.

It was just after eight when there was a tap at the door and a voice announced room service. Tripp checked the peephole and saw a man in a room-service uniform with a tray balanced on his hand. When Tripp opened the door, the man shoved against the door and dropped the tray of food, which went flying across the room. Three men quickly stepped into the room with weapons drawn and closed the door behind them. Raul Soto, José Soto, and Igor Petroff stood side by side, looking at Manuel.

"Señor Favela, it is good to finally find you," Raul said in an ominous tone. "And of course you have your American friends with you: Agent Manning and Agent Tripp." Without turning his head, he snapped, "Check them for weapons."

José and Igor patted the three men down, removing Tripp's Glock and Manning's Sig Sauer.

Tony and Carmen had heard the noise next door and stopped to listen. When they heard Soto talking, they slipped over to the door and quietly set the lock.

"Where are the girl and boy?" Raul asked with a malevolent sneer.

"They are not here. They have returned home," Manuel said without hesitation.

"He is lying," José snapped.

"Never mind. We will find them later," Raul said. He then turned and looked at Tripp.

"So you must be Agent Sean Tripp," Raul said.

When Tripp didn't respond, Raul continued, "I have often wondered what kind of man would allow such a beautiful wife to do such dangerous work."

He paused a moment, watching Tripp. "She was actually quite brave, but it would seem she had a coward for a husband. I almost hated to kill her, but I won't feel such compassion when it's your turn."

It was all Tripp could do to keep his emotions in check. The enmity was overpowering, but he knew what kind of men he was dealing with and he fought to keep silent. When Tripp still did not respond, Raul turned back to Manuel.

"We are out of time and patience, Manuel Favela. I want the money."

Raul cocked his weapon and pointed it at Manuel's head. "And I want it now."

"The money is not here," Manning said. "It is in a locker at the airport."

Manning knew the trunk was in the adjoining room with Carmen and Tony; he hoped one of them had locked the door.

"Search the room," Raul barked to José and Igor.

The men searched under the bed, in the bathroom, and in the closet, but found nothing. Igor then walked toward the door to the adjoining room. Tripp felt a miasmic press of dread as Igor reached for the knob, but the door failed to open, and Igor turned back to Raul.

"There is nothing here."

"Then we will go to where the money is," Raul said.

"My father's last directive was to return with Manuel and his two children," Igor protested.

"Right now all I am interested in is the money," Raul responded. His eyes shifted first to Manning, then to Tripp.

"We are going to escort the three of you down the stairway to the back parking lot, where you will get in the car and take us to this airport locker. I suggest that you not try my patience. Should any of you make one false move, we will kill you."

José led the group out of the room, toward the back stairway. In their room, Carmen and Tony were standing next to the adjoining door, where they could clearly hear the men leave.

"We've got to call the police," Carmen said in a strained whisper.

"They will be long gone before the police can get here, and we will probably never see father again," Tony said. "We've got to follow them and call the police later."

He unlocked the adjoining door, stepped into the room, and looked around. Dishes, silverware, and food were strewn across the room, but Tony spotted what he was looking for. On the dresser he found the keys to the motor-pool car. Carmen and Tony left the room and sprinted for the garage. With Tony behind the wheel, they pulled out of the garage and turned toward the back parking lot. It was a dark evening, but the parking lot was well lit, and Tony spotted the men walking toward the lot.

Tony's initial plan was to follow the men, but then he looked up and saw Igor Petroff only yards away. As if in a movie, everything from Morro came rushing back to him. He looked down at the stub of his finger and a deep-seated anger enveloped him. With a rush of adrenaline, Tony floored the accelerator and sped at Petroff. As if in slow motion, Tony watched as the car slammed into Petroff, sending his gun skidding across the pavement. Tony felt the crunch of impact, and then the hard thumps as the car barreled over Petroff's body. Tony hit the brakes and the car slid to a stop.

Raul and José had dived to avoid the oncoming vehicle, giving Tripp the opportunity he was searching for. In an instant he seized the gun Petroff had dropped and leveled it at Raul.

"Drop your weapons now," Tripp yelled, his eyes burning into Raul.

Raul looked at Tripp and studied him. Tripp stared back, ready to pull the trigger for any reason. Very slowly, Raul and José set their weapons on the pavement. Manning and Manuel each walked over and picked up a gun.

Tripp walked to Raul and stood over him with the gun leveled at his heart. He could feel the blood leaving his fingers as an icy-hot anger settled in. He thought about Katie and the pain of losing her. As he stared into eyes as empty as the deepest abyss, his finger began to tighten on the trigger. Manning shoved the gun he had picked up under his belt and walked over to Tripp.

"Not this way, my friend. To kill a man in anger and hate will not stop the pain or bring Katie back. If you do this, it will always be with you, inside you. You will only destroy yourself from within."

Tripp looked at Manning and knew his friend was right. He then saw Carmen and Tony, who had stepped from the car. Slowly, he released his finger from the trigger and turned away from Soto.

In an instant, Raul reached down, pulled a revolver from his ankle, and lifted it toward Tripp. Before he could level the weapon, a shot rang out and Raul's chest exploded in a burst of crimson. With his arms still outstretched and smoke trickling from the weapon, Manuel stood and looked at the man he had shot.

Seeing his brother dead on the pavement, José stood and charged at Manuel. Without hesitation, Manuel turned the gun on José and pulled the trigger. José's lifeless body fell next to his brother's.

Manuel slumped to his knees and released the weapon. As Carmen and Tony rushed to their father, Tripp stepped over and stared down at the lifeless body of Raul Soto.

CHAPTER 56

-Four days later-

Christmas morning found Monterey Bay bathed in sunshine and clear blue skies. Tripp awoke to the sound of coffee brewing in the galley and a soft voice humming "I'll Be Home For Christmas." He roused himself from bed, slipped on a robe, and made his way to the galley. Carmen was at the sink, rinsing strawberries and wearing only an old sweatshirt she had found in Tripp's closet. Her midnight-black hair draped softly down her back, and even his old sweatshirt couldn't hide her shapely figure. Tripp stood watching her for several moments before she felt his presence.

"Do you like strawberries in your pancakes?" Carmen asked with a warm smile.

"Right now, I can't seem to remember," Tripp said as he sat at the table.

Carmen dried her hands and began to pour Tripp a cup of coffee.

"Then you'll have to eat whatever you're given."

Carmen set the cup on the table and settled in his lap. She slipped her arms around his neck and kissed him warmly.

"Merry Christmas," she said as she pulled back and looked into his eyes.

"Merry Christmas. I wish I had a gift to exchange, but I never had a chance to do any shopping," Tripp said.

"Oh, I don't know, I thought our exchange last night was pretty nice," Carmen said demurely.

Tripp reached up, stroked his fingers down the side of her face, and flashed a coy grin.

"It was very nice, but I've always enjoyed exchanging gifts on Christmas morning, too," he said.

"The others won't be here for a couple of hours," Carmen said as she stood and led him to the bedroom.

It was almost noon when Tripp and Carmen showered and dressed.

Tripp, wearing khaki slacks, Top-Siders without socks, and a white polo shirt with a light-blue sweater, made his way up on deck to start the grill while Carmen went to the galley to get the steaks. It was a gorgeous day, with clear skies and calm waters. And although they would not be having a white Christmas, it was still cool enough to know it was that time of the season. Tripp closed the grill and looked out over the Pacific. Carmen, wearing faded jeans, sneakers, and a red sweater over a white turtleneck, stepped on deck and set the platter of steaks next to the grill. With the steaks in place and beginning to sizzle, Tripp and Carmen turned to watch a family of sea lions splashing and playing in the bay.

A moment later they heard the sound of a car pulling into the marina and watched as Manning, carrying a gift bag, stepped out of his Corvette and made his way on deck.

"Merry Christmas, my friend," Manning said as he handed Tripp the gift.

As Tripp looked in the bag, Manning kissed Carmen on the cheek and said, "And Merry Christmas to you, too. You look absolutely beautiful this morning."

"Thank you, and Merry Christmas to you," Carmen said.

As Tripp pulled a bottle of Chivas Regal from the gift bag, he managed a crooked grin, and said, "Thank you, old friend, but you really didn't have to go to the trouble."

"You're welcome. It was no trouble at all."

Before Tripp could respond, Carmen grabbed Tripp by the hand and said, "I think I see Tony and Father pulling into the marina. Why don't you check on the steaks, Sean."

Tony and Manuel made their way on deck and greeted everyone with a warm season's greetings. A few minutes later, Tripp pronounced the steaks ready and the group prepared to sit for a Christmas dinner of salad, steak, pumpkin pie, and champagne. They had just sat down when a voice rang out from the dock.

"Permission to board?" came the voice of Stony Barker.

"Permission granted, come on aboard," Tripp said as he stood to welcome Stony.

When Stony stepped on deck, Tony stood and embraced his friend.

"Mr. Tripp told me how you went to him for help when I came up missing. I guess I have you to thank for my life and for the lives of my father and sister."

"I think Mr. Tripp had a little bit more to do with it than I did, but you're welcome," Stony said.

Tony introduced Stony to Manuel and Carmen, who greeted him warmly.

"We're just about to have Christmas dinner. Come and join us, Stony," Tripp said.

"Thank you, but I have to get back home. We have a house full of family who are probably ready for dinner too. I just wanted to stop by and welcome Tony back."

Tony turned back to his friend.

"I will always remember what you did for me and my family," Tony said.

Stony smiled and said, "You're welcome, Tony. It's good to have you back."

After Stony left, the group began to dine. A few minutes later, Tripp looked across at Manning.

"So, what's next for you?" Tripp asked.

"Assistant Director Jenner's got me back with the terrorism unit. Basically, I'm taking up where I left off," Manning said. "He read my report, and asked me to give you a message."

Tripp took a sip of champagne and set his glass down. "And that message is?"

"He said it sounds like you're ready to get back in the game. He wants you to come back to work."

Tripp glanced at Carmen and said, "That time may come, but not now."

Manning caught the eye contact between Tripp and Carmen and said, "And what about you, Carmen? Will you be going back to work?"

"The airline said I could take as much time as I needed, so I'll spend next week with my family in New York before I return to work."

"What are your plans, Tony?" Manning asked.

"I'll finish my senior year, and probably go on to a local community college," Tony said.

"With your father's newfound wealth, you could go to any university in the country, Tony," Tripp said.

Tony glanced at his father, but didn't respond.

Manuel set his fork down, patted his mouth with his napkin, and cleared his throat.

"Gentlemen, and my dearest Carmen, I have an announcement to make. The trunk you helped me retrieve contained almost fifteen million dollars in gold, silver, and currency. Yesterday, I donated the entire amount to Amnesty International, with the condition that the majority of monies be spent for the purpose of improving human rights in Cuba."

Manuel was silent for several moments before he continued.

"I have heard that what makes one a man is the choices he makes. I've made bad choices in my life. I only hope that in some way the money will serve to help the people of Cuba, especially those who suffer in the prisons."

All eyes were on Manuel as the table fell silent. Finally, Carmen got up, knelt next to her father, and put her arms around him.

"I love you, Father, and I'm so very proud of you."

Manuel stroked her hair and held her for several moments. "So you see, gentlemen, I won't be able to help Tony much with college, but I will do all I can."

Tripp looked at Manning and nodded.

"I think you will be able to help Tony more than you think," Manning said.

Manuel looked questioningly across the table.

"You see," Manning said. "There was a five-hundred-thousand-dollar reward for each of the Soto brothers."

Manuel stared back, not believing what he had heard.

"For a man that makes good choices, a million dollars can go a long way in helping his family," Tripp said.

The shadows began to grow long as the group enjoyed their day together. Throughout the afternoon, Manuel looked over at his son and daughter, and thought about his wife.

As the boat ebbed in the gentle current of the Pacific Ocean, Manuel looked out to sea and whispered, "The kids are safe, my wife, and I will always watch over them."

EPILOGUE

Swiss Alps, Switzerland, 2008

-one month later-

Tony and Manuel pushed off from the chairlift and glided slowly to the lip of the run, where they planted their poles and paused to set their goggles. To get to the top they had taken two gondolas, a tram, and two T-bars, but the breathtaking panorama before them made it all worthwhile. To their left was the majestic Matterhorn and runs that could carry them across the Swiss border into Cervinia, Italy, and to their right was a snow-covered wonderland of mountain peaks extending as far as they could see. They looked down the Piste before them, which ran for miles into Zermatt, and felt the sun-sparkled snow urging them to jump in.

Tony looked at his father with a wide grin and said, "Last one down's a rotten egg."

With that, he pushed off with his poles and began schussing down the mountain, followed seconds later by Manuel. The two made long, slow turns, enjoying the exhilaration and freedom of the mountain. At this height there were no trees, which allowed them to glide along with unobstructed views. At times the trails would be small ribbons along steep cliffs, while at other times there would be wide plateaus. Each and every turn provided a different breathtaking view, and they soon became one with the mountain. The morning sun was warm on their faces, and the clear skies provided for a perfect day.

Tony reached the lift at Trochener Steg first and stopped to watch his father glide in next to him.

"What took you so long?" Tony asked with a grin.

Manuel nodded toward the restaurant across from the lift, where dozens of skiers were dining and sun-bathing.

"How about some pizza and a bit of a rest?" Manuel suggested as he lifted his goggles on top of his head.

"You won't have to twist my arm. I'm always up for pizza," Tony said.

They skied over and made their way up to the pizzeria Cervino on the second floor. The restaurant was crowded, but the smell of pizza cooking in the wood-fired oven was inviting. They ordered the biagio, a pizza with mozzarella, oregano, parmesan, and ham, and Coca-Colas to drink. They carried their order out on the sun terrace and sat at a table facing the Matterhorn. The Trochener Steg restaurant, which stood at the foot of the Theodul Glacier, was an authentic Swiss chalet with a unique and charming atmosphere. The terrace was filled with skiers on holiday, each eagerly discussing their last run.

The two ate quietly for several minutes as they took in the majestic scenery. Finally, Tony looked across the table at his father.

"It really is beautiful here, Father."

Manuel smiled at Tony and said, "I have been thinking about buying a home here, Tony."

"Are you doing this to escape from Cruz and Castro?"

"No, Tony. I spoke with Omar last evening, and Cruz is currently occupying the same cell I was in. Castro will not bother us anymore since he knows the money has been found."

Tony didn't respond, but continued to look at his father.

"When you were a small child, I used to promise you I would take you away from Cuba. We'd live part of the time in America and part of the time in Switzerland. It was my dream for you."

Tony smiled warmly and said, "Yes, I remember that, Father."

"Would you like to live that dream?" Manuel asked.

"Yes, I would like that very much. It's even more beautiful than I imagined."

Tony and Manuel finished their pizza and made their way down from the terrace. They snapped their skis on and grabbed their poles. A light snow began to fall as the two disappeared down the slope side by side.

Larry Thomas was born in the Dallas area in 1954. He was educated at the University of Texas at Austin, where he graduated in 1977. He taught school for twelve years before receiving his Masters of Education degree from East Texas State University. For twenty years he has worked as a high school principal. Larry Thomas devotes a great deal of time to research, mainly in fiction. As a boating and diving enthusiast he has spent much of his time around and under the water. He lives in the Austin area with his wife and son.

VISIT US ONLINE
www.larrythomas-author.com